FIRST
STEPS

ALSO BY NED LIPS

The Reset Series:
First Steps, the prequel
Reset
Entwined (coming soon)

Other Books:
Freed (coming soon)

FIRST STEPS

NED LIPS

Elliptic, LLC

St. Louis

Published in the United States by Elliptic, LLC, St. Louis, Missouri

First Edition

Library of Congress Control Number: 2019911357

ISBN 978-0-9980325-6-6

Cover design by Jamie Wyatt, imnotskippy.com

Edited by Karen L. Tucker, CommaQueenEditing.com

Dedicated to my patient wife, Barbara, and my two wonderful daughters, Jessica and Christine. I am grateful for their loving support.

ONE

The light from the work lamp glistened on the smooth surface of the flint knife as Sarah turned it in her left hand. Her eyes, tear-filled and tired, struggled as she examined it for any remaining imperfections. The stress of the evening rolled through her. She put her right palm down and rested her left fist on the bench, clutching the knife, supporting her weight. She felt its razor-sharp edges cut into her skin.

The years of physical and emotional abuse coursed through her system. Her body became heavy, as though lead bricks were being piled upon her back, pushing her down, trying to crush her soul, to break her. But, as she had for so long, Sarah endured against the burden, took a deep, cleansing breath, raised her head, cleared her eyes and stood erect, staring into the darkness above the light.

"I've spent too much of my life hiding in the darkness, hiding outside the light. Today is the day that changes forever." Her words echoed through the emptiness and felt every bit as hollow. The ever-present odor of motor oil and garbage reached her consciousness. "This is my haven from my world? How did I deserve this?" The garage was stifling, hot and confined. Her hands were grimy, cut with a bit of smeared blood. Her shirt was soaked in sweat, streaked with dust from the flint she'd been working and blood from her hand. Her hair was as dull, lifeless and entangled as her life.

Instead of feeling unkempt, Sarah felt stronger, emboldened. She loved camping and living off the land and had always felt more comfortable in old well-worn jeans than in fancy dresses. She breathed in her own scent, deep and purely human, free from artificial perfumes.

Sarah stared down at the tools strewn across the workbench, hand-made from stone, antler and bone, of varied lengths, thicknesses and tips, each with its own purpose. Tears began to cloud her vision. Stress pulled at her muscles. Sarah took a deep breath, wiped her eyes with her sleeve and chose the perfect tool, created from a piece of deer antler. She took another deep breath, focused on the knife and deftly applied the antler's sharp tip to a slight imperfection. The flake of flint would be nearly imperceptible to anyone not as skilled as herself. *Jazz would've noticed.*

The events of the evening raced through her mind. Her stomach churned, and again she relied on the bench for support. "Have I done the right thing?" she said aloud to the empty, dark garage. She opened her fingers and watched as the knife slid then tumbled onto the cut and worn wood surface. She felt a bit like that slab of wood: beaten and bashed but still strong. The sting on her cheek where he'd hit her had resonated in each strike on the rock as she'd rendered that knife from its rough stone birthplace. Her left hand moved to her cheek, touched it gently, then looked at her fingers. No blood. It was a habit. She knew this time there would be none.

She half-fell, exhaustion gaining hold, into an old metal folding chair, which clanged and rattled, echoing through the garage, threatening to collapse under her. The tiny work light focused its attention on the workbench. Chunks and chips of the rock and their many tools lay strewn across the old wooden surface. Sarah sat outside the circle of light, gazing at the glistening knife in the middle of the chaos.

She flexed her right hand, the hand that had driven a straight punch into her husband, sending him crashing onto their glass coffee table. She'd finally hit Robert back. Sarah leaned forward into the light, picked up the knife, examined its jewel-like perfection and smiled. "It was time, Sarah," she said aloud to herself. "It is the right time." She wasn't sure she'd convinced herself, but she knew she'd had enough. Bruises, broken bones, excuses and stories to protect him and their family.

He'd come home drunk again, angry and looking for blood. *Her* blood. She closed her eyes and replayed the evening in her mind.

***

"Sarah, goddammit." The door from the garage flew open and slammed against the kitchen wall, the solid wood door bending under his staggering weight against the doorstop. He bounced off it, careening into the end of the cabinets, grabbing for the quartz countertop of the island, sending the salt and pepper shakers skittering across the smooth surface. "Sarah!! Where the fuck are you, goddammit?"

Sarah pushed herself deeper into the darkness of the living room. Their kitchen, a mere 12 feet away, began where the long hardwood in the front foyer ended. The chandelier in the foyer was off. No lights on upstairs or in the living room behind her. The only light came from the small desk lamp in his study, glowing across that foyer floor onto the edges of the plush, beige living room carpet. Save for his stumbling and her own pounding heartbeats and shallow breaths, both of which sounded deafening to her but were imperceptible to her husband, the house was deathly quiet.

She crushed herself into the front corner of the living room, feeling the rough, fashionably textured wall on her right arm as she squatted safely behind an expensive but uncomfortable chair that no one ever sat in. She could just see the open door to the kitchen. He'd struggle through that space soon. If she could see him, she knew he'd be able to see her, but she was banking on his drunkenness to miss her in a dark corner where he would have no reason to look.

Hands clammy, she remained hushed, calming her breath and heart as she'd been taught by her mother and spiritual teachers. Her girls, she hoped, were asleep upstairs. They'd heard their father enter the house from the garage many times in this way and had long ago learned to sleep, or at least pretend to sleep, through it.

"Sarah, you fucking bitch, where's my dinner? Where's my drink? Goddammit, where the fuck are you?" Robert was stumbling through the kitchen. She heard him open the fridge. "SARAH!" His next move was to

3

stagger into his study to find a bottle where he'd drink himself into a stupor and, if she was lucky, fall asleep on his couch. Just as often, however, he'd get that drink, stumble upstairs and find her. That was never good for her. He'd broken their door down even after she'd replaced it with a solid wood exterior door. He was a big man—6'4", about 245 pounds, naturally strong—and, when numbed by alcohol, could break down nearly anything. He'd dislocated his shoulder several months ago coming after her but still managed to hit her until she bled.

"Sarah!" She could see him now as she pushed herself deeper against the wall. Her heart raced despite her training. Her deep, calming breaths were too loud. If he saw her, he'd destroy her. She sucked herself deeper into the shadows. *The darkness will protect me. He'll go left into his study, not right into the living room. The booze is in his study. This* had to work.

He fell against the doorframe leading from the kitchen into the foyer, then knocked over the vase on the foyer table, both broken so many times that she'd bought the current vase and table from Walmart. Once a stickler, he no longer noticed. Sarah held her breath as the cheap vase scattered across the floor toward her, a large piece settling onto the living room carpet not three feet away. She put her hand over her mouth. He righted himself, right hand on the wall, and stared blankly ahead. She switched her breathing technique to tiny, shallow breaths. The light from the desk in his study lit his way. It was the guide she hoped he'd follow.

He gazed up their elegant stairway, now dark and hollow. He was holding onto the polished oak rail and finial with both hands. He was close to bellowing her name again but stopped. *Will he head up there? What would he do when he can't find me? My girls.* She prepared to pounce if he began to head upstairs, if he approached their doors. She'd protect them, but it would mean a long, difficult battle for her. *Please go into the study. Please.*

He just stared up into the darkness.

Then, like a moth drawn to a flame, he turned and headed toward the light, stumbling from the railing to the wall until he could grab the doorframe. Robert steadied himself, lost his balance, an awkward step backward in her direction. *Don't fall.* She pulled back from the chair into the shadows. Robert then righted himself once more and took a step into the study, then another.

Sarah closed her eyes and took a breath. *Quiet, like a hunter, Sarah. You can do this.* Her heart pounded in her chest as she crept from the shadows, sliding around the wall, back against the front door bathed in the light, along it, silent as a cat, then back within the shadows of the wall beside his study.

He wavered in place, searching the study.

As she crept closer, he grabbed a bottle from the file cabinet drawer to his right, opened it and took a long drink. He took another step, one hand on top of the cabinet. She could see his addled mind trying to determine how to navigate to some other object for support. He took another swig. He let go and took one feeble step.

Now!

"Robert!" Sarah jumped into the light at the door of the study behind him.

"Whaaa—" was all Robert could say as he turned around to face her. "You whore!" He slapped her—harder than she'd been prepared for—across her face with his right hand. It shocked her, but she retained a strong footing. "You bitch." The swing staggered him as well. He took a step back, regained his balance. "Where's my dinner?" His body rocked toward her, his right hand raised to strike. Just the window she was looking for.

For the first time in their marriage, she used every pound of leverage her 5-foot, 8-inch athletic frame could generate, from her powerful legs through her sinewy right arm, to drive the heel of her hand deep into and through his shocked face, wishing it was possible to carry through the back of his head.

He fell like a stack of newspapers thrown from a truck, back and through his glass coffee table. His head slammed against the floor. His eyes lost their focus. His nose bled down his cheeks.

Robert struggled for a minute among the broken glass but only managed to cut himself more deeply. He lay nearly motionless on the floor, bottle safely in hand. *Of course.*

She was glad he went down. She didn't want to hit him again, though he deserved it. His left bicep was bleeding heavily from a nasty gash. A pool of red began to form beneath it, stark against the pure white rug. The shard of glass from the table that had inflicted the wound still hung from his arm. Who knew, or cared, what other injuries befell him.

Sarah stood over him for a few seconds. "You're an abusive sadistic asshole, Robert. We're done. From this moment on, you're on your own!" His eyes betrayed his astonishment. "I'm calling the cops. Get the fuck out of this house! And I mean *now*!"

She stormed out of the study, slamming the door behind her. Sarah stood alone in the silent darkness of the foyer. A sense of joy rose from within her and she raised her fists to the chandelier hanging from a ceiling two stories above her. "I've finally done it!" she whispered. She'd hit him back, and hard. Her smile was small and uncertain but present for the first time in a long time. *He'll think twice about hitting me again, if he even remembers tonight.*

The elation was brief. *Now what?* The emotion of the moment and the finality it represented rushed through her. *No plan. How could I not have a plan?* She ran up the stairs, wiping at her tears, leaving Robert to tend to his own wounds. She knew he wouldn't. He'd continue to drink until he passed out.

The tirade and crash woke her girls. "Mom?" It was Jasmine, their oldest, 11, tall for her age and slender, with Sarah's dark black hair and deep green eyes. Sarah ran into her room. Janie, 5, long auburn hair flying in every direction behind her, sprinted in, and as Sarah turned, Janie leaped into her mother's arms.

"What happened, Mommy?" Janie asked.

Sarah gathered her girls into her arms, tears streaming down her cheeks. The three snuggled together in Jazz's double bed. The two girls cried themselves to sleep as she hugged them close. Sarah stared at the open door, ears tuned to any movement, ready.

TWO

It was well after midnight when she'd slipped out of the bed, locked the door, closed it and snuck down the stairs and into her refuge, the garage. Sarah had made the flint knife in a little less than half an hour, and it was perfect. It was the symbol of her freedom, freedom that she'd claimed today. She sat back in the rickety metal chair, knife in her right hand, stretched her arms to the ceiling, leaped to her feet, turned and snapped the knife across the garage.

It drove its sharp tip deep into the aluminum inside of the garage door. The loud crack it made as it struck, followed by the rattle of the disturbed door, somehow reassured her that she was strong enough and that her decision to end it with Robert was the right one. That it protruded from the door right in front of Robert's Mercedes would serve notice that she was serious—dead serious. *He'll notice that! That bastard will think twice before he hits me again. This is the end! No MORE!*

With a deep breath, she took one more look at her handiwork across the garage. Sarah started for the kitchen door, the same one Robert had struggled through. *He's still in there.* She stopped. Sarah turned back to their workbench and surveyed her options. She grabbed a stone long knife Jazz had made, her handcrafted bow and three flint-tipped arrows, just in case, then headed back toward the door. *It'll be self-defense.*

She reached the kitchen door, took a deep centering breath, slid the bow around her left shoulder and arrows in her left hand. She held the knife, tip down, in her right hand. The doorknob turned smoothly, and the door opened without a sound under her control. Sarah crept; crouched as low as possible in case he was waiting for her, she reached the entry to the foyer and peaked around it. Nothing.

The door to Robert's study was still closed. She moved quietly to the center of the foyer where she'd stood after she'd laid him out, now feeling more like a warrior than a victim. She squeezed the long knife, feeling the smooth wooden handle Jazz had fashioned, heart racing, adrenalin coursing through her. Sarah almost wanted Robert to come at her. She imagined him as the huge cruel beast he was, claws raised, teeth bared, coming at her. Sarah saw herself driving the long knife deep into his heart, falling to the floor on top of him, staring into his shocked face, watching life drain from his eyes. She turned and glared at the door to the study and thought about going in and ending it right then. He'd be passed out in the study with that now-empty bottle of booze nearby. It'd be easy.

After several seconds, she dropped her right hand to her side. *I can't do it.* Instead, she turned and plodded up the stairs. Her mind began to run scenarios, most of which ended badly. She stopped on the stairs and turned. *He has the size. He has all the money. They're all his family, friends and connections. I'll be alone and penniless. If I don't kill him now, he'll win.*

Sarah, if you kill him, you go to jail and you lose your girls. Follow your heart and you will survive. She was not sure who was speaking.

"Mom?" she said into the darkness. Nothing. She plopped down onto the stair behind her. Tears welled up. After several minutes contemplating her fate, she reached for the rail and pulled herself up. Jazz's door was still locked. She trudged down the hall a few more feet into her bedroom.

Their master suite was spacious. Sarah pushed the heavy wooden door closed. It broke the silence with a whoosh, thud and a click. She thought about locking it, but she wanted her girls to be able to enter. She thought about getting them, then turned and stared into the darkness, the door holding much of her weight. Hands shaking. Breathing fast and laborious. Heart pounding in her chest, soaked in sweat.

Sarah closed her eyes and breathed deep. *Settle.* Another breath helped slow the panic. Then another and her heart slowed to a still-rapid rhythm. Another. She was lost. Her world began to fall in around her. The knife, arrows and bow slipped from her hands to the carpet. Another breath. She slid down the door to the floor and pulled her knees to her chest. *Should I run?* Sarah was paralyzed. She hadn't thought out her plan past fighting back. *Should I gather up the girls and get out of here?*

She drew a deep breath, trying to center herself. Eyes closed. Heart racing. It was no use.

A sense of griminess crawled through and around her. Enwrapped in guilt, she fell onto her side, curled in the fetal position, tears flowing from her soul down her face and out into the universe. The bow, arrows and knife lay near her. She could reach the knife. It was sharp enough. Perhaps the world would be better off without her. Perhaps she should join her parents.

She closed her eyes. Jazz and Janie. *What have I done?* Weight pushed her into the floor. *I'll lose them. He has money. I have nothing. His family is their only family, my only family. I have nothing. My sisters are his sisters. Without him, will I have anyone? Will I have anything?*

She heard stumbling downstairs. Her senses returned. *Robert! The girls.*

Scrambling to her feet, she opened the door just enough to peak out. *What if he comes up here to hurt them because of me? Right when he gets to the top of the stairs, that's when he'll be most vulnerable.* She snatched the knife from the floor.

She heard a jangle of pans. *He's in the kitchen. He's getting a knife. He's going to try to kill me!* Sarah's eyes grew wide and frantic. Scanned the room. Her dresser. She could push it in front of the door. *What if he threatens the girls instead?*

SLAM. It was the kitchen door. He went into the garage. *What does he want out there? Oh, damn it, I bet he's got a gun in his car. I was out there. Why didn't I check? Now what?*

Rumble, rumble. *The garage door is opening?*

The grumble of a diesel engine. *He's taking the Mercedes.* She ran to the window that overlooked the front lawn and driveway.

Crash. He's backed into a statue, one he so had to have. It teetered and fell into the tiny pool, the pedestal broken and the rear of his Mercedes crumpled in. Blood on the side of the car reflected in the security light. *Where's he going? He's going to the bar. He's going to Pappa's to drink more. Or maybe to the hospital, or the police. No. No way he goes to the police. Not with my bruises. He hates hospitals. He's going to a damn bar. But it's 3:30 in the morning. Nothing's open.*

Sarah sat on the soft cushions that lined the four windows that made up the large bay, her legs tucked under, her head in chaos. She couldn't think. *Settle down, Sarah. He's gone.* Deep breath. No use. *He'll be back. When? Should we run?* Her heart raced, her blood felt cold, her mind dazed, unable to concentrate. She shivered and held herself, rocking slowly back and forth, staring out the windows onto the empty drive.

He seemed to creep inside her. Frozen daggers. The stench of bourbon. Shaking. Muscles locked, her body felt dirty, slimy, to her soul. One thought got through: *Get clean, Sarah. Wash him out.*

The shower's hot water chastised her skin, stinging, burning but soaking deep into her muscles. Grey water with hints of red. Soap, lots of soap, bubbling, slippery, warming, cleansing her skin and her mind. Hands on the tile, she let the hot water pound down onto her head, pour over her, drag her demons away. Her brain was empty. She let it all pour out. The tears mixed with the water, indistinguishable. Soon, they were no longer. Soon, there was only the water, rushing down her clean, sleek frame and taking her misery with it into the drain beneath her toes.

She began to breathe, deep and sudden, as though she'd been suffocating. Forced to struggle for every molecule of oxygen required to survive, but now, eyes wide open, she could breathe. Deep, moist breaths, inhaling air through the water falling around her.

Clean air.

New air.

Her air.

Free air.

THREE

Sarah slipped into her nightgown. *No.* She took it off and dressed in socks, a T-shirt, sweatpants and sweatshirt. She put her shoes beside her bed, long knife on the side table, and bow and arrows leaning against the wall. *Prepared.* She crawled into their luxurious king bed. Her pillows were soft. She slipped under the Egyptian cotton sheets, pulled a pillow into her arms and curled up. All of this because of his wealth, his family's wealth. None of it she needed or even wanted. But it was from *his* family, the only family she had. The only family the girls had ever known. Even though she was exhausted, she couldn't sleep. Her mind wandered.

For years when she was growing up, she'd spent weeks in the wild with her parents, learning how to survive. When they died in that world at the end of her first year in law school, she'd blamed everything they'd shared, that she'd loved, for taking her parents from her. She blamed God, a concept that had always escaped her; nature and the universe of spirits, which she knew well; the doctors and everyone involved in planning and executing the trip. But most of all, she blamed herself. On her last trip home, when storing their gear, she'd discovered that one of their main ropes was frayed. She'd meant to tell them, and she did leave the rope out on the table, unpacked, but she was running late and had forgotten. She meant to leave a note, but it had slipped her mind. Her punishment: she was left alone and penniless. Adrift. An orphan. And it was all her fault. A powerful pang of guilt hit her, even now, so many years later as it always did when she thought of them.

Robert had saved her, been her knight in shining armor.

Her face still sore and her right hand still throbbing, albeit relieved that Robert was no longer in the house, she realized how different her world would have been had Robert not been there to help her get on her feet again. *Did I love him? Of course, I loved him once.* Sarah worked hard to convince herself. *I'm sure of it.* She was not.

She'd met his wonderful family and fallen in love with Mother, his father—who everyone called Herb—three brothers and two sisters and a host of others. She'd gotten pregnant with Jasmine later that summer. They married in December of her second year in law school.

He was a year older and started work in May. Jazz was born in June. He'd been present at her birth and they spent time together, but the life of a first-year lawyer was grueling. She understood, but the next year, caring for a baby and going to law school, was tough. Mother and her sisters, especially Mallory, were so helpful.

He was loving, in his way, when he was there. Wasn't he? It all seemed right, but the honeymoon didn't last long. *When did it all go wrong?* Her mind drifted back, searching. *We were married a little over a year. Things were kinda crazy. We didn't see each other much. It was dinner at the Club. I should have known then, shouldn't I have?*

***

Sarah's final semester was easy academically, which gave her time with Jazz, a precocious 20-month-old at the time. Walking and talking and getting into everything. Sarah, Mother and Mallory grew closer, sharing the joys of keeping up with her and exploring the world of Jazz.

Sarah smiled as the memories poured back to her in the darkness of her spacious bedroom.

Robert barely knew their daughter. He worked long hours and most weekends. It was expected of young associates in big D.C. firms. Sarah understood. She was proud of him.

Sarah received offers from several prestigious firms in D.C. To celebrate, Robert took her to dinner at the Club. She was thrilled to have him to herself. He talked about work incessantly, and she listened intently, asking thoughtful questions and supporting him at every turn. It was a fun evening, though she realized that he never once asked about her life or about their daughter.

As the conversation hit a lull, Sarah took a deep breath and spoke, "Hon, I've got less than a semester left. I have to make a decision about where I should practice after I pass the bar."

"Martin, Schoenberg, van Peebles. It's a great firm, and they offered you the most money. Easy decision."

"Well, if I go there, I'll have to work ten to twelve hours a day and weekends like you do. We have a baby. How can both of us sustain that kind of schedule and raise a child?"

"Mother and the girls will help out."

"But Robert, Jasmine is *our* child. It's our responsibility to raise her, not theirs. Plus, at some point, we're going to get our own house, move out of the family house, and then what?"

Robert put his fork down and looked at her from across the elegant table. "What do you have in mind, then?"

"Well, I was thinking . . ."

"That's your first mistake. Let me do the thinking." Robert picked up his fork and speared a chunk of steak.

"Robert, I'm going to be an attorney. I'm going to finish in the top five percent of my class—higher than you, if I remember right. I can think for myself just fine."

Robert's eyes grew thin and his face reddened. The fork fell with a clank onto the plate. He looked like he was going to explode. *That horrid competitive streak,* she remembered thinking.

"Honey, I'm sorry. I didn't mean that." She put her hand on his and he settled down a bit. He tossed back his glass of wine and called for the waiter.

"Bourbon, neat. Make it a double, Jonesy, and your good stuff, please."

"Yessir."

"OK, what were you saying? Something about raising Jasmine."

1 3

"Right. So, you're making over six figures. What if I did something simpler. Perhaps starting as a public defender? It doesn't pay much, but it would be a normal 40-hour week, and I'd be able to spend time raising Jazz."

"First, I hate that nickname. Her name is Jasmine, not Jazz." He tossed back the drink when it arrived and ordered another. "Second, there's no way my wife is going to work for a bunch of lazy, good-for-nothing freeloaders." His voice was increasing in volume. "That's out of the question. What would our friends here say? Would you have a bunch of poor, low-life criminals around for dinner? Those people choose to live the way they do. They could get jobs. They're a bunch of freeloading, lazy drug addicts. They can fend for themselves."

Sarah looked around the room. Everyone was staring at them. "But Robert . . ."

Robert was standing now, staring down at her from his imposing 6'4" frame. "This is NOT a discussion. I said NO, and NO means NO, goddammit." He leaned over, his face so close to hers that she could smell the alcohol on his breath, his right hand on the table. "You take the job at Martin, Schoenberg, van Peebles. I pulled a lot of strings to get you that interview, and you're taking that job." He stood back up.

Mr. Jones brought the drink. Robert threw it back, slammed the glass on the table, grabbed the folder with the check and signed for the meal. "You do what you need to for Jasmine. We'll get a nanny. End of discussion. We're going home."

People were staring. She hadn't expected that outburst. Mother thought it was a great idea and that Robert would go for it. Boy was she wrong. The valet brought the car. The ride was quiet, and she was frightened both because of his outburst and his drunken driving. She prodded him a couple of times as he swerved.

"Robert, do you want me to drive?"

"No! I'm fine."

FOUR

She remembered, as she sat in the big bed, that when they'd made it home, she'd gotten out and waited for him.

***

Robert sat there for several seconds, staring straight ahead. Sarah walked around to the front of the car and looked through the windshield, her hands up in a "what's up?" gesture. He glared at her, started the car and gunned the engine, which made her jump back. Then he sped backward out of the driveway.

She stood dumbfounded, hands on her hips, watching the car disappear from her view. "Where are you going?" she yelled, with a conflicting mix of emotions: anger, sadness and fear.

Mallory ran out of the house and stood beside her. "What was that all about?"

Tears began to roll down her cheeks. "I have no idea, Mal. We were discussing my life after law school and he flipped out."

Sarah and Mallory walked back up to the big house as Sarah recounted the evening. Then she did it again for Mother. They were both so understanding and as confused as she was. The three discussed the evening, Robert, their future and Jazz all evening. Sarah crawled into bed with Mallory and cried herself to sleep. Although it was the first time in her marriage, it would not be the last.

Robert trudged up the front steps early in the morning, disheveled and forlorn. Sarah was out on a run with Arnold, the family golden retriever. Mother apparently lit into him as though he were still 12, Mallory standing triumphantly behind her.

Sarah jogged up as the scene was ending. Robert turned on the top step, which was as far as the women had allowed him. He was still in his suit, though he looked a mess.

He trod down the steps. Sarah stopped in the yard. Arnold stood in front of her, facing Robert as if to protect her from him. Mother called the dog. He looked back, and Sarah nodded. Arnold growled at Robert as he passed then stood beside Mother and watched, refusing to go inside.

"I'm so sorry, honey." He'd begged Sarah for forgiveness. "This will never happen again. I don't know what came over me last night. I had a long, difficult day, and I guess I wasn't prepared for that discussion."

"Will you at least consider my proposition?" Sarah asked as he came closer.

He took her hands and stood in front of her, looking into her eyes, fully present. "I don't think it's a wise idea, sweetie." He paused, looked down for a moment, then back into her eyes. "Honey, I don't want you to stunt your brilliant career because of Jasmine. We can handle this. We can do it together, and you'll never look back and think that you didn't get your chance to be a great attorney." He said it with so much conviction that she'd actually believed him. She acquiesced, as she would so many times.

***

Even then, she'd known deep inside that working at Martin, Schoenberg, van Peebles was the wrong decision for her, but they'd started a life together and had a young daughter. He was much better after the incident, more attentive to her and Jazz, even accepting the nickname. He agreed that they needed their own house, so they began searching. He laid out very strict guidelines for what he wanted. They were buying his dream house, not hers, but she went along.

The big firm seemed like the logical decision. It was the easy decision. It fit his vision for their life, and she was too emotionally invested in him and his family—now her family—to fight about it. She feared that a rift with him would tear them away from her, and she couldn't deal with that.

As the memories unraveled in her mind, Sarah tossed and turned in the big bed, getting tangled in the sheets. Frustrated, she abandoned sleep entirely and sat up against her pillows, forced to think, to try to figure out when she knew. When should she have realized that Robert was becoming a monster?

He asked her to forgo the rallies for equality and justice that had been so important to her. These, and other issues, were simply not discussed in the household. Herb and, thus, Robert were adamant opponents, considering the protestors to be unpatriotic. When she pointed out that the Constitution protected their rights of free speech, Herb made fun of her "legalese jibber jabber." Robert laughed, perhaps with Herb, but it seemed more *at* her, as she looked back.

Mother and Mallory came to her defense, but they were not really supporters of her causes so much as they supported her. Whenever Mother would stand up for Sarah, Herb would get up with that big belly laugh and come after Mother. She'd squeal and run around the table. Mother would mock complain, "Herb!" as he reached her and gave her a big mustachioed smooch. Everyone would laugh, and Sarah would be forced to smile.

Then Herb would give Sarah a big hug, gazing down at her with his sparkling brown eyes. They separated with a big pat on her back, which would knock her forward. She came to believe that Herb loved her as much as he did Robert. Robert never came to her aid. He'd take a drink and watch, as though he knew she'd be guided into behaving properly. He was right, of course. It didn't take long for her to suppress those thoughts in favor of peace and harmony in the family. Mother had even told her that she appreciated it.

In those early years, she spent one Saturday afternoon a month with Mother, Mallory and Brenda, Robert's other sister, at a homeless shelter, bringing them blankets and clothing Mother had gathered through the church. One Tuesday night a month, they volunteered at a food pantry. Both were rewarding, and she took her participation seriously, but she felt like the rich handing down used leftovers to the underclass.

Robert felt no need to participate and even resented her being away. When they moved out into their own house, this house, and the children grew, it became harder to get away. When Mother got sick, Sarah's charity efforts ended completely. Another "easy" decision.

That's going to change. I'm taking my girls on a march. I need to get back to the causes I believe in. She felt so disconnected from the outside world.

As she stared at the big red letters on her bedside clock, 4:12, she closed her eyes, but all that rattled around in her mind was how many times she'd convinced herself that this life was what she'd really wanted. She'd lied to herself so often. So many choices were made for good, rational reasons—the girls, the marriage, her relationship with Mother and the family—instead of for her. When had she stopped doing what she knew in her heart was the right thing to do? Maybe all these decisions were right in the moment. Looking back now, it was so difficult to determine.

FIVE

Her mind continued to comb through her past, trying to make sense of it all. Her eyes welling up with the memories of the last seven years of her life, she began to cry.

Well before Janie, they'd stopped making love. He'd come home late and drunk, after she was in bed, and force himself on her. She'd fight back, but he was huge. Most of the time, he couldn't perform. He'd get mad, blame her, call her fat and ugly, feign a slap, get up and storm out of the room. He'd apologize in the morning and promise it would never happen again. For a few days, he'd behave and join her in bed without trying to have sex with her. By the third day, they might even cuddle a bit. That taste of normalcy, like the tiny shot of whiskey that sends an alcoholic back into the gutter. Some semblance of normalcy, of family, was her addiction. Then something would snap in him. It was like riding a roller coaster.

Then the serious physical abuse began. It was Jazz's fifth birthday party. He'd missed everything when he stumbled in drunk.

***

Incensed, Sarah sprinted from the backyard as she heard him arrive. "Robert! Where have you been? You've missed the entire party. Jasmine's been looking for you. You made her cry at her own party. What's wrong with you?"

His big right hand came from nowhere and smacked her hard across her face. Shocked, she stumbled back, falling onto the ottoman. Mother,

19

who'd followed her in, had seen the whole thing but did nothing. Sarah watched as she turned and strode through the sliding glass door into their backyard. She turned back as Robert ducked into his study and slammed the door.

Sarah sat there, dazed, in the middle of her living room, feeling the sting on her left cheek, staring at the sliding glass door. *What should I do? Whom can I tell?* "I'll lose them," she whispered to no one. A moment passed that seemed like hours. She stared at the fine beige carpet with, as Mother had put it, "a touch of yellow for warmth." Then she stared back at the sliding glass door. *I can't tell anyone. I can't leave him. I have nothing. They're my only family, Jazz's only family.* She turned from the glass door to the six-paneled door that led to his study. *And he's my only connection to them.* The walls felt closer, the air thicker.

She ran up the stairs as tears poured from her eyes. She stared into the mirror. *You can do this, Sarah Robinson. It's one time. He was drunk and mad, and you started it.* Somehow blaming herself made it better, something she could handle. She took a deep breath, dabbed her eyes, pulled out her makeup and covered the rising bruise as best she could. *Sarah, you can get through this.*

As she entered the backyard through that same sliding door, Mallory's eyes grew large. "Sis, what happened? Your face is all swollen."

Mother popped in, "Oh my, Sarah. Looks like an allergic reaction to something. Did you get stung by a bee, or perhaps it's the soap you're using?" Mother guided Sarah back inside, through the living room and foyer, into the kitchen, where Mother sat her down. "We'll take Jasmine, sweetie. I'll end the party. It's almost done anyway. You get some rest. That'll be gone in no time. Ice is good. Put some ice on it."

Mallory stood a few feet behind Mother. The look in her eye told Sarah that Mal knew. Mother patted Sarah, spun, gathered Mallory in one arm and whooshed her outside. Through the open kitchen window, Sarah could hear Mother's soft voice politely letting the mothers know that the party was over. Within minutes, everyone had left through the exterior gate and Mother had Jasmine ready for an afternoon out. The world around her was deafeningly quiet. She was alone.

Later that evening, Robert emerged from his study. Sarah was petrified, but Robert was pleasant. He apologized profusely and promised never to do it again. He even got her some more ice and held her. *Normalcy?* She forgave him. What other choice did she have?

She made them dinner, which they ate in the dining room, talking politely, if at all, like nothing had happened, but that was the day she realized she was trapped.

SIX

She stared at the glow of their front lights and the streetlights through the blinds. It was dark and quiet. Something that should have been peaceful was not. He didn't change. Her life did. His behavior worsened. Her fear of him submerged her desires for anything, for life. His temper grew hotter and his fuse shorter.

Still, they'd had some good times, hadn't they? When he was home, Jasmine loved him, and he tried to behave around her. He didn't hit Sarah again for over a month. Their arguments increased, but "isn't that the way it is with married couples?" she'd rationalized.

He slapped her again, this time quite a bit harder, one night when he came in late, drunk and smelling of someone else's perfume. She'd started it. He'd finished it with a hard whack across her face, sending her scrambling onto the carpeted floor of their living room. She hit her head on the coffee table. A glancing blow, but it drew blood. He'd run to her, apologized again, held her, helped her to the kitchen and tended to her wound. He was legitimately concerned and loving and again promised never to hit her again. A tiny shot of normalcy.

She forgave him. She remembered that she was touched by his tenderness. It'd been so long since he'd held her, been that way with her. She missed it. He carried her up the stairs to their bed and they had sex. It wasn't making love. It was all about him and lasted maybe 5 minutes, but she felt like maybe she was getting her man back.

She was wrong.

Sarah became pregnant with Janie. One warm moment with her drunken husband after he'd hit her, knocked her down and drew blood. *What kind of love was that?*

Over the next few years, usually after outbursts in front of the girls, Sarah implored him to stop drinking and get help. "For the girls," she'd explain. It was always then that he'd order the girls to their rooms and then at least try to hit her. Sometimes she escaped. Sometimes she'd defend herself and the beating was minimal. Other times . . .

After an issue at his office, he was forced to go to an AA meeting.

***

The girls were upstairs, and Sarah was reading in the living room, hoping against hope that the meeting had opened his eyes.

The kitchen door slammed open and Sarah leaped to her feet. He appeared in the opening from the foyer to the living room, massive and drunk. "That was a fucking waste of time. What a bunch of pussy drunks, complaining and telling sad-ass stories. I got the fuck outta there before it was over. Some dude tried to 'help' me. He touched me, the gay queer. I slapped him silly." Sarah stood, her hands now on her hips. Robert moved toward her. "Fucking lightweights. I can handle my liquor."

"Robert, dammit. Your company, the firm, your bosses made you go to this. You're going to lose your job."

"I am NOT an alkie like those punk-ass weirdos." He was closing in on her. She took a step back and began to look for options. She was cornered in the back half of the living room.

"Honey. Sweetie. I don't know why you can't see how untrue that is?" His eyes grew thin. "Honey, maybe you could try again, for us, for your girls, for me?"

"Fuck no!" he lunged forward, swung with his big right fist, which she deflected with her left arm but still knocked her sprawling to the floor against the wall. She curled into a ball as he towered over her. He kicked her once and then turned away. "I'm not a fucking drunk!" The study door slammed behind him, letting her know it was safe to get up.

***

The first time he put her into the hospital and the police investigated, he'd whispered an apology, hugged her in front of the cops, and with Mother standing right there, Sarah had defended him. She claimed it was someone else, that he'd come to her aid and chased the guy away. That neither of them could describe the man was suspicious, but it ruined any domestic abuse case they could bring. The family patted Robert on the back in the hospital room after the story. All except for Mallory, who knew better. Sarah made Mallory promise not to tell anyone. Mallory had agreed. It was their secret, and it brought them closer. She felt that Mother and Herb and the entire family loved her, sometimes, it seemed, more than they loved Robert. But all of them, except Mallory, refused to see what was really happening. Robert was family, the oldest boy, the heir apparent, the prominent attorney, the golden child, and Herb, in particular, loved him.

Other times, she felt that everyone knew, and the special attention was designed to keep her imprisoned in her little golden cage and to keep all this unpleasant business hidden, where it belonged. The possibility of losing them—losing them for her girls, especially—prevented her from fighting back, from telling anyone, from blaming him and from leaving him . . . until tonight.

SEVEN

Sarah got out of bed and sat on the cushions of the bay window, gazing to the east for any sign of sunrise, but it was still almost two hours away. She opened the blinds a bit more and stared at the broken statue. A deep breath helped a little. She wanted to forget, but memories kept coming, as though she had to air them all out. *Why?*

The weekend that kicked off her journey to last night rose into her memory like it was happening again.

Her world became unraveled following a few particularly rough days during which Robert and Sarah had fought constantly. He'd gotten into a fistfight at the Club that resulted in their suspension. Herb intervened on their behalf, which was the only way they'd avoided being expelled. She'd demanded several days in a row that he stop drinking or they'd lose everything.

Finally, he became enraged, as usual, chased her, demeaned her, and even though she tried to defend herself with a frying pan and the fire-place poker, he'd managed to hit her several times before storming into his study. That was on a Tuesday night in October 2014, but that was not the catalyst. That was just another fight—one, like the others, she could handle for the sake of her girls and their connection to the family.

When she woke up early Wednesday morning, she read from a bloodied Post-it stuck to her chest, "I'm gone. Fuck you." She prayed that he'd meant gone for good.

The girls were off school on Friday for a teacher's professional day and Monday for Columbus Day. Mother was struggling, only a few months before her final prognosis. Sarah decided to stay at the big house and spend time with her.

***

Sarah treated her wounds and carefully hid them as best she could before heading over on Thursday after school. She'd gotten quite good at this. Thursday evening, the girls played board games with their grandparents. Sarah stole away to their bedroom and applied ice to her swollen cheek and aching ribs.

Friday morning, as was her custom, Sarah got up early and ran with Arnold, the golden retriever. It had been a while, and Sarah had to shorten their run considerably as Arnold seemed to labor. When she returned, Mother was, as always, sitting on the porch drinking coffee. Sarah took her seat beside her, picked up the cup Mother had prepared for her and tuned into the wonders of nature around them. This time was only for Sarah and Mother, and very little was said. That first Friday morning, in the quiet, Mother reached over and took Sarah's hand and squeezed it tightly, without turning from the view of the river. Sarah perceived a glisten of a tear in her eyes.

She knows, she remembered thinking. *Should I say something?* She didn't. Mother didn't want to admit that she knew the truth. Sarah realized she hadn't remembered to put on any makeup and thought that it couldn't have been more obvious what was going on. Sarah was sure Mother wanted to let Sarah know she knew and was loved.

On Saturday after Sarah's run with Arnold, Brenda and Mallory arrived, and the three sisters began chatting and preparing the big brunch. Mother couldn't help, but she could talk, and she did. Robert was not mentioned. Not in any context. It was as if he didn't exist. Mallory, of course, noticed Sarah's bruises, but Sarah gave her a look that shushed her before she could say anything. Mother was ill, after all.

The siblings and their families began to show up for brunch as usual. Robert didn't join them. Sarah sat in her place at the table, to Mother's left. The seat opposite her was left empty for their wayward son.

After brunch, Mallory and her husband took the girls for the extended weekend. Sarah helped Mother work in the gardens. Sarah, lost in contemplation of her future, hardly noticed the sweet aromas wafting up from the flowers that she'd once loved.

"Mother," Sarah broke the silence. Mother, sitting on a stool for support, used a cane to sit up from the flowers she was cutting. "I think it's time I go back to work. Janie's old enough for preschool. Jazz is starting elementary school."

"What are you going to do, hon?" she asked.

"I'm not sure yet, Mother, but I feel it's time." Although unsure of her plans, when things finally ended with Robert, she needed to be prepared. She wasn't going to share that with Mother, so why bring it up? Did she need her approval?

"What do you think?" she asked.

Mother waved Sarah over to her. Removing her work gloves, she put a hand on her shoulder. "I think it's time, dear," she said with a tortured smile. "As long as you can care for your husband and girls, I think it's fine." There was a pleading in her eyes, combined with a bit of fear. "I think I should head in, don't you?" Sarah helped Mother up and into the house. That was the end of the discussion.

Dinner with Mother and Herb was quiet and simple. Sarah tried to read. Tried to watch TV. That night, sleep was fitful but eventually came.

Sunday morning, she awoke early, as usual. Sarah prepared for a run on the same path she and Arnold always ran. "Arnold," she whispered, trying not to wake anyone. It was usually enough to bring the happy dog running to see her. Arnold didn't show up. Sarah searched for the dog she loved so deeply, whispering his name as she entered the kitchen. There he was, asleep under Mother's chair in the screened-in porch. "Arnold," she whispered a little more loudly. He didn't move. When she touched him, he still didn't budge. She moved around to his head. Those beautiful, normally happy eyes were lifeless.

Sarah moved Mother's chair, took her old friend into her arms and cried. When Mother appeared, her eyes wide, she dropped her cane, hobbled over and fell to her knees beside Sarah.

"Mother, he's dead," she sobbed.

Mother patted her on the back and tried to console her.

Through the sobs, croaking out each word, Sarah cried, "Everything's dead, Mother." Mother guided Sarah into her arms and put her hand around Sarah's head, holding it to her breast. It felt so warm and nice. Sarah breathed deeply and felt her soul become more centered. Tears slowing, Sarah continued in a quieter voice, "Everything I've loved, dreamed about, it's all dead." She pulled away and turned her tear-filled eyes to the older woman kneeling beside her. "What am I going to do?"

Mother didn't hesitate, staring directly into Sarah's eyes. "Carry on, dear. It's what women have done for centuries. You can handle it. You have two wonderful daughters you love more than anything else in the world. They need you. You have Herb and me and your brothers and sisters, who love you like family. And more than ever, your husband needs you. You have a lot to love and who love you. Carry on, my dear. It is the only answer. Simply carry on."

Mother took Sarah in her arms and held her close. Her parents, dead. Her career, nonexistent. Her marriage, dead. Mother sick, perhaps dying. And now her running partner, dead. Her nightmare was tied to the family she so relied upon and couldn't leave. The only advice Mother had for her was to endure, to carry on, to live with the hurt and destruction. It wasn't lost on Sarah that Mother didn't mention that Robert loved her or that she loved him—only that he needed her.

Sarah pulled away from Mother and sat back on her calves. Mother's eyes weren't loving and nurturing, as Sarah was expecting. They were deeply sorrowful, conflicted and distant, almost apologetic. At a moment when they should have grown closer, instead, something deep was lost between them that they would never get back.

On Monday morning, one day after Sarah had carried Arnold outside and buried him behind the gardens, Sarah and Mother sat in silence in their old chairs, looking out over the stream. Sarah sat there because it was expected and watched the wildlife through clouded eyes. Sarah hadn't been able to bring herself to go for a run without her canine companion.

Mother reached over and took Sarah's hand without changing her gaze. The woman's hand seemed terribly frail. Shaky. Hesitant. Even cold. After a second, Mother let go.

Sarah's cell phone broke the silence. She looked up at Mother. "It's Robert. What should I do?"

"Answer it, dear. He's your husband."

Sarah flipped back her hair, took a breath and pressed the button. "Hello, Robert."

Silence at first.

"Robert?"

She could hear sobbing. "I'm sorry, honey. I'm so sorry."

Sarah had no reply. She held the phone to her ear and waited. She knew Robert would start again, which he did.

"Honey, when are you coming home?"

Again, Sarah was not sure how to answer. She had no desire to go home.

Mother looked her in the eye and spoke, without faltering, "Dear, it's time. You need to go home and make things right. Help Robert get his life together." She paused and took Sarah's free hand, squeezing it with the strength of her youth. Her look was stronger, not pleading but demanding. Then she said in a pleasant voice, "You can do that for me, can't you?"

Sarah's eyes teared up again. *There it was.* It was finally clear to Sarah precisely where she stood in the family. She was "like family," not a part of it. Her job was to stabilize their oldest son. Perhaps he'd always been a problem. Perhaps he'd always been aggressive. Perhaps he'd had a drinking problem before they'd met. How would she know what an alcoholic looked like? Sarah's heart sank, her stomach rebelled against her, and it took everything she had to avoid running off and bawling. What had she been enduring all of this for?

"Go on, dear. Tell him you'll get the kids and be home soon. It's time. You need to go home to your husband."

Sarah froze. Gazing into the woman's eyes, she saw something very different than she'd ever seen there before. Power. Demanding power. Sarah felt a deep obligation, though she didn't know why, and turned her attention to the phone, keeping one eye on Mother. Her stern gaze, a hint of fake love behind a manipulative smile, did not change.

"OK, Robert. I'll get the kids from Mallory's and be home in an hour or so. But when I get home, we have to talk. Robert, things have to change." Mother's face morphed as she beamed with delight. Sarah was playing the role Mother wanted her to play: the savior for her eldest son.

EIGHT

As Sarah sat in her big empty bedroom, she shook her head as she realized that again her own addiction had kicked in.

***

As she drove to Mallory's that Monday, she thought, *Is this the time? Is he finally going to love me enough to change, to love all of us enough to change and save our family? Has he hit bottom?* Her addiction was rekindled. A ray of hope. A touch of normalcy. "Maybe Mother's right," she said aloud as she pulled into Mallory's driveway. "Maybe things will change."

When she and the girls got home, Robert had been drinking. Not completely drunk, but definitely not sober. Sarah sent the girls up to their rooms "to do their homework." Robert and Sarah sat facing each other in two large armchairs on either side of the fireplace in the living room. He had a bottle of bourbon in his left hand and a shot glass in his right, filling it and throwing it back in rapid succession.

"Honey, can you please stop drinking?"

He put the bottle down. Within seconds, he'd picked it up and re-filled the little glass. "Just one more to calm my nerves and help me think."

Despite the words that came out of his mouth, they were getting no-where. As she took her turn to talk, he leaned back into the big easy chair and, in the middle of one of her sentences, snored. Out cold, he clenched the empty bottle to his chest. The shot glass lay on the floor below his right hand.

***

Things did change after that weekend, but not with Robert. Sarah began to take charge of the parts of her life she could control. She began to teach Jazz and Janie all the things she'd learned from her own parents and grandmother. How to meditate, do yoga and connect with the spirits of the universe and of nature. She taught them how to make stone tools from flint, how to recognize plants that were safe to eat, how animals behaved and interacted with their world, to make fire, understand herbs, barks and other natural sources of medicines and cures.

Robert spent the following weekend away. Instead of heading to the big family house, she took the girls on their first of many weekend trips into the wilderness. It turned out that little Janie, at only two years old, loved plants. As she grew older, she devoured anything she could find on them. She was young but very bright.

Sarah converted a part of the garage into a work area to make stone tools the primitive way. Jazz was a natural with stone: knives, spear tips, axe blades and eventually incredibly delicate arrow tips. Sarah was experienced and gifted, but soon her girls were nearly as talented in their areas of passion.

Sarah loved the wilderness. She'd lost that in Robert's striving for wealth and glory. It was rejuvenating for her to return to it and to find that her daughters loved it like she did.

At Mother's insistence, Herb made a call and found Sarah a job in the district attorney's office as a prosecutor. As one of the newbies in the office, she handled petty offenses. She worked hard but refused to work long hours, making sure her girls were safely on the bus in the mornings, she was home for her daughters in the early evenings, and they could go camping nearly every weekend.

***

It was December 22, 2014, a couple months after Arnold had died. Robert had been better. He'd slapped her only twice in that time and had apologized both times. Other days, when he was home, he was pleasant enough until he'd pass out in his study. Maybe normalcy was possible. Sarah's addiction was in full swing. She did everything she could think of to keep Robert happy.

Robert was in an unusually good mood as he emerged from his study that Monday morning. "Sarah, Jazz and Janie," he yelled up the stairs. The two girls arrived at the top. Sarah appeared behind them. "Today is the day I become a partner in the firm. The vote was over the weekend, and all my sources tell me I'm a shoo-in this year." He'd bragged this to anyone who would listen all weekend and had been on his best behavior, especially at dinner with Herb and Mother at the Club.

Sarah bought champagne and made his favorite meal. She and the girls were waiting for him as the time came and went that he should be home. She called him. No answer. An hour passed. A few more calls. No answer.

"He's probably out with the other partners, celebrating," Sarah had said to Jazz and Janie. The garage door opened. "He's here."

Sarah ran to the kitchen door to the garage and flung it open. The car door slammed open into the shelving along the wall. A male hand curled its fingers over the top edge of the door. Robert rose like Godzilla from the ocean, eyes bloodshot, tie askew, shirt unbuttoned and stained, no coat.

Sarah pushed the girls behind her and backed into the kitchen. She knew that look.

"SARAH! Goddammit. Get the fuck out here."

Sarah turned and said, "Girls, upstairs; lock your doors." Jazz and Janie, tears in their eyes, ran out of the kitchen. Sarah reached for a carving knife from the rack. She held it in both hands, facing the door, knees bent and eyes wide open.

The car door slammed shut and soon the huge man filled the doorframe.

"Robert, what's wrong? You got what you always wanted. You're a partner, right?"

Robert ran at her, so she turned to run. Before she could get away, he slammed his left hand into her hip, sending her crashing into the edge of the island. She spun out of control. The knife skittered across the Italian ceramic tile floor. Sarah grabbed the countertop and was able to land on her knees. Her back was to him, so she instinctively curled up into a ball on the floor.

He hit her once with his open hand then kicked her in the ribs. "Get up, you backstabbing bitch. It had to be you. Who else?" He grabbed her hips and yanked her to a standing position.

She took several steps and turned toward him, looking desperately for anything to defend herself. "Honey, I don't know what you're talking about. I made your favorite to celebrate." She pointed. "Medium rare Porterhouse steak, sweet potato and asparagus." The meal was perfectly laid out on the dining room table. "And I got champagne." She pointed to the bottle chilling in their silver ice bucket.

His shoulders seemed to drop, though his eyes were still filled with rage. He raised his fist to strike, but she ran out of the kitchen into the foyer. She considered heading upstairs, but the girls were at the top. "In your rooms!" she shouted as Robert followed behind. Open champagne bottle in his left hand, he drove his huge right paw into her ribs, sending her skittering across the floor to the living room carpet. The girls saw. Janie screamed, and Jazz grabbed her and pulled her back. Sarah rolled away from the girls then onto her hands and knees. Pain ripped through her ribs. They were broken, she was sure of it.

Crash! Something smashed into the side of her head: cold liquid, tinkling glass. She felt the thud of her body against something. Brightness. The room was spinning. She could sense his shadow and put her hands up in its direction. A blow followed to her gut. She folded in two, struggling to breathe.

"You stop hitting Mom, you bastard!" It was Jazz.

"NNOOOOO!" Sarah yelled through the pain. The big shadow moved away. She heard a scream and then footsteps up the stairs.

"Girls," was all she said. They were always her priority. She reached blindly, knocking over a candle on the coffee table. She used the table to struggle to her knees. *Focus.* Blinding brightness. A menacing dark shadow. *I can't let him get to them!* It took all her faculties to get to her

34

unsteady feet. Disoriented but determined, she staggered toward the dangerous darkness. Something stopped her right leg—the ottoman. She fell onto her knees. Using the arm of one of the big chairs, she found her footing and stood. The darkness moved left and was gone. *The stairs are that way! Move, Sarah!* Using furniture and walls to guide her, she reached the foyer. She heard his sobs. In the light of the chandelier above them, the world refused to stand still. She could make him out above her, sitting on the steps, head in his hands. He was crying.

"I'm so sorry, sweetheart. They fired me. They let me go. Those fuckers were supposed to make me a partner. Everything would have changed for us. Masterson was given a partnership. I'm twice the attorney he is, goddammit."

Sarah stood holding onto the frame of the entry between the living room and foyer and listened to him jabber on. He stood up but didn't seem to notice her. Still, she prepared to run, not sure she could. He stumbled down the stairs, grasping the rail with both hands, staring at it as though it was his lifeline.

"I'm going out," he said as he rounded the balustrade and headed into the kitchen. She heard the door open and close, the car start, and the garage door open and close. Only then did she begin to breathe.

"My girls," she said out loud, ascending the stairs one at a time, focusing downward, grasping the rail as best she could. They'd locked themselves in Jazz's room. Holding onto the top of the rail, she croaked out, "Hey girls, it's me." She heard the click and then the door opened.

Both girls' eyes widened. "Mom, oh my god!" Jazz was first to speak as she ran to her side. Jazz's maturity shined through. Janie moved behind her sister. Sarah realized she probably looked like she'd lost a heavyweight bout, which she had, and not a close one.

"Mom, come with me." Jazz moved under Sarah's arm and guided her into the hallway bathroom.

When she looked into the mirror, she didn't recognize her face. Her right eye was a slit, swollen, cut and bleeding. Her left cheek was swollen and purple. Lip bleeding. Hair a mess, sticky with her own blood. She had a large bump that was bleeding on the back of her head. Her left shoulder hurt, and her left ear was bleeding. Her ribs were on fire, and she could hardly breathe. She could barely see, and ringing in her ear blocked her hearing. She lost her balance and crashed to the floor.

Lights in her eyes. Strange voices. A poke in her arm. She was being moved. Then nothing.

***

This time the police got involved, and this time Sarah was not so quick to make up a story about what had happened. Unfortunately, she was anything but clear about what had transpired. Her testimony would not be very useful, she was told. As a prosecutor, she understood. She worked hard to remember the night. Robert came home. Fists and arguing. She believed it was Robert, sure it was Robert, but her statements kept changing. She remembered him crying and then leaving. She remembered seeing her face in the mirror. She recalled nothing more, and she couldn't get the sequencing right, what happened when.

Mother had gotten to the girls and had convinced them not to tell on their father or he might go to prison. "You don't want that, do you?" she'd told them. So they said they didn't remember anything. The reality was, Sarah didn't want to drag them through a legal proceeding against their father, so she didn't try to change their minds. Mother would be pleased. Sarah realized that she still needed her approval. *Why?*

Robert denied he'd done anything. The police asked why the girls had to call the police. Why had he left the scene and gone to a bar? Why didn't he call it in?

Herb told him not to say anything more and hired an expensive attorney. Robert pled to a misdemeanor, was fined an amount he carried in cash in his wallet and was released. He'd been drunk in court, but no one noticed or cared.

Sarah spent the night in the hospital. Fractured ribs, but no other broken bones. She was tough and a quick healer. Always had been. She looked a bit better the next day, was coherent and subsequently was released.

NINE

Sarah rose from the window seat and tried to gain some confidence over the situation. The big red numbers read 5:19. She dried her tear-filled eyes and climbed back into bed. The next memories made her smile.

Sarah took her girls on weekend trips into the wilderness at every opportunity, sometimes on a last-minute whim. The three of them took long vacations during the summers throughout the Appalachian and Rocky Mountains. They camped, explored, learned and experienced a close relationship with everything in nature. Sarah and Jazz interacted with the many animals, great and small. Janie felt and found the myriad edible and unique plants. They sat quietly and just smelled the varied scents, felt the breezes, listened to the sounds and interacted with the spirits all around them. Most of all, they enjoyed complete freedom from Robert. They learned everything Sarah's parents had taught her, and the three discovered new skills together. She found deep personal peace and solace, and she felt her parents were alive again within her.

One of her favorite adventures with the girls had been a visit at the Hopi Reservation in Arizona to learn the natural healing arts of that ancient culture. Robert thought the entire trip was ridiculous. That was fine. She'd made it clear that he wasn't invited. She'd hurried the girls out early to avoid him and ignored his phone calls and those from Mother.

***

Sarah and the girls read about an authentic Hopi medicine man who had a shop in the little town of Keams Canyon along Route 264 on the ridge above the Pongsikya box canyon. The tiny speck of a village, where just over 300 people lived, was composed of the Keams Canyon Shoppers Center, a gas station, a government support center, several government-style portable houses where most residents lived and The Red Moccasin, the shop they were looking for.

They pulled off the road into the ocher gravel lot in front of a small building that looked as though it would fall over at the slightest breeze. The old grey-worn wood had been whitewashed many years earlier. Above the simple porch, "The Red Moccasin" was hand-painted in faded red letters. It was clean enough, and the woman inside was pleasant. They browsed a bit.

"So, could we meet the medicine man?" Janie asked the woman.

She squatted down to Janie's level. "Sure. He loves visitors." There was a gleam in her eye as she rose. She scribbled some directions onto a large Post-it and handed it to Sarah. "You'll find him here." The woman smiled, turned and walked into the back of the store.

They followed the rather cryptic directions east out of town on a gravel road. They made a couple of turns as instructed, finding themselves in the middle of desert, scrub grasses and bushes, reddish rocks and dirt. The Hopi land was hardpan, orange-grey sand and dirt, scrubby cactus and dry brush. It had some of the most remarkable canyons in the country. The Hopis had made the most of what the white men had left them, but it was not an easy life, even now.

Then, as the road turned gently north, an old fence, with weathered grey wooden posts and rails connected by 6-inch-square wire mesh with barbed wire strung along the top, appeared on their right. Dust clouded up behind the rented Jeep as Sarah followed the fence line. She approached an opening marked by two tall wooden posts, between which was a sign. When they got close enough, the faded letters read "The Red Moccasin Ranch." Sarah turned through the front gate, clattering over the cow guard, and along the short driveway to an ancient clapboard home, a barn and another building. An elderly man, a younger man and three boys were waiting on the front porch as if expecting them.

The younger man jogged toward her side of the car. He was ruggedly handsome, with skin darkened from exposure but not yet wrinkled. Two of the boys were given a hand gesture to get down and open Jazz's and Janie's doors. They scurried down in compliance.

The old man stepped down onto the dirt drive, smiling with the wisdom of age, and walked over to Sarah as she got out of the Jeep. He was wearing a wrinkled, off-white cotton shirt and blue jeans. They all wore blue jeans. The boys wore various T-shirts: Def Leppard, Arizona Diamondbacks and Superman. They reminded her of the secondhand clothes she and Mother had delivered to the homeless shelter in D.C.

The younger man looked like a cowboy, broad-shouldered, bright smile and deep brown eyes, and wore a tan button-down and simple pointed-toe, brown-leather boots that'd worn to fit his feet perfectly. His darker brown cowboy hat was the right amount of tattered at the edges. He removed it as he greeted her. His offered right hand was strong and rough as she took it for assistance she didn't need to get out of the Jeep.

She smiled at him and took his measure. He did the same as she stood. She was only slightly shorter in her newer boots with heels. She wore tight Levi jeans and a white tank top under a loose-fitting, unbuttoned cotton shirt that flapped in the wind as she moved. She reached into the Jeep and retrieved her unworn cowboy hat, slipping it onto her head so she looked as much the part as possible. There was a vibe between them that was quickly thwarted by a female voice from the porch.

"Yes, dear, I'll get it. Excuse me." He left. Sarah turned and saw two short, somewhat plump Hopi women on the porch, one older and smiling, obviously getting a kick out of what was transpiring, who Sarah correctly guessed was the old man's wife, and the other younger and definitely not smiling woman was the young man's wife. She waved at both and said, "Hello. Thank you for allowing us into your home." The two just nodded.

The old man held out his hardened hand and she took it.

"I'm Fred. Very glad to meet you. That was my boy Martin; that's Joey, Mark and the young'un there on the porch is Matt. They're Martin's boys. Come down here, boy, these people won't bite." The boy jumped off the porch and stood behind Fred.

"Very nice to meet you as well," Sarah answered. "I'm Sarah. This is Jazz, and this bouncy little scamp is Janie." The girls nodded at the boys, and the boys nodded back at the girls. Joey was several years older than Jazz, Mark was a few years older than Janie, and Matt was maybe three, Sarah guessed.

The two women returned to the house. Martin sauntered in behind them a few minutes later with whatever his wife had sent him for. Fred took Sarah and the girls on a walking tour of the small ranch and old simple wooden buildings in which he lived and worked.

They entered a big barn, once painted red, and were greeted by the strong and varied smells emanating from an amazing array of herbs and plants. Sarah and Janie breathed deep and tried to identify anything they could. Some were drying or dried. Others were kept in water or oil in jars. Janie was in a candy store, overwhelmed with desire to understand everything the shaman had stored or created.

Fred began to talk in generalities, but very quickly, Sarah got him down to specifics, talking in detail about each plant, where it came from, what it was good for, how it was to be prepared. She and Janie were engrossed as he began to teach them the medicinal qualities of native herbs and plants in his warehouse and how to prepare them. As Janie asked some very difficult questions, the old medicine man was duly impressed by her extensive awareness of the plants in their tiny part of the world. He knowledgeably answered all her questions, and at times, the two talked beyond even Sarah's ability to keep up.

Jazz was not interested in herbs. Sarah interrupted, "Fred, Jazz loves to work with flint and stone, making points and other tools."

Fred stood and said something in their native tongue to Martin, who'd just arrived, and Joey, who was following Jazz around. They nodded.

"Follow me," Martin said. He and Joey guided Sarah and Jazz outside and into the next smaller building. Though generally used to store tack for the horses, there was a bench where the Hopis made flint tools. Jazz was immediately transfixed by Martin's skills with flint.

As Joey, who was very accomplished and closer to her age, took over the work with Jazz, Sarah and Martin stepped out into the bright, hot sun and made small talk. The air was clean, tinged with the red dust from the ground, sweet scents of wild rabbitbrush, earthy smells from natural sagebrush and aromatic juniper leaves.

He noticed her breathing in the air, smiled and patted her on the shoulder. "Nice air, here. It rained last night and that brings out the smells. I don't much notice 'em anymore."

"I imagine if you came to my house, you'd smell things I'm no longer aware of."

Martin nodded. Their eyes met. He averted his gaze and shuffled his feet, uncomfortable in the silence. She sensed that Martin had a thing for her, and though it wouldn't go anywhere, she was enjoying the attention.

TEN

"Lunch is ready," came a woman's voice through a window in the house. Sarah could sense Martin's relief.

"Better gather up the others," he said and headed to the first building. Sarah headed toward the second, the one where Jazz was working, feeling desirable for the first time in a long time.

The three Robinson women followed their male hosts into the main house. They sat around a solid wood table, obviously handcrafted and, despite its apparent age, in remarkable condition. Fred's wife, Martha, and Martin's wife, Shanna, had prepared several native dishes, including rattlesnake. They'd also made hot dogs and hamburgers, just in case. Sarah, Jazz and Janie ate their fill and eschewed the American fare. The Hopi boys eagerly gobbled down the dogs and burgers. Martha muttered, "Boys. They'll eat us out of house and home one of these days."

Fred smiled. The boys grinned with full mouths.

Jazz showed them the small spear point she'd made. "Very impressive," Fred noted, making Jazz grin from ear to ear.

Janie prattled on about the herbs until Sarah quieted her.

Finally, Sarah prodded, "So tell me about that lone horse in the corral."

"That horse's wild. Brought it in two days ago. Haven't even begun to break it," Martin said.

"I want to ride it."

Fred, Martin, his three sons and the two women all laughed, until they saw that she was dead serious.

"No way, lady, you'll get killed," Martin implored. Fred produced a wry smile. The boys were chattering with one another in Hopi.

"Boys!!" Martha warned. "Behave. I don't care if they can't understand you!" She lightly slapped the oldest on the side of his head.

"I'm sorry, *So'o'*." She gave him a look that convinced him to obey.

Sarah said, "I'll sign a waiver. I'm an attorney. I'll even draft it. Come on. I'm riding that horse either way." And she got up and walked out. The Hopis knocked over chairs to follow her. Jazz and Janie, both a bit worried, followed close behind.

She was impossible to refuse, and the old man sent Mark and Joey into the corral. After a few attempts, they managed to surround and rope the palomino and guide it to the weathered grey fence. It was not happy, and the boys held on tight. Martin wrapped an old rope tightly around the horse's chest, gave her heavy leather gloves to hold on with, took her by the waist and helped her onto its back, which she enjoyed a bit more than she should have, all the while warning her that this was a very bad idea. Fred stood nearby, watching and smiling. Martha and Shanna watched from the porch with young Matt.

The horse had no bridle. She wouldn't be guiding this horse anywhere anyway. It snorted and complained about the weight as she settled onto its back, pulling the boys forward and back. Jazz and Janie sat on the top rail of the corral fence. Fred nodded to her as if to say, "You've got this."

"Alright, is that tight?" Martin asked. Sarah nodded. "OK, remember, lean into the horse when it rises up and back when it kicks. Lean into the turns. Hold on tight and pull yourself as close to your hand as possible. If you feel yourself losing it, jump off. The goal is to try to land on your feet and not die. Got it?"

She nodded. His eyes displayed his deep concern. Their chemistry was undeniable. The boys were beaming with anticipation. She saw Joey look over at Jazz, who was half-smiling but also nervous. Janie, like always, was beaming. After one more frantic plea from Martin for her to get off, the boys released the horse. It drove forward, made a violent left turn away from the fence, and she almost fell right then. Martin yelled, "Jump!" She pulled herself back onto the horse. It kicked its hind legs high, and she leaned back into it. The palomino landed, hopped to the right and turned violently to its left again. This time she rolled with it, holding on for her life. It kicked and she leaned back, then it turned right, all in nearly the same motion, but she was still on, barely.

The girls were cheering. The Hopi boys were dancing around her in the corral as though they might be able to catch her when she fell, their ropes flying about like crazed snakes looking to strike. One more quick right and a kick of its back feet and off she flew headfirst into a scrub of cacti. Martin sprinted to her and helped her to a sitting position. The palomino raced to the other side of the corral, complaining and snorting. The rope that'd been around its chest was laying a few feet from her in the dirt. The two boys headed after it in what would be a failed attempt to retrieve their ropes.

As Martin confirmed she was OK, the girls and the other Hopis tried to stifle their laughter. Her face and clothes were dirty. She bent forward, trying to get the sand out of her tank top and bra, nearly exposing her breasts to Martin, but it was no use. It was everywhere and had even gotten down her pants. She smiled as she held back the pain and Martin helped her up, dusted her off and handed her hat to her. When she went to put it on, pain shot down her side, and she lost her balance. Martin caught her. The younger Hopis laughed again.

"She held on for a bit over five seconds," Fred announced without consulting a watch. "Longer than any of you." The women on the porch clapped and then started toward her in case they were needed. Fred stayed where he was, that wise smile gracing his leathery cheeks, duly impressed. He waited as she stood tall and walked resiliently out of the corral. Fred held out his right hand, which Sarah accepted. "Thanks for the show." Sarah just smiled.

They spent the better part of twenty minutes extracting cactus barbs. After several minutes in the bathroom stripping down to clean dirt and sand out of everything, she put herself back together and returned. Martin smiled, noticed Shanna was watching and quickly turned the smile toward her. Fred and Janie had prepared a salve for the wounds. She pulled her shirt down well off her shoulder to expose the spine holes in her upper breast in front of poor, conflicted Martin. She felt guilty at once, and after Janie did the lower wounds, she pulled her shirt back up. Oblivious, Janie systematically applied the salve to each puncture.

Martha and Shanna brought out a jug and served her a unique homemade ale. "This'll reduce the pain," Martha explained. It did as promised as well as made her more than a bit woozy. She was not driving anyone anywhere. Martin drove her to the tribal hospital where she discovered she had a few cracked ribs, but she'd dealt with that before and was happy to earn their respect and the pride of her girls. She wouldn't have traded that for anything. Martin sent her a text a week later. They'd broken the horse within a few days and told her that her ride probably helped.

Mostly, though, she knew that horse had helped to break her out of her past, free her from her own perceived limitations and taught her that she could do anything and survive. That day went a long way toward preparing her mind and soul for this day.

ELEVEN

As she sat, now on the side of the big soft bed she never wanted, in a huge master suite she never wanted, in a massive two-story house she never wanted, she remembered her times with Jazz and Janie and smiled. Over the last couple of years, she and the girls had gone on "adventures" that spread over weeks or mere weekends, each indelibly logged in her mind. They were *her* times—her rejuvenation time with her girls.

Until Mother was hospitalized, they spent at least one weekend a month at the big family house, allowing the girls to have valuable time with their grandfather and ailing grandmother. She'd run alone and spent much less time on the porch with Mother, if any. She made up reasons to get away from the house after brunch, often only returning to pick up the girls on Sunday.

Now what? she contemplated from their bedroom. Get the girls to school, leave for work, figure it out then. Perhaps she'd pick them up after school and run away, as far as possible. She started to play out scenarios in her head. *What about Mallory and her relationship with the girls? What about Mother and her failing health? What about Herb? He'll be lost without Mother, already is.* No, she was doing this for her wonderful girls. For herself and for them. *We cannot continue to live like this!*

She fell back against the luxurious pillows and tried to collect herself. Then she sat up, grabbed one and whipped it across the room, as though that would help. Deep centering breaths started to help. She stopped crying. Everything was going to change, and that change would start today. First step: get through this morning. There was nothing to stop her anymore.

TWELVE

Before long, the alarm clock announced that it was 6:00. Janie pushed the door opened and bounded across the room and onto the huge bed. Jazz followed at a sleepy saunter and climbed in next to Sarah, who put an arm around her.

"Janie woke me up again, Mom." She saw Sarah's face. "Are you OK? What happened last night?"

"I'm fine, really. Your father and I had another fight. I'm so sorry to put you through all of this. It's going to end soon. Our lives will change a lot, but it'll be so much better. I promise."

Janie chimed in, "Can we go camping this weekend? Just us girls?"

"Yeah, Mom. It's been forever," Jazz added. "I made some new points yesterday. Have you seen 'em?"

"Yes, I did. I checked them out last night. They're exquisite. You're quite the little stonecutter, young lady. I made a knife last night myself. Darn sharp too."

"I wanna see it." Janie jumped to standing on the bed.

"Not now, honey. Time to get ready for school. I'm going to pick you up. We can go over everything then. I promise we'll be in the wilds, all by ourselves, very soon. Now scurry off and get dressed. I have to get ready for work." She kissed Jazz. Janie plopped down on top of them, Jazz rolling out of the way just in time. Sarah grabbed Janie and kissed and tickled her. "Now off, you two." Janie scampered to her room as

Jazz trudged out the door. They brightened her heart and gave her strength.

The study where the fight had taken place looked like a war zone. The table, figurines and Robert's blood were splattered across the white rug and polished oak floor. Bloodied footprints led to the liquor cabinet and back to the sofa, then out the door, down the hall and into the garage. Where he was now was a mystery. She grabbed a mop and cleaned the blood from the floor up to the door of the study then closed it. It wasn't perfect but good enough.

The rest of the morning was busy, getting the girls out the door. She made them a breakfast for the bus so they wouldn't go into the kitchen. Sarah checked the garage. Robert hadn't returned. She heard the girls coming down the stairs, threw their breakfast and drinks into paper bags and ran to the base of the stairs.

"Hustle up, girls. We're running late. I made breakfast for the bus." She guided them out the front door. Janie sat in the grass. Jazz stood near Sarah. Ten minutes. Fifteen.

"Why'd we have to come out so early?" Jazz asked.

On cue, the bus drove around the corner. "There it is," Sarah blurted out.

"Mom, what's wrong? You're all strung out or something." Jazz was perceptive. Janie was lost in her own world.

"I'm OK. Still a little jumpy from the fight with your father last night."

"Where is he, anyway?" The bus creaked to a stop.

"On you go. I'll pick you up after school. We'll talk then." Sarah watched as the standard yellow school bus jerked forward as it always did and then grumbled off between the tall trees that lined their idyllic neighborhood street. Her two perfect daughters were the center of her universe. She noticed Janie was already giggling with her friends, and Jazz was likely gossiping with hers, both in opposite parts of the bus. The older kids owned the back of the bus, while the younger ones were forced to sit near the front. Each year the children moved closer to the coveted back seats.

She mused at how much school buses and school bus etiquette had remained the same since she was a child while the rest of the world had advanced so much. *Kids,* she thought, *oh to be back in those carefree days.*

Normalcy. She brushed aside a strand of hair, blown by the gentle wind of this beautiful May day. She took a moment to gaze at the glorious deep blue sky before heading back to her front door.

The beauty of the moment faded as she faced the house. She stopped in her tracks and stared at it with deep hatred. It was a big, two-story colonial. Everything he'd wanted. Now they owed more on the mortgage than the house was worth, and with Robert unemployed, they were going to lose it. No way to pay for it on her prosecutor's salary.

His sisters and brothers, whom she called her own, loved her. She was pretty sure. Sarah knew they loved the girls. Maybe they'd help her once free of Robert. *Maybe.*

The house was gone. It was only a matter of time. *That's probably the best thing that can happen to us right now!* Although she was rationalizing, no one could stop the huge change that was coming. She could feel it in her soul. They'd be free, and soon. *Today it ends!*

The garage door opened. Robert's Mercedes swerved into the drive then pulled into the garage. *Screech. He ran the car along the side of the garage opening.*

"Damn," she mumbled. She sprinted through the front door into the foyer, grabbed her computer case, phone and purse, and then raced back out along the front walk and into the garage, ducking under the closing door. It stopped and began to reopen. She started the car remotely. Robert was at the kitchen doorway, screaming for her. When the door changed directions, he turned. "SARAAHHH! You bitch!" Robert stumbled down the steps from the kitchen door. Screaming and bleeding, he put his right hand on the hood of his car for support. The car looked terrible, smashed in the front and back. Steam spewed from the engine. He had a bottle in his left hand.

"You fucking whore, bitch. I'm going to sue you and call the police and have you arrested."

"Shut the fuck up! We're done. Everything, and I mean *everything*, changes today, you fucking bastard. You try to hit me again, and I'll hurt you more than I did last night." She pointed to the flint knife embedded in the garage door above his car. That stopped him, just long enough.

She fell into the front seat of her BMW SAV, popped the car into reverse and backed out. Just as she cleared the rising door, he slammed his fist on the front of the car. She hit the gas, yanking the car out from under him. Her tires squealed as she shifted from reverse to drive and accelerated down the same peaceful, tree-lined street the yellow bus had taken moments before.

She saw him stumble into the street in her rearview mirror, still screaming and bleeding. *I hope he dies right there!* She lowered her window, stuck her arm out, finger raised, and screamed, "Asshole!" though she realized he could no longer hear her.

THIRTEEN

Her insides boiled as she battled the traffic. She screamed at a driver who cut her off, another who took too long to exit and another who wasn't doing anything except not tailgating the car in front of it. The radio talk-show hosts blathered on about nothing. She pressed several buttons and then jammed her finger on the power button, silencing the nonsense.

The parking garage was nearly full, as it was most days when she arrived. Unlike her peers, she arrived later than she should, especially if climbing the ladder was on her priority list. It'd never been. Even her first year at Martin, Schoenberg, van Peebles, where the firm's associates were expected to work all hours of the day, night and weekends, Sarah put in maybe 50 hours a week, no weekends and did a lot of pro bono work for indigent clients. She was caring for Jazz, and if she got fired, she got fired. She hadn't.

She found a nice wide spot three spaces from the end of a row on the top floor of the garage and parked her overpriced, Robert's "got-to-have-it," piece-of-crap Beemer she could no longer afford. She was going to sell it and get an inexpensive used hybrid that was good for the environment but had all-wheel drive. The only reason she hadn't already was that Robert would go ballistic. *Class-chasing, juvenile delinquent bastard.*

She adjusted the rearview mirror to check her makeup. She thought for a moment about life after Robert. She'd be single for the first time in over a decade. Sarah stared into the mirror. Despite the lines under her eyes, she was attractive enough. She reasoned, 36 is not old. I'm going to change my look, back to the way I like it. Her hair was shoulder length, in a simple style that was easy to get ready in the mornings. She'd added highlights because he liked them. She imagined her long, flowing black hair, which she loved even if it got tangled easily.

Her green eyes reflected a depth of sadness and lost hope. Her make-up was more complex than she liked. She was going back to a simpler, more natural look. She wore an appropriate grey jacket and skirt with a conservative white blouse. The standard businesswoman's high-heeled pumps to provide stature against the taller men were designer, though she could not have cared less. She wore gold earrings and a diamond pendant necklace he'd given her, a memory bracelet and her wedding rings, which she'd grown to disdain. She struggled to get the rings off and then threw them on the floor of the passenger side. She watched them bounce around like dice and noted where they landed. She looked back into the mirror at her jewelry. "I'm selling all of this crap." The necklace and earrings found their way onto the floor near her rings.

She paused before she got out. She'd once been a rebel with that long crazy hair, T-shirts, no bra and ripped blue jeans fighting to save the natural world she loved. She wanted to be one of those attorneys who saves the world. Growing up, she was trained to hate ostentatious, wasteful wealth, and now she lived in one of those neighborhoods, in one of those houses, with those types of neighbors and family. *Maybe Robert hadn't saved her after all.*

Sarah rested her head on the steering wheel, hands still clenching it, closed her eyes and wished that all these material trappings were gone and that she could just live with her girls in the wilds of nature.

FOURTEEN

The office was on the fifth floor of an old run-down government building. As the elevator beeped, sounding her arrival, she took a deep breath. Out of habit, she changed to her office politic demeanor, ready to nod to the staff and accord her superiors appropriate deference. She stopped in her tracks. *This is bullshit!* She took a moment and changed her attitude.

"Hello, Mrs. Robinson." The voice of the group's assistant was cheerful as usual.

"Marvin, I wish you'd call me Sarah, for crying out loud. Mrs. Robinson is my husband's mother, and she's old." He called her Mrs. Robinson multiple times every day and would again later this day, she was sure, and every time she'd correct him. She was changing her name back to James. *Put that on the list.*

"Yes, ma'am."

Marvin was a mouse with mousy eyes, mousy hair and a tiny mousy body. *Boy, am I in a crappy mood.* She wanted to apologize to Marvin for how she thought of him. "Marvin, it's OK. Whatever makes you happy. Have a great day, OK?"

Marvin stared at her. No response. So, she winked and headed past him, around a corner and into her office. She plopped into her simple, well-supported "secretary's" chair and sat there for a minute. The diplomas and honors hanging on her wall stared back, mocking her. Juris Doctor with High Honors from prestigious George Washington University in D.C. Order of the Coif, beside her admittances to the Maryland, Virginia, D.C. and New York Bars. Why she'd bothered with New York was still annoying, but she remembered Robert being adamant at the time. It was important to Robert because "all the great attorneys practiced in New York." There they all were, right there on the wall, shouting, "I am very important! You should listen to me!" Few did.

She prosecuted petty criminals. Most were caught up in a world where hope was a four-letter word, dope was their replacement, and life was built on a different foundation. Her boss chastised her for not putting more of these repeat offenders behind bars, at least for a while, to "teach them a lesson." She knew it was the law, but she also knew what was right. For some, the little misdemeanors could mean a parole violation, many more years in prison, lost jobs and families, and children without a mother or father or both.

Sarah kept her job by taking care of these small matters, the cases no one else wanted, with no complaints. More important, she was clearing more cases each week, no matter how it happened, than any other assistant prosecutor at her level. She was not likely to move up. She didn't care. She helped people, spoke with the accused, got them help with psychological or addiction issues, securing employment, improving their credit, reconnecting with families, cleaning up messes and otherwise finding a way to help them move forward with their lives. Those were her plea bargains, always approved by the judge. For those few who couldn't commit to a different life, she secured a conviction. Overall, her system worked, and she felt good about it.

The morning was routine. No court appearances. She sorted through files and met with a couple of defendants and their court-appointed attorneys. She listened to their sob stories and worked out some rehabilitative pleas. She looked through the evidence in one of her files, which was, as always, fairly scant, though plenty for a conviction. She wrote a few memos to the court and looked at her phone: 11:45 A.M. She had things to do. She'd already put in for the rest of the week and the next one off. She was out of the office in minutes and headed back to the house.

Hopefully Robert wasn't home. She guessed that if he was, he was passed out in his study. She checked her phone. It was just past noon. The girls got out at 3:00.

She called a cleaning company. She'd helped the owner with a criminal charge and to start his business. She smiled into the phone as she said, "Charlie, it's for me, personally, and it's an emergency."

"For you, Sarah, anything. We'll be there in under an hour."

"Thanks, Charlie. I'll remember this."

She called another former defendant, then an accused thief, now a locksmith. "Hardcore Lock. Can I help you?" The voice was gruff, and she recognized it immediately.

"Bobby? Sarah. I need your services, ol' buddy. Personal matter. It's urgent. What's your day look like?"

"We'll be there no later than 2:00. Whatever you need."

"Thanks, Bobby. See you then." Bobby was very good, and thanks to her, he was still on the straight and narrow.

She stopped at the bank. The lobby was empty. At the counter, she spoke to a nice young man and asked for the balances on all their accounts. She closed them all. She took $3,000 in cash and the balance in a bank cashier's check—a total of just over $12,000. She drove to a different bank and deposited the check into a new account in her name only.

As she finished the short drive to their house, she called all three of their credit card companies and canceled the cards immediately. She wanted all transactions from that moment forward blocked. She promised to get them paid and scribbled down the current balances of all three. They totaled over $20,000. Nothing from today, which surprised her. She secured two new cards, also in her name only.

FIFTEEN

When she arrived at their house, the cleaning company and a police car were parked in front of the house. She opened the garage door and pulled into her spot. Robert's car was gone. *Thank heavens.*

Two policewomen and the cleaning crew got out of their respective vehicles and walked toward her. The police led the way. She met them at the top of the driveway.

"Ma'am, I'm Officer Smith and this is Officer Mars. Do you have a minute?"

"Absolutely."

"We're here about the incident this morning."

"Right. How can I help? Whatever you need."

"Can you tell us what happened?"

"Sure, well, while we're out here, you can see the blood trail leading out into the street, then back this way. He chased my car. When we get there, you'll see the blood on the hood of my car where he pounded his fist as I was trying to escape." She turned her attention to the cleaning crew. "Guys, thanks for coming. You may as well follow. As soon as the police say it's OK, you'll need to clean the blood off everything."

"Ma'am, here's an empty bottle in the grass." One of the cleaning people was pointing at the ground.

"It's likely his," Sarah said.

Officer Mars took a couple of pictures, picked it up and bagged it.

Officer Mars took pictures of everything outside. The cleaning crew took their own pictures. Officer Smith was also taking notes and walking around.

Sarah went through the entire story, the fact that he was drunk and had been driving drunk. She took them in through the front door, showed them the unpaid bills and the notice of foreclosure. She explained that he'd hit her again, and for the first time, she'd hit him back and he'd landed on the table. The bruise on her face was covered with makeup. She wiped some off and could see the women cringe at the colors. She told them about her fitful night of sleep, how he'd returned home drunk and had chased her with the bourbon bottle in his hand. There was another bottle on the couch in his study. They took pictures, picked up the bottle and some bloody glass and bagged them as evidence.

They took pictures of the bloody footprints from the table to the liquor cabinet and back to the couch. There were new bloody footprints in the kitchen and foyer. She explained that she'd mopped up the bloody prints from the night before when he'd left so that the girls wouldn't see them. These were from this morning. She showed them the bloody mop. It was easy for them to figure out exactly where he'd walked and even the bottles he'd touched as he'd chosen the next one.

They went over the relatively calm morning and getting the girls off to school. Then she reenacted how he'd chased her outside to her car, where she'd narrowly escaped his wrath.

Officer Mars dictated to Officer Smith, who wrote everything down: "Based on his footprints, he got a bottle of bourbon last night after the altercation. At some point he cut his feet and returned to the couch. That bottle is empty and bagged in bag 1." She marked the bag. "He left the house sometime this morning. We have a police report that he was found sleeping in Rosemary Park this morning. They let him drive home for some reason.

"At that time, he came back, chased Mrs. Robinson to her car. As she left the scene, he pounded his fist on the car then followed her out onto the street. He finished another bottle of bourbon, or at least whatever was left in it. That bottle was found on the front lawn and is bagged in bag 2." She marked that bag.

"He returned to the house and to his study. Still barefoot, he cut his feet again but was probably feeling no pain. He bled a great deal."

Sarah interjected, "His bottle of 18-year-old Macallan Scotch is gone. One hundred sixty bucks a bottle. He'd been saving that for a special occasion. I guess this was that occasion."

Officer Smith looked up and then continued, "He returned to the study, secured the bottle of expensive scotch found at the scene of the accident, walked back into the garage, got into his Mercedes and left."

They'd followed his footprints back out the kitchen door.

"Accident? Where'd he go?" Sarah asked.

"Another officer found him, ma'am. He ran the car into Pappa's. Do you know the place?"

"Of course. I've had to scrape him off that bar floor many times and drive him home, only to get yelled at and usually beaten. Recently, he'd be so drunk I could escape into our bathroom until he left our room for more liquor and passed out on that couch in the study. Last night was the last straw, and I finally hit him back." She still couldn't really believe she'd hit him back and that hard. It frightened her, the rage that he'd generated inside her last night and the power that it released into his face.

"Well, we don't know when he got there. Pappa's was closed, of course. It doesn't open until 11:00. The Macallan was broken on the sidewalk. He was passed out and still bleeding, half outside his car door. The officer called for an ambulance. The paramedics put him on an IV right away. They took him to St. Francis Hospital. Do you know where that is?"

"Sure."

"He was alive when the paramedics took him, but beyond that, we don't know much about his condition."

"That's fine. Thank you. Do you need anything else?"

They looked at each other. Checked their notes. Officer Mars turned to Sarah. "No, ma'am, that's all. The prosecutor may want to talk to you, but we're done here. Thank you for your time. Sorry for disturbing you."

"No problem, Officers. Happy to help. Can I have the crew clean all of this up? Is that OK? Do you have all the pictures you need? My daughters get out of school in a little while, and I would hate for them to see all of this blood in their home."

"We understand." The two officers looked at each other. "No, go ahead. We don't need anything else. We have your phone number if we need to call. Get this cleaned up."

The leader of the crew was standing right there. He turned to his team. "Alright boys and girls, let's get this place back to new." He barked out commands, then the six workers jogged to the truck and gathered their gear to start cleaning.

Sarah turned to the leader of the crew. "Please, take that couch, all the glass and broken stuff and anything else in the study that has blood on it and get rid of it. Take all the liquor in there with you as well, except one bottle. I'll get that."

"On it, ma'am."

Bobby, the locksmith, arrived as the police were pulling away. She felt like he'd been waiting nearby for them to leave.

"I want every lock changed and keyed alike." He nodded. "And I want that key when you're done. Got it? How long will this take?"

"About a half hour, maybe 45 minutes."

"Great. Get on it. Thanks, Bobby. I appreciate this."

She walked into the house, emotionally exhausted. She went into the study and got the bottle of 50-year scotch in the brown leather box that Herb had given him at their wedding. It was to be saved for their 50th anniversary. That wasn't going to happen. She planned to sell it. She carried it into the living room and fell into one of the big armchairs flanking the fireplace. She breathed deep and let it out slowly then said aloud, "This is really happening."

"What? Ma'am?" a worker cleaning the foyer asked.

"Oh, sorry. Nothing." The interruption helped her to refocus.

The next call was to a realtor Mallory had recommended to her. Her name was Margaret.

"Mrs. Robinson—"

"Sarah, please. I'm not going to be Mrs. Robinson much longer."

"Sarah, then. Sorry. What can I do for you?"

Sarah briefly explained the situation and her wish to sell the house quickly. "We'll get your house on the market as soon as possible," Margaret said, also agreeing to meet her first thing the next morning. They discussed the loans, and Sarah told her she'd go over that with the bank. "We'll do it in the morning," Margaret assured her. "Don't worry about it tonight. We'll handle all that in the morning."

"Thanks, Margaret. See you then."

She found the foreclosure notice and called the name at the bottom, Roger Benton. She explained the situation to him, and he went over their options. She told him about Margaret.

"Well, the bank would prefer the house be sold by the realtor. So long as the sale is a legitimate arm's length sale for an appropriate price, the bank will usually forgo the difference," Roger promised. "Based on our estimate, Mrs. Robinson, you're only underwater on the house by maybe $10,000—$20,000 max. The house might cover. The market's rebounded, and that difference is not as great as it was a few years back." His voice drifted. He seemed to be doing some math. "You might just cover."

"Thank you, Roger. I'll call you in the morning with my realtor."

"Great. We'll go through it then. I'll get everything together on our end. Have a great evening, Mrs. Robinson, under the circumstances."

Next, the divorce. She called Shawny Jameson, a divorce attorney who only represented women. "Sarah, how the heck are you? I'm sure since you're calling, you're finally kicking that good-for-nothing husband of yours to the curb."

"How is everyone so ahead of me on this?"

"Girlfriend, Robert's a dick. Everyone knows it. This'll be the easiest case I've ever handled. He might be in jail when I'm done with him, but for goddamn sure, he's gonna be broke!"

"Let's not get too far ahead, Shawny. Do you have time to meet in the morning?"

"Suuure. How's 10:30? Here at the office?"

"I'll see you then. Thanks, Shawny."

"Girl, I've been looking forward to this case for a long time. Can't wait to see you." Shawny also did criminal defense work for women, so they'd worked together on a few cases. Being a defender of women, Shawny had noticed Sarah's bruises and had never accepted Sarah's lies. Shawny was naturally gregarious and always made Sarah smile. She was a tall, light-skinned African American woman with long curly hair and a fierce pro-woman attitude. Something had happened to her, or her family, Sarah thought. No doubt she was the right attorney for this case. Robert was in for the battle of his life.

Last call, the hospital. "Hello, St. Francis. How can I direct your call?"

"Hi, I'm Mrs. Sarah Robinson. My husband Robert is there somewhere. Can you tell me anything?"

"Mrs. Robinson, just a moment." There was a pause. "Here he is. Ma'am, your husband Robert came into the ED this morning by paramedic. He was in very bad shape. He's still in surgery, according to the notes. Other than that, I have no news on his condition that I can release over the phone, and right now, no one to transfer you to. You can come in, Mrs. Robinson. We can see if we can connect you to someone when you're here."

It amazed her how little she cared after all these years. She wasn't going to the hospital, but she saw no need to tell the nice woman that. She thanked her and hung up.

It was a race against time. He'd get out. *Then what?* Sarah breathed deeply.

SIXTEEN

As she waited outside the school for Jazz and Janie, she contemplated how she was going to explain all of this to them. A lot had happened in the last 24 hours, and everything would change in the next few weeks. Next week was the end of the semester and their last one at this school they loved so much. They'd switch to public school next semester for the first time. *It'll be a shock for them.* More rigid, more distractions, less demanding. She was not even sure what district they'd be in by then.

After the bell rang, children began to pour out of the huge front doors of the old stone school. Jackson Rose Montessori was the oldest of its kind in the D.C. area. She stepped out of the car and waved to Jazz as she sauntered down the big stairs with some girlfriends. Janie skipped across the broad concrete apron that led to the school.

"Hi, Mommy. How fun. I love it when you pick us up." And she jumped into Sarah's arms.

"I love to pick you guys up." She gave Janie a big loud smooch on her cheek. Janie giggled, and Sarah put her down.

Jazz smiled as she ambled toward the car. She had to maintain her cool and couldn't look too excited to see her mother. However, Jazz couldn't hold it in as the distance shortened. A broad smile graced her pretty face. She was looking more and more like a woman. She ran the last several steps into Sarah's arms and gave her a huge hug.

"I've been so worried all day, Mom. How are you? What's going on?"

"Me too, honey. I'm fine. That last question is going to take a while to answer. Let's go home, and we'll go through everything. Is that OK?"

The girls nodded.

As they settled into the SAV, Sarah asked, "So, how was school?"

Jazz said "fine" like always. That'd be about all she'd get out of her oldest.

Janie, as always, had lots to say. She launched into detail about what they did in each subject and who said what about whom and who pushed whom on the playground and on and on. Janie filled the entire trip home with one-sided dialog. Sarah and Jazz were grateful. Silent pauses would be quite uncomfortable with all the unspoken issues swirling around them.

All the contractors were gone when they returned. There was no blood on the driveway or garage floor. In fact, the garage floor looked cleaner than it had in years. The knife she'd made had been removed from the garage door and was sitting on her workbench. Her knife was still perfect. It hadn't broken. There was something comforting, reaffirming in that.

"Is that the knife you made last night?" Jazz picked it up. "Wow, Mom. This is great. Sharp, well balanced. Nice work, old lady."

"Hey, how about grand master!" They all laughed. Jazz handed the knife to Janie, who was not the stonecutter either of them were so, to her, it was just a nice knife.

"I saw your points," Sarah said as she picked one up. "These are exquisite. These arrow points are ridiculous. They're so tiny. How long did it take to make each one?"

"About an hour. I broke a couple."

"I bet. I'm not sure I could make something this tiny. We're going to have to make another bow and some arrow shafts this weekend and try these out." She remembered that the existing bow and arrows, tipped with sharp chips as was most common rather than perfect points, and the long knife were still in her room. Jazz noticed the long knife was missing and looked at Sarah. Sarah gave her eldest a knowing look, and Jazz seemed to understand that her mother had used it to protect herself. As Jazz nodded, Sarah realized that had been its intended purpose. She and Jazz always seemed to have an innate connection that she didn't share with Janie, or anyone else.

"We're going camping?" Janie screamed, breaking in.

"You bet. I'll figure out a great place tomorrow, and we'll be off to the wilds of nature right after school. We're going to take Monday off so we can stay a little longer."

The two girls were thrilled. They loved camping and exploring the depths of nature while making things with their mother. It'd been a while since they'd gone.

"OK. Let's go inside. We have to talk."

No blood anywhere. The door to the study was closed, but she was sure it was clean as well. It was often closed. The study was Robert's place. Even she didn't know what he kept in there. She'd find out later.

"Girls, go put your books away and change out of your uniforms. I have to make a phone call."

The two scampered off up the stairs. She called St. Francis again. This time she was transferred.

"Hello, ICU, can I help you?"

"Yes, this is Sarah Robinson. You have my husband, Robert Robinson, there. Can you tell me about his condition?"

"Just a moment as I pull up his file. Yes, he was admitted through ED at 8:48 this morning with a severe laceration on his left upper arm, bleeding from both feet, dramatic blood loss and a toxic blood alcohol level. He was unresponsive and on a standard IV. He was given a blood transfusion immediately along with high-glucose IV and broad-spectrum antibiotics. He entered OR to close several lacerations. The doctors have also set a broken right clavicle and severely dislocated right shoulder. The blood alcohol levels made the surgery quite risky. He went into the OR at 11:42 and was transferred here at 14:58—that's 2:58 P.M. He's been sedated since and given painkillers, blood, IV nutrients and antibiotics. The doctor should check on him again in the next hour or so."

"Can we see him?"

"Ma'am, of course, but he's out cold, completely unresponsive. Would you want to see him that way? He'll be kept in a coma at least through the night. His blood alcohol levels are at very toxic levels. They'll keep him in that state until his vitals normalize and the wounds appear to be healing. His blood is so thinned out, the surgery sites are oozing. Getting his blood to a level where any healing can take place will likely take a while." She paused. "He should make it, but it's a good thing the officers found him when they did. Another 30 minutes and he likely would've died right there on the sidewalk."

A brief note of disappointment hit her when the nurse told her that he would have died if they'd found him later. It would've made things a lot simpler. "OK. Thank you. I appreciate the update." Her tone was dispassionate. She had no feelings for him whatsoever.

SEVENTEEN

The girls bounded down the stairs and joined her in the kitchen. *It's a lot to cover. May as well start it out on a good note.*

"Are you guys hungry? Want a snack or something?"

Sarah prepared some cocoa, and the girls got out crackers, peanut butter and cheese. Janie asked if they could have cookies, and Sarah relented, "just this once."

The three sat around the kitchen table, the girls with cocoa and Sarah with reheated coffee left over from the morning, eating a buffet of fruit, crackers, cheese, spreads and cookies. It was a pleasant way to start this family meeting, even if it would spoil their dinner.

"Alright, ladies, let's talk about last night. I don't know if you know this, but your father hits me from time to time."

Janie blurted out, "We know. He can be mean."

"Has he ever tried to hit either of you?"

They looked at each other. Jazz spoke, "Yes. Sometimes. Only when you're not home and he's been drinking too much in his study, and we peak our heads in and disturb him."

"We're pretty quick though, and Daddy usually can't catch us," Janie said.

"We don't bother him anymore, so he hasn't tried to hit us in like a month."

"When he's drunk, Daddy's mean."

"I had no idea. I should've realized that if he'd hit me, if he's drunk enough, he'd hit you girls as well. Why didn't you tell me?"

"Why didn't you tell us he was hitting you?" Jazz countered.

"I think we were all sorta afraid of him," Janie added.

"Janie, I think you're right, and that's going to stop right now. Actually, I finally stopped it last night. He hit me, and I reared back and punched him so hard I knocked him onto the coffee table. I couldn't believe I finally stood up for myself."

"Yay, Mom!"

"Thank you, Jazz. Yeah, yay me," she said without much enthusiasm. "Alright, here's the rest of the story." She told them about the previous evening's events. "So, your father, bottle of booze in hand, drove drunk to Pappa's Tavern, over the curb and into the side of the building. Then he apparently fell out of the car and nearly bled to death. Some nice police officers found him. He's in a coma in the intensive care unit at the hospital."

"What's a coma?"

"Good question, Janie. The type of coma your father is in was brought on by the doctors putting your father to sleep on purpose so that their medicine can work to make him better. Alcohol is a poison, and your Dad drank way too much. Enough to kill him. He'll be out in the coma at least all night. We might be able to see him tomorrow after school, if you want, before we head out of town for our adventure. We can decide then."

The girls looked at each other for a few seconds.

"You don't have to decide now."

Jazz stared first at the counter then glanced at Janie before staring directly into Sarah's eyes. "Mom, I don't think I want to see him, even if he's awake in time."

"Jazz, I understand, but take a moment to think about it."

"Mom, I'm not going." Jazz's voice turned stern, her eyes angry.

"Me neither," Janie followed.

Sarah looked at Janie and then back at Jazz, still steadfast in her gaze. "Alright, that's decided."

After a pause, the tension settled in the room. Sarah considered exploring the subject but decided to leave that for the weekend. She took a deep breath. "So, Mom and Dad are going to get a divorce. I can't live like this anymore, and the two of you shouldn't have to live like this. Your father doesn't know it yet, but tomorrow morning, I'm going to see a woman who helps people with divorces, and she'll help me start the process. Do you understand why this has to happen?"

She assumed they'd cry, but they didn't. Janie teared up a little, but Jazz said in a straightforward manner, "Mom, it's about time. Dad's a jerk, and we need to get as far away from him as we can as fast as we can."

Sarah was not prepared for the venom Jazz had in her heart for her father. There had to be something more that Sarah didn't know about.

Janie nodded. "Mommy, we love you. I don't think we love Daddy anymore. Can Grandma and Grandpa come with us?"

She hugged them close. They were all in, but there was the rub—the rest of the family.

"They'll always love you, sweetie." Janie smiled and that seemed enough for her. Sarah was not sure what would actually happen with those relationships. "I'll get the divorce started as soon as possible. I promise. I'm so sorry it took me so long. I had no idea how miserable you two were around your father."

Jazz asked, "Mom, what does the divorce mean for us? We're not going to have to stay with Dad like on weekends and stuff like other kids. There's no way I'm doing that. *No way.*"

"Me neither."

Sarah took a deep breath, calming herself as much as possible. "It means that pretty much everything will change. We're going to have to sell this house. I'm meeting with a realtor in the morning. We'll find a place. Your Aunt Mallory told me they'd take us in for a while if we need her to, but that would be temporary. We'll find a place of our own. It won't be as big as this. It'll be a lot smaller, but it'll be safe, and your father won't be able to get to us anymore. The first thing I'll talk to the divorce attorney about is making sure that you two are kept safe. Do you understand that? You are my first priority. I'll do whatever it takes to make sure you're safe from your father from now on." She paused and took a breath. "How do you feel about that?"

They looked at each other again. "This house is too big anyway," Janie said.

Jazz smiled with relief at her little sister and then at Sarah. "Thanks, Mom. We're in. Whatever it takes. I agree with Janie. There's nothing in this house or anything else right now that would stop me from getting away from Dad."

They were taking it well so far, better than expected. In fact, they seemed way ahead of her. Sarah realized that this was a lot, and she had a long time to deal with changing schools, so she decided to save that topic for later. "Girls, we're going to be fine. Just fine. We'll go camping on weekends and head out West later this summer and do all the things we love to do."

Janie beamed, and Jazz gave her an uncertain smile.

"Alright, if we're going camping for a long weekend, you two have some packing to do and your homework." It was after four o'clock. She would deal with dinner later. "I'll clean this up. You two scurry on up-stairs and get started."

"Yes, ma'am!" Janie said as she leaped from her chair and flew up the stairs to her room.

Jazz rose slowly, gave her mother a kiss and said, "It's going to be alright, Mom. This is the right thing to do. We both have seen this coming for a while. Daddy's had a hard time, and he's taken it out on the three of us. I hope he can get better, but he's going to have to do it on his own first. Then we can see about whether we can let him back into our lives. I don't want to see him tomorrow. I know you don't. If we don't mention it, but focus on the adventure, Janie won't miss it either. It'll be OK." Jazz turned and strolled nonchalantly out of the room and up the stairs.

Sarah took a deep breath, fell back against the chair and exhaled long and slow. *That went better than expected. Maybe we should have had this conversation a long time ago?*

EIGHTEEN

She'd slept like a rock. When the alarm burst her dreamy bubble, she slapped at it, trying to turn it off. Within seconds, though, Janie burst through the door and jumped on her bed. Jazz trudged in smiling, which was new.

"We're going camping, we're going camping." Janie jumped up and down on the bed. Jazz crawled in beside Sarah and into her arms. Janie vaulted onto Sarah with a thud.

"Ugh. Girlfriend, you are getting big. That almost knocked the wind out of me." She hugged them both. "Girls, today is the first day of our new life together. Just the three of us. I'm going to pick you up from school, and we'll be off to the wilderness somewhere, which I'll figure out between now and then. Are you both all packed?"

"Of course, Mommy. We totally got it down." Janie stood back up and bounced on the bed.

"We used our checklists. We have everything." Jazz was so much more reserved than Janie.

"Can I have that checklist? I have no idea where mine is. I'm packed sort of, but a checklist would be great."

"I'll get mine." Janie launched herself off the bed, sprinted out of the room and returned in a flash with a piece of notebook paper fluttering in her little hand. Janie used the bottom of the bed as a trampoline, and Sarah rolled just in time to avoid being smashed again.

She tickled her youngest, who squirmed until she fell off the far side of the bed. She peaked over the edge. "Is it safe up there, Jazz?"

Jazz nodded, smiling from ear to ear. Everything was brighter this morning. Certainly when compared to yesterday, but really when compared with every morning for years. A huge weight was off their shoulders. The big threat downstairs was absent and soon would be gone permanently—*one way or the other,* she promised herself. She hugged her girls close and felt like she would never let them go.

"Alright, you two scamps, who I love more than anything in the entire world, you have to go to school. Off with you. Get yourselves together while I get ready." Janie took off like a superhero. Jazz kissed Sarah again then walked off with a slight bounce in her step. Jazz was happy, but Sarah was more than a little worried about her. She didn't know the whole story between Jazz and Robert, but she'd find out over the weekend.

Sarah got up but changed her entire routine. She usually went to work and ran or worked out at the gym in her building over lunch. Today, she'd run in the bright sunshine of this beautiful morning after the girls were off to school. She pulled a comb hastily through her hair, which was a mess and reminded her of her college days. She slipped on a sports bra, T-shirt, shorts, socks and running shoes. She walked into the bathroom. *No makeup today.* She smiled into the mirror. She sighed as she saw the ugly colors of the bruise on her cheek. *Well, just enough so I don't frighten people.* After pulling her hair back into a ponytail, she was ready for the morning.

She beat the girls downstairs. No quickie meal this morning. She made them scrambled eggs, bacon and toast, which were ready when they rumbled down the stairs.

"I'm impressed. I like this new Mom." Jazz slipped into her chair, and Janie climbed into hers. Sarah poured orange juice for all of them and brought her second cup of coffee over from the counter. She sat, held one of each of their hands, and Jazz reached across the table to hold Janie's. "I'm so thankful every day for my two wonderful girls. I'm so happy I was finally able to stand up for myself, for all of us, and start us on a new path together. It'll be different—a lot different—but we'll make it together. It'll be our journey."

She let go of their hands, and they both smiled. It wasn't really a prayer, mostly because she had no sense of who to pray to, but it was spiritual. It felt good.

NINETEEN

The meeting with Margaret, the realtor, and conference call with Roger at the mortgage bank had gone as well as it could have. They at least had a clear understanding as to what the bank would require and allow. Margaret glided through the house, making comments on knickknacks and personal items that needed to be removed. She opened the door to the study. The couch and any evidence of the fight were gone. No table, figurines, glass, liquor bottles other than the leather case, and no trace of blood. *They did a nice job.* The two of them moved a few pieces of furniture from the living room into the study. "Fill in this empty space while decluttering that other room," Margaret said in a businesslike tone. Margaret gave her some additional instructions, which Sarah wrote down. Margaret continued to move and remove things as Sarah found a few boxes in the basement and garage. When done, Margaret took pictures of each room from every conceivable angle.

"We'll have a videographer come in to create a virtual tour of the house we can put up on over 40 websites. This house will sell in no time."

They listed it for enough so that if she got her asking price, it would cover the bank debt, commissions and closing costs. She and Robert would get nothing, but at least they wouldn't owe anything.

The next meeting was with Shawny, the divorce attorney. They discussed the case in some detail, and Sarah filled her in on what she'd done so far and on what she knew of Robert's current condition. Sarah called the hospital to check on Robert. He was still in bad shape and still in a coma.

Shawny told her she'd call the police and get copies of all the reports relating in any way to Robert over the years. They scheduled another meeting for the following Wednesday to go over the complaint to get the process started. "I'm assuming Robert will likely be somewhat cognitive by then. We need him awake to serve him papers."

When Sarah returned to the house she no longer considered home, she entered the study and sat at Robert's desk. She began to sort through the papers and organize them into stacks on the floor behind her: bills that needed to be paid, bank statements and a few other odds and ends. She found nothing unexpected among them.

She opened his drawers and searched through them. Mostly junk. She began to throw away or organize the items on the floor behind her. The lower left drawer, a deep file drawer, was full of empty liquor bottles. After she filled the waste basket with them, she carried it outside to dump in the recycling bin. She needed a moment out of that room. The cloud of past encounters with Robert was suffocating.

The similar-sized drawer on the other side was filled with files. She sorted through them: old legal files. She took each one out and flipped through its contents. Nothing exciting. She put those in a Bankers Box and moved them to the garage for a future storage unit with Robert's other belongings.

In the top left drawer, carefully stored away, were all the cards and letters she'd ever sent him. Little gifts, notes and trinkets. He'd saved everything. He even had the file for the sale of her family home in Cleveland and the resolution of her parents' estate. He'd kept her law school graduation tassel, wrapped around his. He had his typed wedding vows along with hers, carefully handwritten, along with their wedding invitation. It was all there. Everything that documented their life together, he'd saved it all. She realized that she hadn't kept anything.

She teared up as she removed each item. She paused over each memento and remembered what it'd meant to them. She worked her way through the years. As time passed, there were fewer and fewer items, and they contained increasingly bland sentiments. Over the last seven years, there were only birthday, Christmas and anniversary cards that she'd simply signed. On most, she hadn't even written "Love, Sarah," just "Sarah." She found a large manila envelope and slid the contents of the drawer into it, retaining only the file pertaining to her parents' home and estate. She wasn't sure what she needed it for, but it was hers, not his. She set it on the floor with the other items she needed to deal with later, stood and walked out to the garage. She placed the envelope with their entire married life inside into the Bankers Box to go to the storage unit. She closed the lid, took a deep breath. *That's that.*

As instructed by Margaret, she straightened up the books, packing many of them in boxes. She removed the old bottle of scotch and put it in the garage for the auction.

The garage was half full of small pieces of furniture and strewn with knickknacks the auctioneers would sell. She perused the contents and felt no attachment to any of it. It was all Robert's decorative junk.

The big desk was clean, the bookshelf neat and tidy, the liquor cabinet empty. It looked like an office. It would show well this way. The room looked bigger.

She sat at his desk and turned on his computer. She knew his password. He never changed it. Sarah searched through his files. Most everything was innocuous.

She searched his internet favorites, and there she found it. Anderson Financial. Maybe these were accounts that she didn't know about. It was password protected, of course. She searched the papers on the floor and found several scraps. Two had seemingly random letters and numbers. There were two sets on each—one she presumed to be the username and the other the password. *Why didn't I notice these before?* She shook her head.

She tried the first one. No luck.

She tried the second set. *Bingo.*

There were three accounts. One was marked "Janie's college account." It had $22,000 in it. The second was marked "Jazz's college account." It had $30,000 in it. The third was labeled "Gifts for Sarah." It had just under $5,000 in it. Nothing had been deposited into these accounts since January 2015. She remembered he'd proudly won a case back then and set these up with some of that money. He'd made sure to save money for the kids and for her.

She felt her own addiction to normalcy tug at her heart. "Could he be saved? Could they have a normal family?" it begged.

"NO!" she said out loud.

The last withdrawal was two days before her birthday almost two years ago. He'd given her a lovely set of emerald earrings. She remembered telling him that they didn't have the money for this sort of thing. He'd forced them on her, saying, "I've got this covered. I always have my family covered, honey." She'd accepted them with a smile and put them on, placing the ones she'd been wearing into the box. They were stunning. It was that sort of crap that had fed her addiction. She'd always hoped that maybe, just maybe, that guy would emerge again. He never did. Even that night had ended in disaster.

She took a screen shot of the accounts and wrote down the name of the account representative. While she was logged in, she changed the username and password and wrote them down. She didn't want him draining those accounts once he found out about the divorce. She crumpled his scrap of paper and tossed it into the trash can. She texted Shawny the account information so she could contact the account rep at Anderson to freeze those accounts. She replied almost immediately that she was "on it."

Now, what is this other set of numbers for?

She searched the computer and found nothing else. She took the scrap of paper upstairs and made a copy. She put the scrap into her purse and the copy into an envelope to take to Shawny. All that old stuff and the accounts for her and the girls might have softened her resolve. But his alcoholism and the violence against her girls were reason enough not to go back.

She tidied up the rest of the house for the weekend in case Margaret had any early nibbles. The cleaning crew had done a remarkable job. The house would be listed this afternoon.

She checked her phone: 1:30. Time to prepare for their weekend.

TWENTY

The car was packed as she arrived at Jackson Rose Montessori a few minutes before school let out. Robert was still in a coma. His blood alcohol levels were still high, nowhere near a "safe" level. His liver, pancreas and kidney functions were impaired, and they were not ready to bring him out of the coma. "Probably not for a few days," the nurse had said.

She climbed out of the car to a clear blue sky. She breathed deep and smelled the soft May air, the air she'd ignored for so long. Sweet honeysuckle growing all along the school's fence dominated her nostrils, and she loved it. The girls burst through the door seconds after the bell rang and sprinted together to Sarah. Jazz was happier than she'd been in months, maybe even years. Sarah hugged them both.

"Ready?"

"Yes," Janie squealed as she pushed her mother out of the way and jumped into the back seat. Jazz climbed into the front passenger seat with a big smile. Sarah jogged around the front of the car, also feeling like a kid again.

"Where are we going? Where are we going?" Janie pleaded.

Jazz turned in her seat and Sarah lowered the windows. "Smell the air, girls." They both breathed deep and smiled. "That's the smell of freedom."

"Actually, that's honeysuckle, Mommy. It's an invasive species that . . ."

"I know, sweetie, but it smells nice." She turned and winked at Janie, who giggled. "How does Mountain Lake Wilderness sound?" Sarah handed Jazz the information she'd printed out from the computer. "Or we could go to the Brush Mountain Wilderness. They're the same direction in the southwest Virginia Appalachian Mountains, and we've never been to either one. Jazz, read us what's on those sheets, and we'll figure out which sounds best. We can also call the Rangers and see how things are at each one to see what they think."

Sarah smiled as she declared, "Wagons ho!"

The two girls laughed and looked at her like she was crazy. "What?" she asked. Sarah relished in the release of their laughter.

As they drove, Jazz read aloud the information Sarah had given her. Jazz did additional research on Sarah's cell phone and made calls to the respective Ranger stations. They chose Mountain Lake. The gruff female Ranger told them of a pristine clearing that was hard to get to but next to a small pool formed in the course of a significant creek leading to Mountain Lake. It was not near any marked path, providing the seclusion they were seeking, and had a decent supply of flint nearby, the Ranger assured them.

They parked at the Ranger station, which had to have been built in the 1940s, and checked in with the same crusty older woman who'd taken Jazz's call. After Sarah paid the fees, secured clear instructions on how to get to the campsite and stated clearly that they were not to be disturbed, she returned outside and spread her arms wide to the girls.

"Done and done. Let's get outta here."

They unloaded their gear, laced up their hiking boots, helped one another with their backpacks and headed out on the two-and-a-half-mile hike. As accomplished hikers and outdoorswomen, they knew how to pack efficiently and manage their respective backpacks, sized precisely for each of them. About an hour and a couple of rests, explorations, beautiful views and wonders of nature later, they turned from the established trail into the Appalachian underbrush toward their destination. The hiking became more difficult. Sarah helped Janie up two steep ridges, traversed the creek that they would camp beside and fought through some dense underbrush using only handmade flint long knives until they arrived at the clearing the Ranger had promised.

The three stood in awe. "It's perfect," Jazz said in a subdued, almost reverent, tone.

The creek pooled into a good-sized pond that was several feet deep in the middle. The pond then cascaded down a three-foot waterfall into a smaller pool that led to rapids that ran off into the dense woods. Somewhere the stream entered Mountain Lake, which the website said was beautiful. They would take a day trip there.

They always "cheated" on the first night, bringing food with them for their first meal. It would be the only one they wouldn't catch or gather themselves from the wilderness around them. While the girls pitched the big tent they'd all share, Sarah focused on getting a fire started. She found a flint and a piece of iron pyrite to start the fire. She'd brought a piece of steel, just in case, but never used it if iron pyrite could be found. It was a lot more difficult to get the spark started with pyrite, but it was part of their dedication to living off the land rather than relying on man-made supplies.

She gathered dry logs, kindling, small sticks and grasses. She cleared an area for their fire pit with a flint hand shovel they'd previously made and had brought with them, encircled it with stones to keep the fire from spreading, stacked the kindling and logs so that the fire would draft nicely, and prepared a small heap of the dry grasses into which she would send a spark from the flint and pyrite.

The girls finished and joined her to watch as she began this slow task. She struck the pyrite on the flint. The first strike produced nothing. She gazed at the pyrite, selected another face and struck it again against the flint. A tiny spark flew into the dry grasses. It smoldered but didn't light. She hit it again in the same spot and a larger spark leapt from the stone into the grasses. This time a small flame was produced.

Janie took over, cupping the flame to keep the wind from extinguishing it; she blew ever so gently, increasing the heat. As the little flicker grew in strength, Jazz added some small twigs while Janie continued to coax the fire into existence. Jazz added more sticks and the fire grew. Janie stopped blowing and allowed the soft breeze to fan the flame. Larger and larger sticks were added until the flame was strong enough to light the kindling at the base of the fire. Once lit, the design of the fire drew the flames into the center, lighting more kindling and eventually the logs. The process took over half an hour, but the three were all smiles as their fire raged before them.

Jazz found two sticks with Y-shaped branches at the top and drove them into the ground on either side of the fire, offset so that the spit she was constructing would not be directly over the flame. She cut a green sapling and stripped it of its bark, leaving a few of the shortened branches to hold the meat in place as it cooked.

Janie gathered some herbs from near the camp and pulled out a paper bag of herbs she'd gathered along the path. Sarah unpacked a small, uncooked whole chicken from an insulated bag. She tossed the ice onto the ground and handed the chicken to Janie, who seasoned it, and then passed it to Jazz, who slipped it onto the spit. Jazz placed the spit onto the two Y-shaped supports. The bag was rinsed in the creek and put back into Sarah's pack.

As the fire began to grow, Janie scoured the perimeter of the camp for some native edible plants. As usual, her hands were full when she returned. At the creek below the falls, Sarah found a shallow, concave stone under one of the more focused cascades. It was about a foot in diameter, oblong in shape, with a one-inch indentation. This would serve as a cooking stone. They built a semicircle of stones and set the cooking stone on top. They carried water from the creek in deer bladders they'd brought with them, and a small amount was poured into the cavity in the stone. The greens and blossoms Janie had found were steamed, a little at a time, with herbs. When done, the fire beneath it was extinguished.

Sarah had brought some apples, which were neither in season nor locally grown. Both girls objected but each still ate their apple. The chicken was roasted slowly and, when done, was removed from the spit and set onto the cooking stone. Jazz used one of her knives to carve off pieces for each of them. Other than discussion about the food preparation, there was little conversation. They used some wooden bowls they'd previously carved with flint knives as plates and ate with their fingers.

TWENTY-ONE

After dinner they washed in the stream. Night had fallen. No cell phones or other forms of technology were allowed on their adventures, so time was irrelevant. They'd lie down to sleep when they were tired. This was a time to talk, and there was a lot to discuss.

"Mom," Jazz started, "so what happens next with you and Dad and us and the house and all that stuff?"

Sarah took a deep breath. She figured this had been weighing on their minds. It was weighing on hers. "Your father and I will start the legal process of getting a divorce. Depending on a lot of things, this could take a long time or a few months. We'll see.

"We'll have to sell the house. We can't afford it any longer. We needed your father's income to pay the bills, and he can't hold a job until he agrees to get help from his disease."

"What disease does Daddy have?" Janie asked.

"Your father is addicted to alcohol. The disease is called alcoholism. What happens to people like your father is that alcohol creates a chemical that builds up in their brains, and they need more and more alcohol for the brain to get enough of the chemical. It demands it from him. So, he drinks more. He has a choice not to, but it is very difficult to resist. Addicts often have to hit rock bottom—get to the worst place in their lives, with the threat of losing everything they love—for them to even admit that they have a problem, and sometimes that isn't enough. We'll see with your father."

"He's pretty stubborn," Jazz said.

Sarah nodded. "Yes, he is. So, we'll see. His brain doesn't want him to believe there's a problem. Does that make sense?"

"Sorta," Jazz answered for them both.

"So, your body is a machine. All its parts, except the brain, can be replaced. Just like in a car: lose a leg, or lose a tire, and we can give you a new one. It may not be as good as the old one, but researchers and the technology are getting better and better."

"So, my heart and lungs and stuff like that are just machines?" Jazz asked.

"Yep. They're your machines, unique to you, but the heart is just a pump. It doesn't think or do anything without guidance. Heart transplants are no longer uncommon."

"What about my hands?" Jazz asked.

"Think about how your hands work. You, the spirit who is you, looks at a piece of flint. Based on the information you've observed and learned, which is stored in your brain as data and programs, you decide how to shape the piece of flint you're working with. Your brain then gets that message from you, accesses all the data and programs you've taught it over the years and then tells your hands precisely how to accomplish the task you've instructed them to perform. If your brain begins to run a program you don't want it to, you, your soul, overrides it and guides it a different way. It may be an entirely new concept that both you and your brain will have to learn, like when you made those tiny arrow points for the first time. It took both you and your brain a while to get that right. Your old programs weren't enough. You had to be creative. You and your brain did that together, but *you* made the decisions. Understand? Your hands are tools at the end of your arms that do things you tell your brain to tell them to do."

"Mom, that's pretty cool. So, is the brain like, sort of, a big computer?"

"Exactly. The brain is a big computer that we begin to program from birth. You've both added thousands of programs and adjustments to your programs, and billions of pieces of data to your brain on everything, including plants and how to create flint knives, points and such.

That way, you don't have to rethink every detail every time. You, your spirit or soul, just like when you're sitting at your computer, have the ability to override your programs and make creative adjustments, but if your brain is doing the work fine on its own, you can often be thinking about other things. Your brain is continually running the existing programs. You do this to walk, talk, eat and many other things without thinking about it. Your spirit may decide to walk to a place, but once you give your brain that simple direction, your brain runs all the relevant programs to get you there.

"Sometimes you start on a journey to one place, but what your brain sees is something it knows well. You're driving and thinking about other things. You sorta wake up and realize that you are driving to the wrong place. Then you smack your head and take over, changing the program to reroute to the right place, hopefully before you get to the wrong one you know so well."

"Have you done that, Mommy?" Janie asked. "Gone one place instead of the right one?"

"I have. Several times. Once I pulled all the way up to Grandma and Grandpa's drive before I realized I didn't mean to go to their house. Grandma saw me. I had to stop and get out and tell her what I'd done. We had a good laugh. Then I left and headed in the right direction. Of course, I was late. So embarrassing, but everyone does it.

"Your soul, which is what makes you *you*, is mostly only involved in starting the processes, making big decisions, overriding simple ones and performing new, creative, imaginative sorts of things—things you've never trained your brain to know. You, your soul, and your brain, which is your computer, work closely together to get you through your day, run your body's machine and figure out solutions to new things."

Sarah paused to see if the girls were following but began again when she realized she had their undivided attention.

"So, your father's system is broken. What alcohol and drugs do is break the connection between the brain and the soul, your spirit. The brain is trained to protect you and to get what it understands you need to survive. The soul, as I mentioned, has the power to change the program and get the brain to stop doing something that the brain thinks is good, but the soul knows is not.

"Your father is now programmed to respond in a particular way to the chemical that alcohol creates in his brain. I'm not. I can stop drinking any time and do. My brain doesn't need me to drink to feel that it's protecting my body from harm. His brain thinks that if he doesn't replenish the chemical, then his body is in danger. Just like if you didn't eat for a long time, your body would crave food to fix the problem."

"I get that. That makes sense," Jazz said. Janie also nodded that she understood.

"In reality, your father's brain is right. Over the next few days, his body will go into shock—withdrawal, they call it. He'll be denied alcohol, and his brain and body will react violently and painfully for a few days. It'll hurt. His brain knew this would happen if he stopped drinking, but this time he drank so much that it almost killed him. The shock of withdrawal and the near-death experience, along with losing the three of us and his home, could be enough to give his soul the strength to take over and override his brain this time.

"He has to stop drinking alcohol in any form—even beer and wine—for the rest of his life. There are groups and medical people who'll help him, but he needs to be fully committed to helping himself before anyone else can do anything for him. Does that make sense?"

"We have to help him, Mommy, don't we? He's sick." Sarah could see the concern in Janie's big brown eyes.

Jazz turned to her sister. "We've loved him and everything for as long as we've been alive, and all that happened was he got sicker and sicker. That's not going to work. We have to do something different or he'll die, like he almost did."

"The doctors will help us when we get back. They told me he'll be out of it for a while, so being away like this is the best thing. The doctors will do everything they can to help him through this, and then it's up to him. We'll see when we get back."

The two girls stared into the fire. Sarah soon joined them. There was nothing more to discuss tonight. The girls had enough to process.

"Mommy, I'm tired," Janie finally said.

"Me too."

They slipped out of their boots, crawled into their tent, zipped it closed, undressed, rolled into their sleeping bags and lay their heads on their inflatable pillows. Their sleeping arrangements were among the few man-made comforts they allowed themselves. Sarah put her arms around her two daughters. Sarah closed her eyes, breathed deeply and connected to the world of nature around her. She asked the spirits she felt there for strength and guidance. It had been a long couple of days.

TWENTY-TWO

They'd fallen asleep to the calming drone of cicadas and crickets and were awakened by the bright songs of the many birds of the forest, welcoming them to a new day in a wondrous place in the middle of everywhere. Sarah crawled out of the tent and stood barefoot in her cotton grey shorts and matching tank top and marveled at the rays of the rising sun streaming through the branches of the trees like laser beams, the active early birds out after their breakfast, the gurgling of the stream that flowed by them over the falls and the rustling of the leaves in the early morning breeze. She stretched her arms to the sky, interlocked her hands and bent to her left, then back and to her right, releasing her hands, arching her back, face to the sky, throwing her arms out wide to each side, breathing in deep the glorious clean air of the wilderness. *This is heaven, if I believed in such a thing.*

Janie and then Jazz crawled out behind her.

"Mom, let's do yoga. We haven't done yoga together in a long time."

"Yeah, Mommy, let's do yoga. Yoga, yoga, yoga." Janie hopped around.

"I think that's a wonderful idea."

On the far side of the clearing was a flat area of soft green grass bathed in the morning sunshine. They all faced the center and sat lotus style. Sarah began one of the soft mantras that they used to meditate.

They chanted, "Om Namah Shivaya," which they all knew was an honor to the divine spirit in each of them, that spirit who made up who they are, and a commitment to positivity in all things. It was one of many they used, but in this instance, Sarah felt the strength of their inner souls and a positive focus in the face of the major changes before them were the best intentions for them to put out into the universe.

All three began to chant the mantra. Soon, Sarah could feel the universe of spirits surround her and them. The souls of the three were dancing together, slow and methodical, with each breath of the mantra. The spirits around them were warm, soft, caressing and positive.

Her soul relaxed. The hatred and anger she felt toward Robert began to swirl among the spirits. She could feel the negativity from Jazz and Janie joining hers. The spirits of the universe guided it away and replaced it with love.

Time was irrelevant. They now chanted the mantra instinctually. Their souls were feeling the spirits of the forest, of the universe, of all time, and it was peaceful, joyful and loving. When it was time, the spirits guided them back into their bodily consciousness. They opened their eyes and gazed at one another but said nothing.

Sarah moved through the series of yoga positions that they each knew so well: graceful, powerful, purposeful, balanced. They were one with the world around them, with each other and with themselves. When they finished, they knelt, put their hands together in front of their chests, stood slowly and bowed to the center space between them. "Namaste," they said in unison.

"Wow, Mommy, that was awesome. We need to do that every day." Janie bounced around and off toward the tent to get dressed for the day.

"Thanks, Mom. That was amazing. I could feel your pain."

"I could feel yours. There's a lot in there, Jazz. Can we talk about it later?"

"Sure. I think I would like that. It felt good to feel it, to see it and to have the spirits take it away, but it's never really all gone, is it?"

"As soon as they guide it off into the universe, we come back to ourselves and make it all real again. We'll teach ourselves to leave it out there. That's the goal. But we have to deal with it here, first, before we can let it go entirely."

"I know."

"We'll get there. So much is so close, so uncertain and so real right now, it's hard to let it go completely, but it's nice to know you can, even if only for a few minutes."

"Yeah, that felt good. I love you." Jazz hugged Sarah tight and held on for several seconds. Sarah could feel her fear.

She knelt in front of her daughter. "Honey, it's going to be OK. Trust me. It's going to all turn out to be the best thing we've ever done. You know the simple rule of life, right?"

"Do what you know in your heart is the right thing to do, and you will stay in harmony with all of the souls in the universe."

"Right. I haven't been doing that for the last few years, for all the man-made, rationalist reasons that I've tried to teach you to ignore. A while back, I decided that the universe is my guide; on Thursday, it guided me to end it with your father. I'll choose to listen to and follow the spirits of the universe, the souls of all who live and have lived, and connect with the spiritual internet that binds us all."

"Today was a good step, Mom. I'm going to do that too. From now on."

"Attagirl. Om Namah Shivaya."

"Om Namah Shivaya."

TWENTY-THREE

"**A**lright, we have to catch breakfast."

Janie was already gathering greens, berries, herbs, mushrooms, morels and flowers. Sarah and Jazz closed their eyes, imagining the spear they'd need, then opened them, and Jazz knew right where to go. She found the perfect long, strong and straight branch. Using a hand axe, Sarah cut it from the tree, striking the top of the juncture of the branch and trunk. When cut through, they pulled the branch from the tree. Jazz used one of her longer and sharper knives to trim off the side branches, whittled the end near the trunk to a rounded butt and the other end to a point. She then split the pointed tip back about an inch, put the split tip into the fire to harden it and inserted one of her long, razor-sharp flint points into the slit. Using strips of the green bark, she tied the tip securely into the slit at the end of her spear. Then she carved back small barbs in the wood behind the tip and was ready to catch some fish for breakfast.

"How's that?" she said with pride as she held up her handiwork.

"Very nice," Sarah answered.

"Great, sis. Now catch us a fish. I'm starving," Janie jumped in.

Jazz smiled and skipped down to the pond. She waded in until her ankles were submerged and watched the fish glide under the surface. She again closed her eyes, envisioned her prey and a successful strike, and then opened them. The fish she saw was a few feet away. It changed course and moved in her direction. With swift, well-trained accuracy, she snapped the spear through the water and deep into the heart of the fish, killing it instantly. She pulled it out of the water, thanked the spirits of the universe and of the fish, and turned to her family.

"Ask and you shall receive."

"Nice work, sissy. That's a good one."

Jazz was as good with her knives as she was in making them. She fileted the trout in minutes, scooping out the organs and tossing them back into the stream, then separating the sweet flesh from the bones in smooth, easy strokes.

Sarah had prepared the cooking stone. They pulled out the same simple wooden bowls. If this had been a multiweek adventure, they'd start with nothing other than the first evening's meal and make everything from scratch in the wild, including flint knives, points, bowls, etc. For these short weekend trips, they "cheated" using man-made tents and sleeping gear, flint knives and points, deer bladders and carved or stone bowls they'd made on other trips or in the garage at home.

They ate and were satisfied. The next step was finding lunch. Jazz again focused inwardly and found the right branch. She and Sarah removed it from the tree, and Jazz prepared a second spear for her mother and then retipped her own spear with a larger point. Sensing the spirits around them, the girls wondered what they'd provide for them today. They'd take only that.

Sarah was a quiet huntress. The girls followed behind her. Completely connected to the wilderness around her, Sarah knew which way to head. She could feel the presence of the birds, reptiles, small mammals and even insects. She could tell Jazz was connecting with the world around them in the same spiritual way. Janie was bouncing along, seeing, hearing and experiencing nature. She was still young, and unlike Jazz, who seemed to always feel the weight of the universe, Janie blithely bounded through life.

Sarah focused on the task at hand, moving through the woods like a tiger—graceful, powerful, knowing. Her spirit felt the animal well before her senses perceived it. A deer. A young buck, grazing just beyond the edge of the trees. She raised her hand. Jazz had already felt it and had stopped cold, lowering herself to a crouch. Janie stopped on command, knelt close to the ground and looked around for what the other two had felt. Sarah and Jazz, both wielding deadly spears, would be involved in the kill. They could communicate without speaking. Janie, who could not, would wait.

Janie understood and was comfortable with that. She was a botanist. Her world was plants, not animals. She could sense a morel under three inches of old rotting leaves. Neither Sarah nor Jazz could do that. Janie knew her special skills and was happy to leave the killing of animals to her mother and elder sister.

Sarah and Jazz moved in unison—Jazz toward the rear of the still-unseen deer, Sarah toward its right side. They moved without sound, one step at a time, in unison. Sarah saw it first. It was a small male, young and alone. That was not unusual. Mating season was essentially over, and adult males tended to travel alone. This one was a runt and likely couldn't overpower any other male, which was the only way bucks managed to mate. He'd likely not live long. Now she knew he wouldn't.

Sarah's movements became even more imperceptible. She could feel Jazz move into position on the buck's opposite side, well back in the tall grass. Jazz crouched as she moved, skimming her left hand along the ground for balance. Sarah stood behind a large oak near the edge of the woods, not 20 feet from the target. She readied the spear in her right hand. She could feel Jazz doing the same from her crouched position.

Together, Sarah stepped from behind the tree and Jazz rose above the grasses, and the two launched their spears at the unsuspecting buck. Sarah was true, her spear driving deep into the side of the deer above his right foreleg into his heart. Jazz's throw was a bit higher, with more arc, and struck the buck in the neck. The deer faltered, took a step and fell. Janie jumped up and down and cheered. Sarah quieted her. Janie put her hands together over her mouth and bowed to her mother. She knew better. Sarah, Jazz and Janie knelt beside the young deer and thanked the spirits of the universe and the spirit of the deer.

They tied the deer's feet together with leather tether Janie had carried and slid their spears under the bound legs. They lifted the deer on their shoulders and hauled it back to their camp. It was heavy and the journey back seemed a lot longer than the journey out. It always did.

TWENTY-FOUR

Sarah and Jazz dressed the deer, being careful to preserve every-thing. It was a lot of meat. Jazz and Janie cut some saplings to make a small smoker to help preserve it. The smoker was about 3-foot square and 4-foot tall. Four vertical posts were placed in holes they dug in the ground at each corner. Crossbeams were tethered with tanned leather from a previous deer hide. More vertical branches were tethered to the crossbeams. Three sides reached the ground. One side was about six inches above the ground where they could add hot coals and airflow could circulate to keep the coals smoking. Across the top, several green branches could be laid with pieces of meat hanging from them into the smoker.

While they worked on this task, Sarah prepared the deer meat, some for lunch and the rest to be smoked for the rest of their meals that week-end. Jazz found another long green skewer for a rotisserie over the fire, chose a nice cut from the deer's hip, seasoned it with Janie's suggestions and began roasting it over the fire. The girls hung the other meat on the green branches over the smoker.

Sarah cleaned out the intestines well then chopped up the heart, liver and kidneys with some fat and deer meat. Janie seasoned the sausage and stuffed the intestines with the chopped, seasoned meat. Sarah and Janie twisted the intestines every so often into links then began to cook them on the cooking stone at the base of the fire.

Sarah cut the hide from the carcass, including from the skull and lower legs, and lay it fur side down on the ground. She gathered up the parts of the deer that they would not use. The three returned to the place where they'd killed the deer and set the remains there for other animals to devour. They knelt, closed their eyes and again thanked the spirits of the universe for their gift.

Janie ran into the nearby woods to gather vegetables while Jazz tended to the cooking sausages, the roast on her spit and the smoking meat. Sarah watched them with pride, gathered the deer's skin, found a soft place to work in the warm sun and began to prepare the hide to be tanned. She would tan it and stretch it as much as possible over the next few days, and by the time they headed home, it would be ready for transport. Tanning it would take several more days, which she'd do at home. It was peaceful work, and she enjoyed working the hide while watching her two girls perform like veteran survivalists.

Lunch was roasted herb-encrusted deer, several different berries, greens and mushrooms. They all ate too much and lay back on the grass in the sun. Sarah decided to shimmy out of her jeans and took off her top. "I'm taking a swim and then getting a start on my summer tan."

Jazz and Janie followed suit. They frolicked naked in the cold water, splashing one another, then laying in the shallower end below the rapids, feeling the rejuvenating water flow across their bodies. Janie got up first, but they were all ready. They used their hands to push as much water off as possible, then lay in the sunny grassy area where they'd done yoga. The rays warmed their cold bodies, happy, at peace together.

TWENTY-FIVE

Jazz felt the presence before the other two, but Sarah was awake in seconds. They both instinctively grabbed their tops and slipped them back on and then pulled on their jeans. Jazz nudged Janie. She woke quickly and followed suit. Sarah was dressed first, jumped to her bare feet and ran to grab a spear, just in case. The spirit that was approaching seemed harmless, even positive. She put the spear down and gazed into the woods. Jazz ran over behind her.

"Feels friendly."

"Yeah, Mom, what do you think?"

"I don't know. I can't tell."

The voice was that of a man. "Hello, there. Didn't mean to startle you ladies. Name's Frank. Maggie asked me to come out here and check on you. We check on everyone from time to time, especially folks like you who like to find out-of-the-way camping spots. Everything OK? Wow, something smells good."

Sarah met his gaze, a bit perturbed. "Everything's great. We were just napping in the sun. You startled us, but yes, we're fine."

He was in his mid-teens, tall, rugged and strong, like every Ranger she'd run across. Who else would become a wilderness Ranger?

Now almost 12, Jazz was smitten. Sarah could feel it. He was cute. Not catalog handsome, but attractive in a rustic caveman sort of way. Messy sandy brown hair under his Ranger hat, one of those "haven't shaved in a week" sorts of beards, which hid some acne. He displayed a big toothy smile, revealing a couple of crooked teeth. His walk was gangly and loping. He stopped at the edge of the clearing, pulled out his credentials and held them out for Sarah. Very official and polite. He looked legit. His walkie-talkie suddenly buzzed and crackled, and the Ranger woman they'd met asked, "Everythin' alright with them girls out there, Frank?"

He picked up the walkie, clicked a toggle and replied, "Everythin's just fine. Probably shouldn't've bothered 'em. Looks like they can fend for themselves."

"Great. Tell 'em sorry we barged in. Park policy. Out." The walkie went silent, and he returned it to his belt.

"Are you hungry?" Jazz asked. "We have some fresh roasted deer meat still on the spit. I prepared it."

"I got the greens and herbs." Janie leaped in between Jazz and the boy. Sarah took her arm and guided her back beside her, shushing her.

Jazz scowled at her younger sister then turned back to the young Ranger. "And we have some greens and berries Janie here gathered. We couldn't eat it all. Happy to share."

"Well, I am a tad hungry. If ya don't mind . . . and don't tell Maggie."

"No problem. We promise," Sarah said in support of Jazz's violation of one of their sacred rules. "Jazz, would you mind preparing Frank here some lunch?"

Jazz blushed, turned and cut the young man a huge chunk of the remaining meat on the spit. She used one of their nicer wood bowls to serve him and added some cooked greens, mushrooms and fresh berries. When she brought it over, she had the soft but wide eyes of a young girl with a crush.

"Here you are, sir."

"Call me Frank. You're Jazz, right?

"Yes . . . Frank."

"This looks great. Do ya have like a fork or anythin'?"

"Nope," Janie burst out, bounding over. "When we're in the wild, we eat with what we have. In this case, our hands."

Jazz looked at her sister with scorn. "Frank, I'll get you something to eat with." She handed him an exquisite flint knife, her best one, mounted on a carved wooden handle to make it easier to use. She pulled out a carved wooden spoon she'd also made.

"Wow. D'you make these?"

"Yep."

"They're amazing." He admired the knife first, held it in his hand, balanced it and felt its edge. "Wow, sharp. This is as fine a flint knife as I've ever seen, even in museums. What'd you use to make it?"

"Flint, chert and bone tools that I designed and made for various parts of the process. I'm glad you like it." Jazz moved a bit closer to the young man. "Eat up while it's hot."

Jazz sat on the ground cross-legged and patted the ground for Frank to sit as well. He obliged. They were facing each other. The two struck up a conversation as the Ranger dug in. Sarah slipped away and motioned with her head for Janie to do the same. Frank ate every bite, and Jazz cut him the rest of the meat from the bone. Sarah watched from the sunny spot where they'd been resting as Jazz laughed at whatever Frank was saying, flipped her hair and gave him several flirty looks. Luckily, he was rather clueless, but he warmed up to Jazz and gradually understood that she was coming on to him.

He glanced over at Sarah, and she shrugged and grinned back at him. It was good to see Jazz smiling, flirting and being a girl for a change. A weight had been lifted from her shoulders, and Sarah could feel her daughter's spirit spreading her wings for the first time in a long time. This interlude wouldn't go anywhere. Frank had to get back to work, and the family had a weekend ahead of them that was sacred and not to be interrupted by foreigners. Sarah let this one slide. Jazz needed it.

Crackle, buzz, crackle. "Frank?"

Frank grabbed the walkie. "Yes, ma'am?"

"You checked the duck blinds down by Mount'n Lake yet?"

"Not yet. On my way," he lied, and he shared a smile with Jazz, who stifled a giggle with her hands to her mouth.

"You walkin' in mud? Get on it, boy. Shouda been there by now. Times a wastin'. Lots to do, intern. Maggie out." The walkie crackled and went silent.

"I guess I gotta go, Jazz. Thanks for the meal. This was fun. Maybe I could come back around?"

Jazz looked at Sarah, who shook her head slightly, making it clear that this weekend was girls only.

"I had fun too, but I don't think that's a good idea. This is a special time for me, my mother and sister. Do you have a cell phone?"

"Sure."

"Here's my number back in the real world. We live in D.C. If you're ever up that way, give me a call."

"Don't you have one?"

"Of course, this is my number. On these trips, we don't bring any technology at all."

"What'd you shoot that deer with?"

"We didn't shoot it." Jazz stood and held up her spear, dipping the still bloody tip down toward him.

"You killed that deer with this? By yourself?"

Jazz snuck a gaze at Sarah, who nodded. "Yep. Made the spear and the tip myself. That's how we Robinson girls roll in the wilds. In fact, you mighta been next if we hadn't been able to tell you were harmless." Jazz had a twinkle in her eye. Frank looked impressed and mocked a bit of fear, then smiled a big toothy smile. "So, you can tell Maggie that we're just fine and can fend for ourselves. Ask her not to send anyone else around and not to tell anyone where we are. We asked her that when we headed out, so if you could reiterate that, it'd be great."

She reached down, took his empty bowl and utensils with her left hand and offered him her right to help him up. He was amazed at her grip and the leverage she used to help him up.

"You're strong."

"Like I said, don't mess with Robinson girls."

Sarah stood and walked over.

"Thank you all very much. The meal was awesome. I had fun. So sorry for interruptin'. Jazz, it was great to meet you. I'll call you if I can get up to D.C. I'll tell Maggie to leave y'all alone."

"Thank you for stopping by." Sarah extended her hand and the Ranger intern took it. Sarah's handshake was firm. The tall youngster nodded at Jazz, smiled at Janie, then turned and headed into the woods the way he'd come in. "He seemed nice."

"Nice enough. He's 16, from Richmond. Goes to high school there. His school ended a few days ago. He's interning for the summer. He just started today. Maggie's got him working pretty hard already. She's a family friend, and he's been coming here for years. He says he knows these woods like the back of his hand. Grew up in a small town near here before his family moved to Richmond for a job for his mother. I guess his dad's not around or dead or something. He didn't mention him. He wants to be a Ranger when he graduates."

"Flirting is fun, isn't it?"

"Yeah, it was fun. It took him a while to figure out I was flirting with him. Boys can be dumb."

"They can be," Sarah cautioned as she put her arm around Jazz, "but, my dear, they can also be sneaky."

TWENTY-SIX

After her comment, she could feel a twinge of darkness descend on Jazz's spirit. It was Robert . . . something to do with Robert. Sarah looked for and found her youngest. Janie, as was often the case, was in her own world, making a ring of flowers for her hair. Sarah returned her attention to Jazz.

Sarah stopped, turned to her eldest and placed her hands on Jazz's shoulders. She looked directly into her eyes. "Sweetie, I can feel a darkness on your spirit. It's something to do with your father. Do you want to talk about it?"

Jazz began to cry. Sarah pulled her close and held her. She moved them behind a tree, out of the vision of Janie so as not to awaken her from her little daydream.

"One night, a while ago, Dad came into my room late at night. He was drunk and ran into my side table, which woke me up. He was naked, standing over me, and I freaked out. He put his hand over my mouth and climbed on top of me. I had the sheet over me, and he started to try to touch me. He tried to pull the sheet down, but I held on tight. Then he fell on top of me. I could feel his . . . you know," Sarah nodded. ". . . rubbing against me. I was on my back and he was holding me down, his hand over my mouth. I tried to squirm and scream, but I couldn't move." Jazz paused and slid down to her knees. Sarah followed, holding her close.

"Mom, Dad started to hump me, rubbing against the sheet and against my, well, down here. He pushed himself between my legs, but the sheet kept him from . . ." Tears poured from her eyes.

"I'm here, honey. He's far away. You don't have to continue." *That bastard!*

Jazz whispered into Sarah's ear, "Mom, it was so disgusting. It got all over the sheet, and he was laying on me. It soaked through to my nightgown and got all over my stomach. It was so gross. Then he passed out on top of me.

"He was out cold. He weighed a ton. I started to panic. I wiggled and pushed him until he rolled off to the floor. I jumped out of bed, grabbed a different nightgown, ran into the bathroom, locked the door, cleaned myself and changed. Then I sat there and cried. I was so afraid to go out into the hall.

"I heard him. He was calling for someone, I think, stumbling around in the hall. I heard him head down the stairs. He missed a step, I guess, and fell down to the landing. He said some cuss words. Then I heard him go the rest of the way downstairs. I peeked out the door. He was gone." Tears were pouring from Jazz's eyes. As she tried to speak again, the words got caught in her throat.

Sarah held her close and let her cry. What could she say that would help?

After a few seconds, Jazz spoke with her head still on Sarah's shoulder. "I ran into Janie's room and crawled in bed with her. Janie woke up and saw I was crying. She asked what was wrong, but I lied. I told her I had a bad nightmare. She hugged me, and I slept there that night. It was horrible." She fell into Sarah's arms and sobbed.

"I'm so sorry, honey. I'm so sorry." Sarah hugged her tight and rubbed her back, letting Jazz cry it all out. She poured love from her soul into Jazz's soul. She could feel the darkness let go, not entirely, but her sobs began to settle down.

"Honey, where was I?"

"It was the night you went to Chicago on that business trip."

That stupid continuing education. She'd traveled one night with her team to a function and this happens. While the team had stayed several days, she'd returned the next morning.

"I'm so sorry. You're safe now. That will never happen again. Never. We'll be away from him soon, and he'll never hurt you again." *One way or the other.*

"Thanks, Mom."

"Do you want to tell Janie about this?" Sarah asked, knowing the answer.

"No way. That'll just scare her more."

"I agree. Just between you and me and the spirits. Let's try to get them to take that darkness away. Let's take some time to meditate. What do you think?"

"OK. I'll try." She smiled and hugged Sarah, who pulled her in so close she felt they could become one. This had been a necessary trip in so many ways.

TWENTY-SEVEN

"**L**ook what I made." Janie popped around the big tree with a very nice flower wreath around her head.

"That's beautiful." Sarah knelt down, directing her attention from Jazz so that the older daughter could sneak away, collect herself and wash her face. "Can you make me one and maybe one for Jazz? Or show us how?"

"I'd love one," Jazz said as she returned, bright faced and smiling. Sarah smiled back at her.

"Sure, come on. I'll totally show you. It's soooo easy." She grabbed their hands and pulled them across the clearing. They made flower crowns, bracelets, necklaces and other jewelry for the next couple of hours, bantering about random, inconsequential things, mostly led by the endless supply of stories and ideas produced by Janie's hyper-imaginative mind.

Sarah suggested they meditate in the warmth of the fading afternoon sun. Both girls agreed. They took their meditation poses, facing the center of the circle created by their spirits. Sarah selected another mantra, one created by the ancient Sikh warrior-saint Guru Gobind Singh to remove negativity from one's spirit and soul.

Sarah began, "Jae Te Gang." The words came out with depth and rhythm. The girls repeated the mantra, knowing what it meant and why one would choose this chant. Sarah could feel the darkness in Jazz's soul.

She could feel the darkness in her own. As they chanted "Jae Te Gang," she felt the spirits descend upon them, bringing brightness and joy, sucking the darkness into the universe. She could feel her spirit lighten. She could feel Jazz letting the darkness go, releasing that horrible memory to the spirits and into the universe. Sarah stayed with the mantra for many minutes; she didn't have any idea how long. She could feel the smiles of her girls, the joy entering their souls and the fear leaving them. She could feel it in herself. The wonders of the spirits guiding her and them into a new life. They would follow. They would listen. They would know.

The spirits swirled away, taking the darkness with them. It took Sarah a few seconds to slowly open her eyes. Janie bounced up and danced around them. "I feel so happy. That was so great. I'm hungry."

To Sarah's surprise, Jazz also jumped to her feet, took Janie's hands in hers and danced with her around the grassy clearing. They each took one of Sarah's hands, and she joined them, dancing in circles. Janie started to sing a song from school they all knew well, so Sarah and Jazz joined in. It was melodic, about a young girl from China who conquered her fears and climbed a mountain forbidden to girls. At the top she met god, who she learned loved her as much as any man. The song told of her life, teaching everyone that god loves them all, male and female, old and young, rich and poor.

When they finished, they stopped dancing but kept holding hands. Sarah turned to Janie. "That's a great song. Thank you so much for sharing that with us." Sarah released the girls and then all bowed to the space between them. "Namaste," they said in unison. Then she gathered them to her and hugged them tight. The love that traveled between their spirits radiated from them throughout the forest. Birds sang and crickets chirped. The quiet woods came alive.

Dinner was deer sausage, greens and mushrooms with herbs, some root vegetables Janie had found and berries.

TWENTY-EIGHT

On Sunday they found Mountain Lake, tracked a wolverine and found its den occupied. They watched from a safe distance as the mother cared for her cubs. Janie related all sorts of facts about wolverines. Sarah sensed the wildlife around them, and by changing course, they witnessed a puma make a kill, watched as a hawk snagged a field mouse from the ground and an eagle rip a huge trout from the big lake. Janie had information about everything they ran across, especially plants.

"Everything has energy, a spirit. Even plants, Mom. You guys can feel the spirits of the animals, and I can feel the spirits of the plants and the spirits that live among the plants."

Sunday night, the girls asked about Sarah and Robert. They wanted to know everything. Sarah realized that it was time.

"Well, first a bit about me before Robert. I grew up the daughter of a union carpenter and a union schoolteacher in a small house in a tightly knit neighborhood of diverse, hard-working people in the Cleveland Heights suburb of Cleveland.

"I have some unique features for an American. They're the result of a diverse heritage on my side. My dark black hair and complexion come from my mother, who was half Indian and half something else. My mother never knew her father, my grandfather. My grandmother, who I called Nānī, never spoke of him. He'd died in some war, she thought.

"Nānī passed down many of the spiritual traditions and skills learned in the practice of her ancestry, the wonders of Eastern religions far beyond the teachings of Hindu. Nānī didn't believe in the many gods but understood them as metaphors. God, to Nānī and to Mom and thus to me, is not a singular, all-knowing being, but rather the connection of all souls to all others."

"Mom, you've told us about what god is. Why do you call it the spiritual internet sometimes?" Janie asked.

Sarah smiled and giggled a little. "When I was in law school, I had a roommate. Her name was Heather. Heather was sweet, but she was not going to make it in law school. She never studied, partied too hard and didn't seem to care enough. She was pretty and from a nice family in New York. For Heather, law school was the next school her parents would pay for before she had to venture out into the real world. I think she dropped out after our first year. Anyway, I tried to explain what we believe god is to Heather. She said, 'So, it's like a spiritual internet?' I always liked that analogy, so I've used it. People get it that way, I think. Heather did."

Sarah and Janie nodded.

"So, Nānī died a long time ago, way before I met your father, but my mom and dad continued to pass her teachings on to me. We would explore the spiritual and natural worlds together, like the three of us do."

"Mommy," Janie asked, "why do you and Jazz have green eyes? You know, less than two percent of the world has green eyes, and yours are *so* green. Like grass."

"It's a wonderful characteristic. My dad's mom was from Iceland, and his dad was from Ireland."

"Green eyes are common in Iceland. It's, like, the only place," Janie added.

"Well, your dad certainly wasn't Hindu then," Jazz noted.

"You're right. Despite being raised devoutly Catholic by his stern father, dad didn't practice or even like that religion at all. He relished researching the concepts of Hinduism, Buddhism and other Eastern belief systems, as well as diverse Nordic and nature-based European traditions. His parents divorced early, and Dad was an only child. My Icelandic grandmother, Amma, never moved off the island. I only met Amma once. She was wonderful and encouraged dad's spiritual exploration. She had these deep green eyes.

"My dad's father disowned him for leaving the faith. He apparently also had green eyes, though I've only seen black-and-white photos.

"What's weird is that my great grandmother, like Nānī, both of whom were born in India, had these vibrant green eyes. They were outcast in their villages, considered *sundar jaadoog aranee*, which loosely translates as beautiful sorceress. Nānī moved to Cleveland Heights when she was pregnant with my mom, but that wasn't an improvement. She was a single mother, spoke broken English with a heavy accent, and her deep devotion to meditation, intense yoga and even out-of-body experiences, common in India, did not help perceptions of her family in the States.

"Nānī used to tell me the women were all jealous of her because all the men in town wanted her." Sarah smiled and winked. The girls chuckled. "Nani was fun. I wish you'd have had the chance to meet her."

Sarah told a few stories about her parents and their trips into the woods—how she'd learned almost everything she'd taught the two of them from her parents, including the connection of souls to all who are willing to receive them.

TWENTY-NINE

"Mom," Jazz interrupted, trying to steer her mom on track, "did you ever really love Dad? Was he always like this?"

Sarah took a deep breath. *Did I ever really love him?* "Well, honey, your father was my knight in shining armor when I needed that very much. I was living in the dorm in law school, studying for a test one night."

***

Sarah and Heather's simple square apartment bedroom was lit only by Sarah's study lamp. She turned to check on her roommate. Heather was sound asleep. Sarah shook her head as she pulled her Con Law casebook toward her and reread what she was sure was the holding in the case they'd hear about in class the next morning. Finals were coming soon—the end of her first year at George Washington University Law School in Washington, D.C.

She stretched her arms above her head and then arched across the back of her chair, staring at the plain white ceiling. Then back erect. She gazed into her parents' eyes in her favorite photo of them. They were camping, of course, living off the land and communing with nature. Their smiles were so genuine and full of their deep love for one another, but also for the world of nature they adored and had taught her so much about. Her mother's bright green eyes sparkled. She smiled, kissed her finger and touched each of their faces.

"Thank you! I won't let you down," she whispered.

Her parents had been so proud of her when she'd been admitted to a top-ten law school—at the last minute, for sure, but she was here, competing with some of the top young legal minds in the country.

Sarah was determined to become the sort of lawyer who'd fight for the rights of the people who, like her parents, were losing ground in the modern economy. They'd taken out a second mortgage on their house and drained their savings to get her here, and she was not going to let them down. She'd pay them back. Every cent!

Her cell phone vibrated across her desk. She grabbed it and turned to see if Heather had been disturbed.

Sarah flipped the phone open. "Hello? Yes, this is Sarah James." The woman on the other end hesitated. "Can I help you?"

"Ms. James, I have some very bad news to give you. Are you sitting down?"

"Yes, what is it?"

"Your parents have passed away this evening. They were in a mountain-climbing accident . . ." The woman kept talking, but Sarah was paralyzed.

"What? What're you talking about? They've climbed dozens of mountains. We practically lived in the wilderness. There's no way. Who are you? Why would you say these things? What's wrong with you?"

"Ms. James, I am so sorry. I'm Dr. French with Bozeman Deaconess Hospital. Your parents were flown here by helicopter several hours ago. Your mother was dead upon arrival. Your father was in critical condition. We did everything we could to save him. We have the best trauma team in the country out here, but his injuries were too severe, and he died about fifteen minutes ago. I called as soon as I got out of surgery. I'm so sorry."

The phone clattered onto the ground, waking Heather.

"What's up, Sarah? Oh my god, Sarah. You look like you've seen a ghost or something."

"Heather, they're dead. My mom and dad, they're dead." The sobs came from deep within her. Sarah fell to her knees, then slipped to the floor, curled into a ball on the thin carpet. Heather leaped out of the bed and ran to her. She put her hand on her shoulder, but there was nothing to say.

Heather heard the voice from Sarah's cell phone and reached for it under the desk.

"Hello, this is Heather. I'm Sarah's roommate. Sarah can't talk anymore. How can I help?"

The doctor gave her the information for the hospital and other relevant contact numbers and details. Heather wrote them on Sarah's Con Law notes. Heather had always laughed at her for using paper and pencil but was happy to have them now.

"Thank you, doctor. We'll contact you in the morning."

Heather lay next to Sarah in the light of Sarah's laptop until it went to sleep. Sarah couldn't feel anything. She was lost. The warmth of Heather's body worked its way into her psyche. She moved her trembling body back into the arms of her roommate.

"Sarah, let me help you into your bed. This floor is hard, and my arm is falling asleep under you, sweetie." Heather slipped her arm from under Sarah and got to her knees. She helped Sarah sit up. Heather was dainty, a socialite not an athlete, and Sarah was not a willing participant. "Sarah, I can't do this on my own. Sweetheart, it'll be better if you get into bed."

Devastation, loss and confusion sucked all emotion from Sarah's face, but she moved with Heather into her bed. Heather crawled in behind her and held her close. Neither of them said a word. Eventually, Sarah cried herself to sleep, but sleep was fitful. At some point, Heather got up and climbed back into her own bed. Sarah awoke to darkness, alone and shivering with fear, anger and loss.

THIRTY

The alarm clock played "A Song for the Lonely" by Cher. It was 6:00. Sarah sat up in bed and stared at the white wall in front of her.

"Screw it! Screw law school! Screw Con Law! Screw it all!" She threw her pillow across the room at her computer. It fluttered and hit the table leg, slid down and landed harmlessly on the floor where she'd lain the night before. "Dammmnnnn!"

Heather sat up in her bed and stared at her roommate. Sarah seldom got angry. Heather's initial look betrayed her desire to sleep, but when she saw Sarah's face, her attitude changed. "Hey, girlfriend." Heather slid out of bed and in behind Sarah, wrapping her arms around her. Sarah was sitting cross-legged on her bed with her blankets clutched to her chest, radiating anger from every pore. Heather whispered into her ear, "Horrible news. What can I do?"

"Nothing! Not a goddamn thing! What can anyone do? I'm done. Screwed. Alone. Penniless. How could they do this, Heather? How could they leave me like this? Where were the spirits of the goddamn universe? What kind of loving soul lets this kind of thing happen? Where were my mom's precious nature spirits? Where were they when she needed them? Tell me that, Heather! Gods and spirits are supernatural. They're gods, goddammit. What can you or I do? We're mortals. We're going to die. Maybe tomorrow. Maybe today. Maybe in the next five minutes. What the hell is it all for? Why do we waste our time? Why do we give a rat's ass about anyone or anything but ourselves? Tell me that, Heather! Answer that one for me!"

In the middle of the tirade, Heather got up, moved to Sarah's desk, picked up Sarah's cell phone and called Robert Robinson. Sarah had been dating him for a few weeks now, in the haphazard way Sarah dated in between studying, her insane workout schedule and all her causes. "Robert? Hi, this is Heather, Sarah's roommate. Sarah's parents died last night in a climbing accident. Can you come over? Sarah's a total mess. Yeah, that's her. Great. Thank you."

"Sarah, honey, Robert's coming over. We're going to get you through this. You are not quitting. I'll call our Con Law professor and let her know what happened and that neither of us will be in class." Heather sat on the edge of the small twin bed beside Sarah and put her arm around her.

"They were everything to me, Heather. They're all I have in the world. What am I going to do? I can't handle this. I just can't." Sarah broke into deep sobs and fell into Heather's embrace.

"There, there," was all Heather could think to say.

The knock on the door startled them both. "Hey, it's me, Robert. Let me in."

Heather raced to the door, unlocked it and let him in. Sarah stood, tears still streaming down her face.

"Oh, sweetheart," he said. She ran to him and sank into his strong arms.

"Oh my god, Robert. What am I going to do? My parents are gone. I'm alone."

"You're not alone. You have me. I'm here. I'm not going anywhere." He kissed her on her forehead. She gazed up into his deep brown eyes. At that moment, she needed him more than she'd ever needed anyone.

"Thank you." She stood on her tiptoes to kiss him. He pulled her closer and kissed her. It was a loving, "I'm all in for you" sort of kiss. She put her head on his shoulder and was finally able to control her sobs. Tears still flowed, but her breathing calmed. He felt so good. She felt so right in his arms. Her huge teddy bear had her.

"Don't let me go," she whispered.

"I won't."

THIRTY-ONE

"**W**ow." Jazz broke the trance Sarah had slipped into as she told the story, reliving the pain. "Then what happened?"

***

Heather called and got her excused from classes. Robert held her, now sitting on her bed, caressing her forehead, moving stray strands to one side, as he listened to Sarah talk it all out, giving simple, helpful, encouraging responses. Heather dressed and left.

Sarah finally was able to stop crying, cuddled on her bed in Robert's arms. His embrace was winning the battle in her soul over the desperate fear caused by the loss of her parents, at least in the moment. Her breathing had calmed. Her heart settled into a gentle rhythm.

Heather returned with a Danish and coffee. Sarah wasn't hungry. The two made her eat. She only nibbled at the pastry but finished the coffee. Tucked against her teddy bear's strong chest, she could feel his breath and heart reaching out to hers. He was warmth and safety in a cold, horrid place.

Her brain reminded her that Robert had to go to class, and as she gained some composure, she pulled back and looked up into his eyes. "Honey, sweetie, thank you so much for coming over. You can't know how much it means to me."

"I'm here."

"I know, but you have classes. Go ahead and go. I'm OK. I need to go for a run anyway. I need to burn this out of me." He kissed her and stood. She realized that he was in a T-shirt and sweats, no socks and a pair of untied tennis shoes. His normally perfectly coifed hair was a mess, and he needed a shave. She smiled for the first time since the call, which felt good. "Boyfriend, you've got to get cleaned up and dressed. You can't go out like that. You're my hunk. If other girls see you like that, you'll never make it home."

He smiled, took a quick look in the mirror, made a futile attempt to fix his hair, kissed her, hovered over her for a few seconds, kissed her again, grabbed his keys and left.

She lay back on her twin bed, her long, silky black hair fanned across the pillow as she stared at the white drywall ceiling in their dorm room. She noticed the cobwebs in the corner and the imperfections at the edges of the drywall sheets. Some of the nails were pushing through. Her mind was blank.

Heather broke the trance. "You OK? You look like you're somewhere else."

"Yeah." A long sigh followed. "I was nowhere, Heather, nowhere. I guess that's as good a place to start from as any, right?"

She could see that Heather was confused. "Sure. Right. You go, girl."

Sarah stared at the ceiling and said, "I'm going running."

"Of course, what else would you do?" That big smile again, mocking. "And then four hundred push-ups and ten hours of yoga just for fun, I bet. Girl, I get tired just watching you. I'm going to Freddy's for a mocha." Heather grabbed Sarah's hands and pulled her out of the bed.

"You can't get my exercise for me while you're lying on that bed. Do you want me to get fat?" Heather kissed her on the cheek and headed out the door. "Want me to bring you back something green and disgusting with grass and stuff in it? I think they mowed the lawn yesterday. Should be fresh."

"Not today, Heather." Sarah gave her a difficult smile. "Thanks. I'll get my own later. Say hello to everyone for me." Heather nodded, waved and was gone. They weren't really friends, per se, but Sarah was happy to have Heather as a roommate and appreciated her efforts to cheer her up.

THIRTY-TWO

Sarah took longer than usual to dress for her run. After she pulled on each garment, she sat on the edge of her bed for several seconds, remembering something else about her parents. They'd gotten her running regularly. They'd run every day together. They'd taught her yoga and meditation. They'd taught her to care about her body. They'd showed her how she could control it, even when she was a little girl. She'd injured herself on a hike, and her mother helped her understand and withstand pain. The tears were soft and gentle as they slipped down her cheeks.

The visions clouded, darkened, faded. They were dead. *"Deeeeead!!"* The scream came from deep within and tore into the nothingness that surrounded her.

Dressed, she bolted out the door, leaped down the front steps and launched herself into a blistering pace along her normal route. She poured her emotions into each driving stride, pounding across campus. Ripping between walkers. Flying past runners. Bumping, jostling, feeling the contact, relishing it, hating it. Her vision was clouded, but she wasn't looking outward. Tears flowed over her cheekbones and back into her hair.

She nearly ran through the last concrete building as she cleared its corner, her cheeks wet with tears, body drenched with sweat, heart pounding. Mind racing, screaming, spinning.

The park to the river opened before her. Two last steps and her right arm whipped through the air, as though it could expel the anger with its violence. Her water bottle exploded against the huge oak tree. She came to a stop, breathing heavily. Something snapped inside her as her favorite water bottle clattered to the ground in pieces. She ran to it and fell to her knees, as if she could put it back together; like her life, the contents bled out into the soft grass. She knelt, grasping the battered bottle to her chest, now only drops of life left inside, as teardrops slipped from her eyes. She knelt, rocking slightly, holding the broken container to her chest until . . .

Sarah, pull your sorry butt together! She stood erect and looked up from the bottle. *Endure, Sarah. It is who you are!*

As her eyes cleared, heart slowed and her mind settled, Sarah tossed the bottle into a nearby recycling container then turned and leaned against its gravel-embedded concrete structure. Before her stood a massive oak, rising high into the sky, reaching out in every direction, flourishing. She could feel the life in and exuding from the old tree. It seemed to call to her.

She walked toward it, drawn to it, needing it. She touched its rough bark, smelled the air around it, soft and gentle. Exhausted, she fell onto the old, peeling wooden bench that wrapped around the four-foot-wide trunk, laying back against the thick bark of the ancient tree. She stared up, up into endless limbs that blocked out all but a few angular specs of pure blue above them. The sun glowed in various shades of green behind the leaves, lighter, brighter nearer the top of the canopy, streams of sunlight angling through the seams. None made it down to her.

Her breaths steadied, long and deep. *Who am I without them? Alone. Penniless.* With two more expensive years of law school to pay for, she faced over one hundred thousand dollars in debt.

She spoke to the old tree, whom she knew in her soul was a wise and comforting old woman she could trust. "Life is about living, right? You should know that more than anyone. You've been here since before 'here' was even here. This is your world and we've invaded, and yet you've survived, endured, even flourished, the grand matriarch of the land." Sarah could feel the strength of the soul of the tree wrap with hers. It made her feel safe somehow. She'd long ago stopped telling others about these experiences. They'd look askance at her. Like her mother and grandmother before her, more than a few people she'd met along the way thought her strange and an outcast.

Without her parents, this crazy law school life was no longer about living. She closed her eyes. "I'm quitting," she told the old tree. The tree had no opinion on the subject. She reached for her phone to make the call. "Damn!" she screamed, not to the tree, but out to the world.

Sarah took a deep breath, then another. She was able to center herself with a few more. She pulled her legs up and sat lotus style atop the bench. She'd learned so much from her mother and grandmother, who were deeply connected to the spirits of nature, but had learned even more about deepening her meditation from a guru, Maharishi Prema, a young, amazingly connected woman whose ashram was simple and unassuming, located, oddly enough, in a small retail strip center in Virginia next to a deli. "Place and time do not matter," Guru Prema had told her when she'd walked in the first time, looking a bit unsure.

Straight back, palms up, she closed her eyes. She chose a mantra for strength and courage: "*Om Hanumate Namah*." She should say it 108 times, though she didn't have her counting beads. The spirits would guide her.

Fears, thoughts and emotions about her parents, law school, money invaded her consciousness. Her heart was racing again. Images burst in and out. She was out of control. Her eyes flew open. Panting and sweating, she refocused. Sarah stretched her arms out wide and then back on either side of the tree behind her, feeling the roughness on her skin, soaking in its ancient strength and courage against the world. She held that position, engaging the energy around her. The ancient tree seemed to be calming her. "Strength against time, and time doesn't matter," it seemed to be saying.

Settled. An understanding. Hands back on her knees, palms up, eyes closed, she took in a deep breath and held it. "Reeee-laaaax," she intoned loudly. Breathing in rhythm, slowing her heartbeat, feeling the great tree and the spirits of nature all around her, focusing on the mantra, the chaos within her began to quell. She forced her consciousness to let her soul take over. She felt panic signals from her brain, but she let them be, exist in time, then flicker and melt away. Lingering on them, letting them become real, created panic. *Strength against time, and time doesn't matter.*

It took several minutes, but peace settled over her then flowed through her from her torso in all four directions, guiding the tension and pain out into the universe. She could feel the powerful spirits around the tree and within this small patch of nature descend and warm her. Each breath took her away from the earthly world, connecting into nature's cleansing purity.

She was no longer alone. Thousands of spirits were with her. The pain of the loss was still there. It would take a lot more than this to set it free. But she felt better. As the spirits let her know she was reaching the count, her soul settled and she was back to reality. She opened her eyes. She felt refreshed. Still frightened, but no longer angry. Her legs untangled, she stood and shook them out, preparing to finish her run.

I will be strong. I can be strong.

THIRTY-THREE

Sarah stretched and then changed her mind. She would go through her yoga sequences right there in the park. She found a soft grassy area where the big oak permitted a few rays to reach the ground. She bowed to the mother tree. *Thank you. Namaste.*

Sarah moved with grace, purpose and strength through her grueling workout, feeling the stress in her muscles loosen their hold. As she finished, she felt even better. The small rays of sun warmed her as she sat, sweating, on the soft grass under that old tree in a tiny park in the middle of one of the most energetic and powerful cities in the world. Peace. *Good will come of this. Watch for it. Sense it. Know it. Follow it. Sarah, you can endure. Strength against time, and time doesn't matter.*

Before she got up, she laid back on the grass and stared through the maze of branches above her. Paths. So many paths. So many options. The only way to find the right path was to connect to the spirits of nature and of all souls, living and dead, to remain in harmony with them. The souls who loved her would guide her along the right path. She needed only to have the faith to follow, to do what she knew in her heart was right.

A squirrel raced through the huge tree, flying from limb to limb, and was gone. It navigated the maze with ease. Animals were always connected. Never off path. No timetables. No places to be. No expectations from others. Just follow the path the universe provides.

Humans create so many obstacles, real and imagined, to block their paths. To block the paths of others. To confuse the voice from the heart that carries the right messages, the vision for the right path. Deep from within her, a voice, her Nānī's soft, gravelly voice: *Be honest with yourself, believe what you come to know, Sarah, and the path will unfold itself for you.*

She began to run at her normal, rhythmic pace. She should have been comforted. She wasn't. Her mind should have been clear. It wasn't. Not clear in the least. Her pace slowed, the rhythm lost. *They're gone. Gone forever.*

The fear and her anger were still there. She couldn't keep them at bay, and they welled up inside her, knocking her off stride. Running, jogging, running, bumping into people, restarting, dazed as the emotions rekindled. She stopped at a table, surprising the students seated there. She leaned on the corner of the sturdy green structure. Support, balance, constancy. She shed a few tears as she stared at the simple grid of the tabletop. She was not far from her building. She raised her head and stared in its direction, at the stairs leading to their small room. Dark, foreboding, hazy.

One of the students stood. "Umm, are you alright? Can we help with anything?" It was one of those reluctant inquiries, provided because it seemed polite but delivered with clear disinterest and hope the entreaty would not be met with any requests.

As Sarah stared blankly at the young woman, she took a step back, her face delivering an extra dose of concern. *Deep green, freaked-out eyes. Wild, sweaty jet-black hair. I'd be afraid of me right now.* Sarah's voiced croaked out, "No. I can do it." She was not at all sure she could. She turned toward the building and walked, feeling a bit drunk and uneasy.

As she crested the last stair, there before her was the blank white door. For several seconds she stood, her left palm flat against it, the other holding the keys in the lock. Several deep breaths. Several more. They weren't working. She closed her eyes and turned the knob.

As she entered the tiny room, she saw their picture on her desk. Smiling, happy, alive. When the door closed behind her with a solid clunk, the room began to collapse around her. Breathing difficult. Heart racing. Her throat constricted. Nausea roiled in her stomach. It was choking her. She was on her knees. The chaos swirled in her head. She bent at the waist, lower, face near the floor, still on her knees. Eyes closed, she tried to breathe, tried to feel herself.

She crawled to a safe place where her dresser met the wall. She couldn't see her desk, the rest of the room, their picture. Breaths came. Halting. Slow. The pounding in her chest slowed. Some control returned. A deep breath. Standing presented a baffling challenge. Her dresser provided stability. Tears blinded her. She held on and breathed, slowly, deeply, until she could open her cloudy eyes.

Hunched but on her feet, clutching the dresser, feeling the need to wretch, she worked her way into the bathroom. Some cold water on her face helped. Her breathing and pulse slowed. After many minutes, lots of cold water and inner encouragement, the panic receded. With great effort, she pulled her clothes off, staggered from the vanity, put her hand on the wall and entered the shower.

Sarah stood a long time under the hot water, thinking, feeling, remembering and considering her future, before washing her body and hair. She felt better. Not good, nothing resolved, but better. She dried herself off, threw on her robe and stood before the closed bathroom door. That room was on the other side. Several deep breaths. Eyes closed, she opened the door, walked through and fell back into her bed, opened her eyes and stared at the dirty white ceiling.

THIRTY-FOUR

A soft knock on the door. "Honey? Sarah, are you in there? Can I come in?" It was Robert. She sat up, pushed her hair back and wiped the tears from her face.

"Come in," her voice cracked.

"Sweetheart, I'm so sorry this happened. Let's get out of here. This room can only depress you more, if that's possible. It's beautiful outside. Let me take you to lunch."

"OK," was all she could say.

He rushed over and took her in his arms, leaned back, looked her in the eyes and smiled broadly. "I know this doesn't help now, but it's going to be OK, sweetie. You're going to be OK. I won't let you down." She smiled and nodded. "Do you want me to wait here or outside?"

"Here's fine." He stood and helped her up off the bed and held her.

"I know everything seems to be lost right now, but I'll do whatever it takes to help you out of this. You will make it, Sarah James." He was repeating himself, but she realized he didn't know what else to say. Then he changed her life. "This, law school, was not only your dream, honey, it was also theirs. You can't let them down. Not now."

She looked up into those deep, soulful eyes that seemed to envelop her entire being, guiding her to him, a safe and secure place. This was not just about her. It was about them and their memory. This revelation hadn't occurred to her. Heather's caring, the run, the ancient tree, the spirits, the meditation and yoga, her shower, and now the security of Robert's strong arms and the warmth of his loving eyes were all starting to work in her. But that one bit of wisdom from Robert refocused her, settled her and made her feel so much better. "I'll be quick. I've already showered."

"Take your time. We have all day."

THIRTY-FIVE

She selected some clothes, a pair of tight blue jeans with worn areas in the thighs and knees—stylish even though they were naturally threadbare—a sleeveless T-shirt and a lightweight GW sweatshirt. She returned to the bathroom and dried and brushed her hair. She loved how it shined as it fell around her shoulders.

Sarah dressed and tried to do her makeup. Her hands were trembling, so she gave up. She didn't wear much anyway, and he'd seen her looking worse. She put one hand on each side of the sink and stared at her reflection in the mirror. *You can do this, Sarah James.* Down deep, the doubt was strong, but she stood, checked herself out and turned toward the bathroom door. The other side, where Robert now stood, was not quite as frightening, although after entering the small room, he swiftly guided her outside, shielding her so she wouldn't even glance into that horrid space. She appreciated the effort.

The air was warm and the breeze refreshing as they walked across the small quadrangle between the dorms and the undergraduate portion of GW. The grass was bright green, and the trees were full of blooms morphing into new light-green leaves as their petals fell like snow on the sidewalk. Students laughed while pretending to study at the various tables and benches. She hadn't noticed any of that when she'd left for her run or as she'd returned. She was so focused on herself, disconnected from the world. It helped to drink it all in, to sense it, to feel the warmth and positivity in the air. She felt better.

She snuggled into the soft leather seats of his BMW as he slipped through traffic. She put her left hand in his lap and stared into space, not paying any attention to where they were headed. She thought about her parents, Robert, school, money, life but came to no new conclusions. The car stopped. She gazed into Robert's gentle, smiling eyes and sat up. A young man came around and opened her door. Robert handed him the keys as he rounded the front of the car and took Sarah's hand. She wasn't entirely sure what was real and what was a dream. She held on tight and followed, her heart and soul searching for balance, while he became the only strength in her life.

They entered a bright and cheerful bistro. It was nicer than anywhere she'd ever gone, and she felt immediately out of place. She let Robert do all the talking. Sarah was a strong woman and was used to speaking up for herself, but not today. Today she was happy someone, anyone, cared for her.

They sat on a terrace beneath a pure blue sky. The waiter handed her the menu. The bistro served "trendy fresh dishes," whatever that meant. The menu apparently "changed with the seasons." Sarah looked up briefly. Robert was staring at her with the sweetest smile. She blushed and opened the menu then peaked seductively over its top, which Robert rewarded with a wink. She lifted the menu so he couldn't see her blush and tried to read it. She was not sure what anything was. She was used to simpler food—the sort her parents could afford.

Sarah lowered the menu, and Robert could tell that she was at a loss. A wisp of a woman, wearing a pastel, multicolored dress that floated about her, moved with amazing energy from table to table, from waiter to serving station to the kitchen and back. Robert called her over.

She glided across the floor to them. "Hello, may I help you?"

"Please help my girlfriend order. Thank you." Robert's tone was one of lord over servant, but Sarah didn't notice. She wasn't noticing much.

"Certainly. My name is Tish. How can I help you?" Her voice was sweet, melodic, with a touch of an accent Sarah couldn't place. For no apparent reason, it relaxed her.

***

it.

"You were a hot mess, Mom, and Dad seemed nice," Jazz added.

"It gets better." And Sarah continued.

***

After a long, leisurely lunch, he opened the BMW's roof, and they took a drive around town and out on the highway, going nowhere in particular. She loved the feeling of her long black hair flying in the wind behind her. The look he gave her told her that he liked it as well. She closed her eyes, shook her head to release all her hair from behind her and felt the wind carry her depression away.

They stopped on an island in the Potomac and walked hand in hand for a bit, perusing a few sculptures, then sat on a park bench. She told him about her life, and he listened. For some reason, that's what she needed. Just to talk. Perhaps because she had almost no friends, at least none who knew her well or cared about her life, or perhaps because she needed him to really know her and still like her, she wasn't sure. He didn't offer advice or solutions. He just listened. By the time they reached the car, she felt better.

As the afternoon waned, he suggested they go to the Kennerly Golf and Country Club in Maryland just northwest of American University Park in the District. "We're long-time members," he mentioned casually. She'd never been to a country club. As they drove, she realized how much she had needed someone to talk to, to listen to her. She'd never let anyone else in, besides her parents. It felt good. She reached over and put her hand on his. He took it and glanced at her. She was smitten as she gazed back into those eyes. She turned and put her right hand on his strong bicep and laid her head on his shoulder.

As they entered the red brick drive beneath the towering front gates, she gawked at the flower-filled landscapes lining the long drive up to the graceful front porch that led into the Club. She must've looked like an alien in a new world, staring one way and then stretching to look another as the marvels of deep historic wealth spread out before her. He parked, opened the door for her, gave her his hand to guide her to her feet and then gently hugged her to him.

"You're safe with me, Sarah. I hope you know that."

Completely under his spell, she nodded as she gazed into those dreamy eyes that seemed to swallow her up. She laid her head on his chest and breathed.

After a few seconds, she reluctantly left his embrace. "Thank you."

"Of course. So, sweetheart, let me give you a tour. What do you say?"

She nodded, and he took her hand.

THIRTY-SIX

"**W**as that the first time you'd been to the Club, Mommy?" Janie interrupted.

"Honey, I was poor. My family was, and outside of your father, I'm still poor. It was the first time I'd been in any club or place like that. It was Wonderland to me."

"Now, shhhhh, Janie. Let Mom tell the story." Jazz was unusually short with her sister.

Janie pretended to lock her mouth with a key and throw it away.

"Then what happened?" Jazz asked. "This is getting romantic."

Sarah smiled. The sun had set. The air was sweet and fresh. The fire burned low beside them, the wind carrying the smoke away. Nature had settled down for the evening, though she could feel the spirits all around, as if they too were listening to the story. Sarah reached out and took each of their hands and squeezed. "It's been a long time since I thought about those times. It's nice. And yes, Jazz, it was romantic."

***

They strolled around the Club holding hands as he talked and she listened, lost in a dream world among the lush grounds, gardens, statues, the golf course, the tennis courts, the pool and the outside grill, which was nicer than any restaurant she'd eaten in. It was unlike her to be girlish, but right now, she wanted him to lead, to do the talking, and without any request on her part, he did. It seemed right. She was floating safely in his world now.

Sarah was wafting among the clouds, walking on the paths of a glistening kingdom with a gallant prince who had ridden in and saved her from the gaping mouth of a fire-breathing dragon. She hadn't read a lot of fairy tales growing up, but she was living her own right now. As they approached the huge, solid oak front door, she stopped him.

She noticed that people, in particular, the women, were staring at her. "Robert, I can't go in there dressed like this."

"Don't worry, sweetheart, we'll take care of that."

The Club had a boutique that sold designer dresses, shoes and accessories. He talked her into trying on a few. It was an easy sell. She was caught up in an escape from reality that she desperately needed. She was almost afraid to touch anything. "How much does that cost?" she asked the kind woman helping them.

Robert stepped in, "She's new here. Honey, don't worry about the prices." He winked at the woman.

Sarah's smile was uncomfortable, but the woman's was genuine, which eased Sarah's mind. "Here, Miss, I think you'd look divine in this, don't you?" Sarah looked at Robert, who nodded. The long, flowing, soft cotton dresses draped beautifully on her athletic figure. She twirled in one and watched as the skirt billowed out around her strong legs like something from a movie. He bought her favorite and a pair of strappy high heels. She thought that maybe she recognized one of the designer names. She had no idea what the bill was, but it had to have been a lot. More than she'd ever spent on a wardrobe, much less one dress and a pair of shoes.

He guided her to the women's locker room to dress and freshen up. The space was opulent. Pink walls, white glossy trim, rich dark wood— even the lockers. Soft chairs. Marble and gold vanities. She undressed and stuffed her old jeans, T-shirt and sweatshirt into a locker. She thought about it for a few minutes before taking off her bra and adding it to the heap. There was no way to wear it under the dress he'd bought her. The robe inside was luxuriant. She put it on and headed to the mirrors with her purse.

A nice woman looked over at her and then down at her Walmart makeup options. After touching her hair, she asked, "New here, honey?" Sarah felt a bit like an animal being sized up at a fair. The woman's sweet smile indicated she was legitimately interested in helping her, and Sarah desperately needed help.

"Pretty obvious, I guess. I'm here with Robert Robinson. We've been dating." She thought about telling her the rest of the story but didn't want to cry.

The woman nodded to two others nearby. "Let us help you, dear." The three women went to work on her hair, her face and nails, taking options from their own makeup bags and discussing them like experts. "Just sit here and hold still." She did.

Sarah did as she was told and withstood the pain the three women inflicted. "No pain, no gain," the woman working her cuticles and nails said as Sarah winced. The women giggled. Sarah could only smile. They massaged and tugged on her hair, adding various potions from bottles until its long black luxurance glistened and fell like silk around her shoulders. They scrubbed and patted products on her face, chest and even between her breasts. They trimmed, filed and painted her fingernails and toes.

Why are these women helping me? But she relaxed and released herself to them. They brought over her dress and shoes and helped her put them on without interfering with their masterwork. One lady pushed her breasts up while another tied a bow behind her back. Sarah gasped.

"Shh, dear. Almost done."

Finally, she stood before the three women who looked at one another, obviously pleased. They stepped back, and the woman who'd started all of this spun her finger in the air, indicating Sarah should turn so she could see herself in the mirror.

Sarah's eyes widened and her jaw dropped at what she saw. She barely recognized herself. The women smiled as Sarah's face split into a huge grin.

She was Cinderella!

THIRTY-SEVEN

"**Y**ou clean up very nicely, young lady," the first woman said.

"Thank you, ma'am. Thank you all so much. I've never been in a place like this. I feel . . ." Sarah hesitated, "pretty." She felt so nice, different, in this place with Robert, and it felt good, secure.

"I think these will be lovely." The woman held up a bejeweled necklace and earrings that seemed to match the dress perfectly, then the three helped her put them on. "Now, my dear, please follow me." The other two women followed them out.

"Mrs. Sandlewood, how are you doing this fine evening?" Robert was deferential to the older woman who led Sarah out of the women's locker room. Before she answered, she stepped aside. Robert's jaw dropped.

"Robert, I believe this fine young lady is with you."

A broad smile crossed Robert's face. "So that's what took over an hour." The women smiled. Mrs. Sandlewood handed Sarah's arm to Robert, who took it in his. The older woman winked, and Robert nodded back. Then she turned to Sarah. "Dear, you look like a proper princess."

***

Sarah broke from the retelling. "He didn't listen to me," she said more to herself than to her daughters.

"What do you mean, Mommy?"

131

"I just realized. I was so taken, smitten, wrapped up and needy, I thought he was listening to me when we were walking. There were so many things I told your father that day that he was astounded to find out about later. It was all a mirage, and I fell for it." She paused. The girls remained quiet. As this revelation dawned on her, she said aloud, "He wanted a princess, even back then, and I fell right into it."

Sarah reflected quietly for a minute. "I'm the one who changed. I'm the one who's different. I'm not myself. I've been dishonest. He's the same person now that I met way back then. Domineering. Controlling. The king looking for a queen to serve at his beck and call. How'd I miss it?"

"Mom." Sarah was shocked into reality by Jazz's voice. "You were vulnerable. You needed him, or probably anyone."

"But he didn't save me, Jazz. If he hadn't been there, I'd be the sort of attorney I wanted to be. He changed me. He and Mother and the family. And I completely let them." She paused. "Girls, do not let that happen to you. Be strong and be yourself, no matter what happens."

The girls nodded, then after a minute, Jazz asked in an uncertain voice, "Mom, if you don't mind continuing the story, what happened next?"

"No, sure." Sarah cleared the fog from her own revelation. "Where were we?"

"In the Club. The ladies helped you. You were Cinderella," Janie reminded her.

Sarah sighed and launched back into the story.

***

Heads turned as they entered the dining room. Although most of the women were similarly attired, Sarah's bright green eyes, golden skin and midnight hair, flowing gracefully around her shoulders, turned their casual glances into stares. She pulled herself closer to Robert.

"They're all staring," she whispered into his ear.

"You're stunning, that's why." He puffed out his chest and stuck his nose a bit higher in the air as he glided through the room to a table for two overlooking the gardens. They had a leisurely dinner during which he did most of the talking. It was the fanciest place she'd ever been. He'd offered to order for them, and she'd let him. He was strong, debonair and in charge. He was in his element. She was lost, her life spinning out of control, but here, with Robert, there was a sense of safety, stability.

He'd changed into a sleek suit and tie from his locker so that he could comply with the dress code. He was quite handsome all dressed up. They ate and drank wine. They danced to a live quartet, and he showed her how to waltz. After a few minutes, she had the basics. Between songs, he filled their glasses, and at his urging, they drank quickly so they could get back to the floor. She swooned as he led her around the dance floor. She'd been alone so much of her life, and now she faced the prospect of being permanently alone. In that moment, it felt comforting to be in the arms of a big, strong man with means who took charge and seemed to care about her.

He held her close during the last slow song. Tipsy and quite relaxed, she snuggled deep into his embrace. As the tune ended and the lights were turned up, he gazed into her eyes.

As he kept a firm hold on her waist, they kissed, long and deep. Deeper than any kiss she'd ever shared with anyone. She melted. She was his. It hadn't even been a day since she'd lost her parents, but he'd brought her most of the way back to life, and that dorm room would only drag her back down. She needed comforting and company; right now, she needed him.

Later that night, she awoke and sat up—startled, lost, alone, afraid. Nightmares had invaded her sleep. She found herself in his big, warm bed. He wrapped her in his arms, delivering soft, gentle kisses as she wept. When she'd calmed down, she slipped into a deep sleep.

Warmth. Safety. Security.

THIRTY-EIGHT

In the morning, Sarah woke up to the smell of strong coffee and bacon. She grinned, enwrapped in soft, luxurious sheets atop a firm bed. She was wearing one of his T-shirts, which was huge on her. She didn't remember changing. She slid to the edge of the bed, the sheet wrapped around her, taking in the lovely features of the room. Dark woods. Soft carpet. Opulence. Something she was not at all used to.

She realized she'd left her clothes in the locker at the Club. "I have no clothes," she said rather loudly.

Robert bounded up the steps. "You're awake. Wonderful. Breakfast is ready. Perfect timing. You look radiant this morning. Simply beautiful."

She doubted him but took the compliment. "Thank you. Um, Robert, I don't have anything to wear. I left my clothes in the locker at your club."

"Hmmm." He grabbed a robe as soft and luxurious as the one she'd worn at the Club. "This should work. Stole it from the Club." He brought it to her, kissing her on the forehead.

She smiled and pushed him away. "Go, you. I need to get dressed. I'll be right down."

She watched him descend the stairs before slipping the robe around her shoulders, tying it at her waist, smiling broadly the entire time. *I could get used to this.*

Over eggs, bacon, fresh croissants, orange juice and coffee, he said, "Sarah, I realize we've only been dating for a little while and you're very vulnerable right now, but I'm crazy about you. I don't know, but I was hooked the moment we first met at the library. Anyway, I can't let you go back to that depressing dorm room. So, I was wondering if you'd like to move in together? I have plenty of space here in the apartment. You can have your own room and everything. We can figure all that out later. But it's yours if you want it, and I'd love to have you move in."

She took a deep breath. He'd swept her completely off her feet, which she needed at this point, and he did it with such style and grace. She gazed into those deep brown eyes and said the only thing she could.

"OK."

THIRTY-NINE

After breakfast, the conversation turned to her parents. Sarah explained that they'd wanted their organs harvested for transplant and whatever was left cremated, both of which were difficult for Sarah to deal with. Robert got on the phone immediately. Within minutes, he'd spoken with the hospital and a mortuary in Bozeman, Montana. To remain viable, organs had to be harvested there and before Sarah would be able to get to Bozeman.

Robert made another call and then called Heather. Twenty minutes later, Heather arrived at the door with Sarah's clothes. "Sweetie, how're you doing?"

Robert kissed Sarah gently. "Hon, get dressed. We're going on a little trip."

Heather joined her upstairs as she dressed. "Dish, girlfriend!" Heather made her smile. She told her about the evening with Robert, and Heather swooned.

"Heather," Sarah added, "I'm not coming back to the dorm. I can't stay there."

"I understand, sweetie. It's only one more month."

Robert arrived at the top of the steps. "Not to worry. I've taken care of it. You're paid up. Heather, the place is all yours."

Sarah hugged Heather. Neither had any idea it would be the last time they'd see each other.

Robert arranged for "people" to stop by and get the rest of her stuff, then drove her to a small private airport. He met up with a friend who'd agreed to fly them to Bozeman to pick up her parents' remains. Sarah was overwhelmed as they climbed aboard the small jet.

She cried the entire trip, sometimes sobbing uncontrollably, sometimes just weeping, often curled up in Robert's arms. She'd never felt so helpless, but he was there for her every step of the way.

By the time they arrived at the hospital, anything salvageable had been removed from their bodies, encased in ice and shipped, including, and most troubling for Sarah, her mother's lovely green eyes.

He'd arranged for her parents' remains to be cremated in Montana and paid extra to have it done quickly. Her parents were now in small plastic boxes. When the mortician handed them over to Sarah, she was surprised both at their weight and then how incredibly light they were in relation to what they'd each weighed in life. Each box had a simple white label with the logo and name of the mortuary and each of her parents' names in simple Times Roman script. She hugged them to her chest. Robert thanked him for rushing the process and put his arm around her.

Within hours, they were back in the air headed to Cleveland. She clutched the two boxes for a while, then set them down. She'd cried herself out but needed the comfort of Robert's big arms. He held her the entire way, brushing his fingers through her hair, caressing her face. He was so gentle, caring, loving. He drank the entire trip. Bourbon, neat, but he didn't seem to get drunk.

Robert and Sarah stayed that Wednesday night in her family home. It was an 1,100-square-foot, 70-plus-year-old brick two-story, three-bedroom, one-and-a-half-bath bungalow with a small finished basement and a nice but tiny backyard with a detached frame one-car garage facing the alley in back.

Robert was astounded she could live in such a cramped house, but to her it was comfortable and home. There was unity and pride in this little neighborhood. It was a community, though one she'd never felt completely connected to. Everything centered on the church and its activities, which they didn't attend. She realized she wouldn't miss the neighbor-hood, just the memories inside this house.

They spent the evening going through pictures, mementos and memories from her childhood. There was only a twin bed in her old room, and she couldn't bear to sleep on the double bed in her parents' room, so they slept in the small bed. He pulled her in next to him. It was nice to be held, and she fell asleep within seconds.

Being in her old house was nice but too emotional and uncomfortable for another night. She gathered some special things from the home, things of only emotional value: pictures, hiking and camping gear, flint knives, points and other tools she'd made, and a few other mementos. Robert had them shipped back to his family home. He'd already called a realtor who met them at the house in the morning. Sarah signed the listing agreement and gave up her keys. When they walked out the front door, it was the last time she'd see her childhood home. Robert handled everything, and she was so grateful for his help.

The visitation was held that evening, a Thursday, two days after they'd died, in a local funeral home. A good crowd came by. No caskets, but the little boxes of ashes were there. Mourners saw only the albums of pictures Sarah had gathered. She was fairly cried out by that point and was able to greet the many friends and colleagues of her parents who attended—people she barely knew or didn't know at all.

She realized how few friends she'd had in Cleveland Heights. Even though she'd sent out several e-mails, no one she knew came to the visitation. It was last minute, they had new lives and hadn't seen her in years, but in reality, she'd never tried to be popular, was even a little odd—maybe a lot odd to her schoolmates—and had been gone nearly every weekend in the wilderness with her parents. They hadn't really been friends then and weren't now. It was a good break from her childhood. This town was no longer her home.

When the event ended, she felt a bit freer. There was no longer a need to hold onto her hometown. As she was shaking the hands of the last people to leave, Robert appeared with the two boxes.

Robert asked, "Would you like to keep the ashes in nicer urns?"

"No," Sarah answered. Robert's face exposed his confusion. "Me and my parents believe that all things are composed of two parts, the physical body and the spiritual soul. Your spiritual soul is you. Your physical body is just a form being used while your soul resides on this earth. When you die, your soul moves on. What's left in these boxes are the remnants of the now useless and empty physical bodies my parents' souls used to live in."

"What are you talking about?" His smile was so radiant and pleasant that it made her smile.

She pushed his arm gently. "Never mind. I don't need nice urns because I want to return them to nature."

She and Robert checked into a hotel near the airport. After dinner, they drove to and walked out into a field not far from the airport on a windy Cleveland evening, opened the boxes and let the wind carry the ashes out over the grasses. She placed her palms together at her heart, bowed and said, "Namaste."

"What'd you say?" Robert asked.

Sarah kept her gaze out across the big field under the clear night sky. "It's a term, a gesture of peaceful spirituality sent into the universe, a term of thank you, in this case to the souls of my parents who loved me, knowing they will bring that peace back to me, if I pay attention."

Nothing else was said.

When they boarded the private plane on Friday morning, she left Cleveland behind forever.

FORTY

"**M**om, why'd you stay with him all these years?" Jazz asked.
"That's easy, honey. For you, for me. I have no family. None. The only family I have, that you two have, is your father's family. He's my connection to them. If I lose him, I could lose them, maybe you guys too, and I was afraid. They're rich. I'm dirt poor. They can hire attorneys. Who'd represent me? It scared me. Still does. But now I'm stronger; *we're* stronger."

"But Grandma and Grandpa are the best," Janie added.

"You're right, sweetie, and I'll never forget meeting them the first time."

***

They landed and headed to his apartment, where Sarah worked on her makeup using her tried-and-true Walmart special buys. She found a decent light blue cotton skirt and white blouse, did her hair and got it looking fairly nice.

"How do I look? Acceptable?"

"You look great, honey." Robert walked over and put his powerful hands on her muscular shoulders, which for some reason did not feel very strong. He looked her right in the eyes with his deep brown ones. "Don't worry, Sarah. My family will love you. Just be yourself." After a quick lunch, during which he attempted to prepare her, he drove her to his boyhood home in Virginia to meet his entire family.

She was excited and frightened. Sarah and Robert had been serious for only a few days, but meeting his family seemed like the right thing to do, even for her.

They turned onto a long drive; tall grasses lined the Potomac tributary to their left. A woodland area stretched off to their right. "That's a nature preserve," Robert pointed out. "My parents bought the land just after they were married before the state took this part. They were poor back then." The tree line ended. They were still flanked by tall grasses. The drive rolled right, up an incline and then left toward the crest.

As they entered the clearing at the top of the small hill, she was greeted with a majestic colonial home: two-plus stories, white with a soft blue trim and shutters. The third floor benefitted from dormers on either side of the peaked roof. She fell in love with the broad wrap-around porch that led to a four-season room overlooking the tributary on the left side of the home. "When Mother and Herb bought it, the house was a run-down old plantation manor. The owners controlled all the land as far as you can see. It was livable, but they rehabbed it, partly using the money from the sale of the park land. They did a lot of the early work themselves."

He got out of the car and walked around the front as she opened her door. He pulled it the rest of the way for her and extended his hand. She took it as he guided her out of the car. He was still talking. "Over the years, they've updated it further, using contractors and professionals, of course." He chatted and pointed as they walked hand in hand up the flagstone walkway.

As they approached, Robert's mother, who everyone, even her husband Herb, called Mother, greeted her with a wave from the big porch. Family poured out the front door. When she reached the top of the stairs, she was embraced with big loving hugs as though she'd been part of the family her entire life. The family whooshed her into the big house.

***

"Your Grandma and Grandpa and all your aunts and uncles are completely different from anything I knew as a family. I was an only child, as were my parents. No aunts or uncles and, so, no cousins. I was all alone in the world when my parents died. From the moment I met your father's family, I had a family—really for the first time. Mom and Dad and I were sorta best buds rather than a family. Thanksgiving was no bigger than dinner the day before. They loved me, but it was just us three.

"Your Dad's family, your family, was large and noisy, and they played and laughed a *lot*. It took me a while, but I soon came to understand them and then became a part of it. I love Mother." Sarah paused, wondering how she really felt at that moment, then continued. "We ended up staying all weekend. No matter how odd it seems looking back, at the time, it seemed so natural."

"I kinda wonder, Mom, if that was all part of Dad's plan?" The distrust and near hatred Jazz held for Robert was deep.

"Maybe, but I sure fell into it, and I wouldn't trade it for the world. I got the two of you out of it and so much more. As I sit here with you this evening, I remember what that old tree said to me."

Jazz broke in, "Strength against time, and time doesn't matter."

"Right. I took too long, true, but I stood strong against time, and now that we're free, the time no longer matters."

"Smart tree," Janie said. "I told you plants were smart."

FORTY-ONE

"Tell us more about when you met our family," Jazz said as she smiled at her sister.

***

As Mother guided her through the entourage of family into the big living room, she took Sarah's hands. "Look at you. So lovely. Robert, this one's a keeper. I can feel it." She turned to him and took him by his shoulders, which were well above hers. Mother looked Robert squarely in the eyes and, in front of everyone, said, "Boy, do not mess this one up. You got it, young man?"

"Yes, ma'am," he responded. Sarah didn't know how to react, but the brothers and sisters she didn't yet know laughed and patted Robert on his back.

Mother turned to Sarah and took her hands again. "Dear, tomorrow we're going shopping. We'll make a day of it."

The evening was rather chaotic, especially for Sarah. Family members and friends arrived at all hours, and Robert made sure they were all introduced to Sarah. A large spread was laid out on the long dining room table, but no one sat there. Herb bragged about the barbecued chicken, forcing two pieces on her. Robert graciously ate one for her. The rest of the spread included salted, crispy new potatoes, steamed broccoli with a bit of fresh lemon, glazed carrots, fresh fruit salad, a large Caesar salad, two

143

loaves of fresh bread—one sourdough and the other pumpernickel—and both chocolate and blonde brownies.

She was overwhelmed. The brothers and sisters, along with the friends and other relatives over that evening, ate in small groups, chatting, watching a Washington Nationals game, and playing board and card games. Watching from a corner, Sarah barely said a word. Robert sat and spoke with her, telling her stories and giving her some background, little of which she could even process.

They spent the night in his childhood room, which was still adorned with his trophies, pictures, articles and awards, mostly from high school. He ignored them, but she absentmindedly poked through them. They slept together in his queen bed. She was not in the mood to make love, and he was respectful. Her mind swirled, but not with anything specific. The demons from her parents' deaths did not revisit her. She snuggled into him, letting him hold her close, and smiled.

In the morning, she awoke, happy and frisky, like a weight had been lifted. They made love. Slow, gentle, caressing love, and he made her feel special. They cuddled and chatted for an hour until Justin yelled up the stairs, "Breakfast's ready."

"Wow, we gotta go. Saturday morning brunch is not to be missed." Robert was in a jovial mood.

She was all smiles as they dressed in jeans and T-shirts and headed down for breakfast. Mother sat Sarah in the chair beside her for breakfast, a spot ordinarily reserved for her youngest son, Danny, who she shooed with a smile to another seat. Robert sat across from her, on Mother's right. The family laughed and teased Danny as he pulled a chair up from the wall. None of the other siblings would let him in until Mother ordered them to behave. "Let little Danny in please." Although she smiled as she said it, she was hoping Danny would assert himself with the family.

The table was long to accommodate the six children, son Justin's girlfriend, Mother, Herb, Mother's elderly mother, who everyone called Gram, and Uncle Burt who, as far as she could tell, was completely unrelated. The table was covered with a lovely lace cloth. A couple of candles in silver holders and a small bouquet of fresh flowers graced the center. "Fragrant and lovely, but not so high that the family can't see over it," Mother explained. The chairs were antique, cushioned, mahogany and hand carved, and they all matched. Little in her family home had matched, and this dining room was nearly as big as an entire floor of her house. She was more than a little overwhelmed.

The two girls, Mallory and Brenda, and Danny left the table and brought back scrambled eggs, bacon, sausages, toast, Danish, croissants, a huge bowl of fruit, coffee, tea and three different juice options.

They passed the food, giggled together, both helping one another and pretending to deny food. Their manners were polite, despite the silliness. Herb, it seemed, was one of the biggest instigators. He worked very hard, and Saturday morning was his time to spend with his brood. No one scheduled anything over Saturday morning brunch.

FORTY-TWO

Mother spoke with her several times and toward the end of breakfast reaffirmed her plans for a shopping trip. "Sarah, we'll have a grand time. Are you ready to go spend some of Herb's hard-earned cash?"

Sarah glanced at Robert, who smiled encouragingly, and then looked back at Mother. "I think I'd like that very much."

"Good. Have you finished?"

She'd finished some time ago. She hadn't eaten much; the two consecutive feasts had been far beyond her own family's modest meals. "Yes, ma'am."

"Great." Mother stood and announced to the table, "Sarah and I will be gone all day. We are going shopping. Herbert, I am quite certain you have this gaggle of heathens under control and that we won't return to a complete disaster around here."

"Oh sure, honey. Got it all under control." He was stealing a piece of bacon from one of the boy's plates, was swiftly caught and the bacon confiscated. Snickers abounded around the table. Sarah noticed from the conspiratorial smile that Herb shared with his children that he had nothing under control; Mother's worst fears would be realized by the time they returned.

Herb got up from the table and made a point to kiss Mother more passionately than she thought appropriate. Everyone laughed. She slapped him gently and feigned a blush. They were so in love, and it showed in everything they did. "Have fun, honey. You know we're only millionaires, so keep it in budget." He knew perfectly well that she had no budget and would spend whatever she pleased. It was all part of their game.

Robert kissed her as she left. "Have fun."

Sarah raised an eyebrow, half-nervous, half-excited about the adventure with Mother.

***

Sarah broke from the story and addressed her girls. "Mother was honest to a fault, loved to gossip, seemed to know everyone, and had impeccable taste. We bounced from boutique to boutique along the streets of Georgetown. I felt like a puppy on a leash. We had our hair done by Rex, nails done by Pi because, as Mother pointed out, 'They're the best of the best.'

"We dined at a table along a quiet street at an expensive French bistro, where Mother convinced me that the escargot 'were to die for.' I tried them but didn't care for them, even though I acted as though I did. We'd been drinking wine, and—"

"What're escargot?" Jazz asked.

"They're snails."

"Yuck!" Janie exclaimed.

"Exactly," Sarah laughed. "Mother hates them too. I don't know why—it was probably the wine—but we laughed 'til we cried over Mother's trying to fool me." The girls smiled.

"Anyway, Mother taught me about makeup, proper posture and even how to walk in high heels." She noticed her girls stifling giggles. "Well, I'm good at it now.

"She never judged me or how I looked back then. She deftly turned me from an emotionally drained girl who wore little to no makeup, with crazy long hair and cheap clothes from the Goodwill, to a woman who stood tall and proud, wore stylish clothing and was well coifed.

"Mother did it with so much love and compassion that I never even noticed." Sarah paused. "Or perhaps I did notice and was happy to fit in and learn how to become Cinderella whenever I wanted."

"You were a princess, Mommy," Janie added with a smile.

"Yes, honey, I didn't realize it, but I was becoming a princess. That's what they wanted for your father—a princess." She shook her head. "How did I miss that?"

"Grandma's taught me that stuff too," Jazz noted.

There was a silence as Sarah thought about what was really going on back then. "Nothing was real for me then. I'd felt like a fly on the wall the evening before and at breakfast with all those people. I followed Mother around and did as instructed. Mother was like that."

"What happened next, Mommy?" Janie blurted out.

***

When they returned to the mess Herb and the children had created both inside and outside the house, everyone stopped and stared. Robert, in grass-stained jeans and an old Colts jersey from their Baltimore days, stood and smiled. He'd seen her this way before.

She was radiant in a long, flowing off-white cotton sundress cut at an angle and three-inch strappy designer heels, which showed off her powerful figure with elegance and grace. The wide-brimmed hat brilliantly framed her beaming face. From her ears hung gold earrings with triangle rubies mounted at the lobe and at the base of the pendant dangling from the delicate inch-long chain.

His eyes told her she was beautiful. The two daughters, who'd remained more put together than the boys, ran to her and patted Mother on her back.

"Mother," Brenda, the younger at about 15, said, "This is your best work ever."

Sarah wasn't sure exactly how to take that, but the young girl followed up, "Sarah, you look amazing, beautiful. Wow. I thought you were pretty before, but now you're off the charts."

"Thank you. I think."

Mallory, who was two years younger than Sarah, smiled with her. "Girl, you look stunning. I don't know what you see in Robert, but he'd be crazy to let you get away."

Mother gave her a mock scowl, as did Robert, but all three smiled. Then Mother addressed the rest of the troops. "Alright, all you hooligans—and that includes you, Herb—clean up this mess right now. Get the house back to some sort of order. Then we're going out to dinner to celebrate. Chantal's. Robert, you are excused from cleaning up. Please go outside and carry my new friend Sarah's clothes up to your room and then get yourself cleaned up. Mallory, you may help him. He's going to need it. Everyone else, please, let's get a move on. I'll make the reservations. We're leaving at 7. Be ready, dress properly, or you don't eat."

***

"There were a lot of bags and boxes. I carried my share, but your father and Aunt Mallory wrestled the others up two flights of stairs to your father's room on the third floor." She paused with another revelation. "Huh. I didn't realize it until just this moment, but other than my picture of my parents and schoolbooks, I never saw any of my own things ever again. I wonder what they did with it all?"

FORTY-THREE

Sarah turned to her girls in the darkness of the forest, her eyes moist and vision clouded. "Those were such good times for me, and for us as a couple. For the first time in my life, I had sisters, two of them, and they included me in all the silly things they did. They had my back. Your aunts included me in their constant pranking of your uncles, and the boys tended to be nicer to me when getting us back than they were to Mal and Brenda. It was a fun little feud.

"I suddenly had three younger brothers, and Herb, who was just as delinquent as the boys. Unlike my new sisters, I loved roughhousing and playing with Robert, Herb and the boys in the pool or yard. I could keep up with any of them and was in better shape than all of them.

"We lived at Grandma and Grandpa's house all that summer and our first two years together. I got into a nice rhythm with the family. It was a short drive to the law school. Your father and I rode in together. We were thrilled to see each other at the end of each day. My fellow female law students swooned over your father and told me how lucky I was. I guess I felt lucky.

"I'd get up early, grab Arnold's leash, and we'd run several miles before anyone other than Mother was up. It took a few days for Arnold to keep up with me, but he looked forward to our runs. He'd look so cute waiting for me at the bottom of the stairs."

"I loved Arnold," Jazz chimed in.

"So did I, sweetie, so did I." A tear slipped sown her cheek, but she regrouped. "So Mother was always there in the screened-in porch when we got back with a cup of coffee with vanilla creamer, just the way I like it. Mother and I would sit, Arnold at our feet, and talk or quietly take in the scenery. We'd see all sorts of birds, beavers, ground-hogs, deer and even the occasional raccoon. Arnold would stare at the animals, but he never barked or tried to chase them. It was a peaceful way to begin the day.

"Eventually, Arnold would nuzzle my leg and I'd get up to feed him. Then Mother and I would make breakfast for Herb, your father, Gram and Uncle Bert. Your dad landed a summer clerkship with a big law firm. He worked long hours and came home tired or would stay at his apart-ment. Hmmm. Thinking back, I never went back there. Ever. But he kept it." She paused, putting that out of her mind as she'd been doing with so much. "Doesn't matter.

"Anyway, your father suggested I take the summer off and spend it with the family, stabilizing my emotional world and finding joy in life again after the death of my parents. I agreed. I needed the time to grieve and heal."

"Mom, I think it was his first effort to control your life," Jazz said.

"Honey, you're probably right, but I did need that time. I spent most of it with Mother, cleaning the house or working in the gardens. Mal and I took long walks and talked about all sorts of things, like boys, relation-ships, marriage, families, having children and creating a home. Mallory wanted nothing more than to have the sort of life and home Mother had. Sometimes Brenda would join us, but she'd get bored.

"I think it was in late June that I took an occasional shift a couple of days a week as a waitress at a little diner in Georgetown. Somewhere Robert would never go. I needed the time away, doing something produc-tive, even if it was simple. I never told your father or your grandparents about the job. Not sure why. Perhaps even then, I sensed he would've dis-approved." Sarah smiled sympathetically at Jazz. "I know, I know. Part of your father's plan to suck me in and control me. Maybe you're right, sweetie. Maybe you're right. But I was in no place to see it back then.

"Life was moving fast. In a matter of weeks, my entire perspective on life had changed. I was living with a man I'd only been dating a few weeks along with his family in their stately home. That this was weird never occurred to me. Not once during that summer, or even the next two years, did I feel as though I didn't belong there with that family. Of course, I had no place else to go and no one else to turn to."

"Mom, I think maybe being with dad and the family made it easy for you, so you didn't have to think about how lonely you were or would be without them," Jazz summarized.

Sarah nodded. "Perhaps."

FORTY-FOUR

Several minutes passed in the quiet of the forest darkness, the fire crackling nearby, a gentle breeze blowing through the trees and the brook babbling its way to the lake until Jazz broke the calm. "But, Mom, did you ever really love Dad?" Jazz was determined, and Sarah could feel she wanted the answer to be no.

"I realize now, girls, that he and his wonderful family had gathered me fully into their lives after my parents died, and I'd let them. I needed it. Perhaps I fell in love more with his family or the circumstance or opportunity rather than with him. Hard to tell now, looking back, especially with how he's been." Sarah paused for several seconds, staring into the fire. "I suppose it's a question I've asked myself a lot lately." Sarah looked directly into Jazz's eyes and shrugged. "I owed him so much emotionally."

Janie had laid down and was fast asleep. Sarah got up, found a blanket in the tent and covered her youngest as the night grew colder.

"This was 2005, right?" Jazz asked.

"Right."

"I was born in June of 2006. So, I was conceived that same summer?"

"Good math, and yes. After all the lows and highs, I got pregnant with you, Jazz. It's a lovely story really." Sarah winked. "You want to hear it? It's kinda mushy."

"Yes." Jazz nodded.

***

A warm breeze flowed across the broad lawns of the Country Club. It came this evening without the humidity that D.C. days of summer often did. She had him all to herself. No late night at work or family function. Just Sarah and her man.

They'd dined on the big veranda at the Club overlooking the gardens and the golf course. She'd suggested a sunset stroll in the perfectly manicured grass along the trees between the first and ninth fairways. Her high heels dangling from her left hand, the sun glowing off her smooth golden skin that contrasted perfectly with her short bright yellow summer dress, she danced ahead of him. She'd loosened the ties at the top of her dress, exposing more of her modest cleavage, and watched as Robert gazed lovingly and lustfully at her.

Her soul soared as he increased his pace. She smiled and jogged backward. According to her plan, he was closing in on her. She wanted him and could feel passion coursing through her.

As she passed a bunker and a subtle rise in the course, she stopped and tossed her shoes in the grass. He jogged to her, and she leaped into his arms. He twirled her around, her bare feet floating through the air. As he stopped, she wrapped her legs around his waist and kissed him. Electricity raced through her body as his big hands caressed her back and then down to her butt, pulling her dress up so he could touch her skin.

Still in his strong arms, Sarah pushed his jacket off his shoulders, and he lay it on the ground. As he set her down, she gave him her best seductive smile and began to unbutton his shirt, kissing his bare chest above each button. She could feel his breathing change, his powerful hands stroking her bare back. She slipped his shirt off those muscular shoulders and couldn't help but run her hands atop them and then down his chest to his tight abdomen, then finally inside the top of his pants. Then, just as he was ready for her to unbutton them, she tickled him, giggling as he tried to tickle her back. She outflanked him, turning him, then pushing him onto the grass between two raised fairway bunkers. She fell to her knees atop him, her soft golden skin glistening in the glow of the setting sun. She looked both ways. No one could see them; she was sure of it.

Silhouetted against the darkening sky, a gentle wind blowing her long black locks, she met his piercing eyes, melting her heart as he lay there looking longingly up at her. His firm hands slid up her sides, peeling her dress up her body, sensuous, slow. As he lifted her dress over her face, eliminating her sense of sight for a second, she breathed in the wonderous aroma of the flowers blooming all around them. She felt the joy of the spirits of nature she'd trusted all her life dancing with them. After pulling the dress up her long arms, his dark brown eyes hers again, he casually tossed it aside.

They made love in the peaceful evening breeze on top of his $1,000 suit jacket under the last red rays of the sun on a beautiful warm August evening. When the sun had set and they were spent, he wrapped her up in his big arms and they lay together until the sky became indigo blue from edge to edge.

***

"Mom, that was so romantic." Jazz was swooning a bit. "How do you know that's the day I was conceived?"

"It was the only time we had unprotected sex, and you were born nine months later. He was my rock back then, and I loved that and, even more so, needed it."

"But did you ever actually love him? What did you have in common?" Jazz was persistent.

Sarah took a deep breath. "Love is a strange thing, Jazz. I'm not really sure when you know for certain that you're 'in love.' I felt in love with him at the time, but there was so much going on in my life. I was frightened and he saved me. I was alone and he gave me a family. I was penniless and he provided financial security. I don't know. He was there for me when I needed him. What's love?"

Jazz offered no answers to the rhetorical question.

FORTY-FIVE

Sarah continued, "Well, things did change. I quit all my causes because he asked me to, but mostly, he said, because he wanted to 'protect the baby,' whatever that meant. He didn't like camping, so I did that alone about one weekend a month. He usually planned a trip with the boys somewhere, then I'd head out. I took you, Ms. Jazz, when you were only six months old. The trip was simple, but you loved it from the first moment."

Sarah smiled. "Everyone was elated when they found out I was pregnant with you. We got married just after Christmas during winter break. It was a long Catholic Mass, presided over by Father Bob. I wasn't and still am not even remotely Catholic, though I did go through premarriage counseling, attended Sunday Mass with the family and came to know many of the parishioners. I didn't care that the religion made no sense to me. I'm sure I said whatever I was told to, and I did love Father Bob. So, maybe that makes me Catholic. Who knows?"

"Knows what?" Janie awoke, sitting up and rubbing her eyes.

"Everyone said I glowed at the wedding. We went on a romantic, two-week honeymoon to Aruba, Bonaire and Curaçao in the Caribbean. We lolled on the beach, snorkeled through amazing reefs, took a four-night cruise on a pirate ship, which required everyone to be barefoot, even at meals. The boat fired blank canons at the passing cruise ships."

"Cool. Can we go, Mommy?" Janie asked.

"I think they went out of business, but I can check."

"Let Mom tell the story, Janie."

Sarah smiled as Janie locked her mouth. "On shore, we dined at the finest restaurants and ate breakfast on our private veranda overlooking the ocean. I ran every morning on the soft sand beaches, did yoga in the bright sun and warm breezes. Your father sat in a beach chair with a drink in his hand and watched. He drank, a lot. I was pregnant, so I stayed sober. He never got so drunk that he lost control. Nothing like the last seven or eight years, but I do remember that he drank a lot on that trip. I wrote it off to the fact that I couldn't join him. Sort of jealousy, I guess.

"Even though I was starting to show a little, he told me I was sexy, and I felt it. The trip was a blast."

"I think, Mom, that you loved him. I think I would have. He seemed like a great guy, fun and silly back then." Jazz paused. "It's good to know that you loved him once, Mom. That he wasn't always like this. That he does have a disease and is not just a jerk." Jazz stared at her lap then back up at Sarah. "That makes me feel better. He'd never have done what he did if he were his old self."

"No, honey, never. I hope this accident knocks some sense into him. We'll see."

FORTY-SIX

The three of them crawled into the tent, and the girls were soon asleep. Sarah stared up at the fabric, thinking about the next few months with Robert.

**

At Robert's insistence, unlike the rest of her peers, Sarah didn't take a legal job the summer after her second year. Jazz was born eight days later than expected. That had stressed her out, but Mother was wonderful. Robert was there at the birth, excited as any new father. Having picked the name Jasmine, he was thrilled to announce it to the family. But once they were home, his work demands interfered. She understood. This was how it was for first-year associates at big firms. Long hours. She realized that in a year, she'd face the same demands.

All the ladies in the family, including her sisters, helped out as she finished her final year. Robert worked late and went in on Saturdays after brunch. He seldom worked Sundays, and after church, they'd often find something fun to do as a family or just the two of them. Sunday afternoons were their time, and she tried to plan something special every week. They had some good times, she remembered with a small smile.

The last semester of law school, Sarah was able to spend a lot of time with Jazz. Always there for Sarah, Mallory was amazing, and their relationship grew. Brenda loved to watch Jazz, but being in high school, she was often off with her friends doing who knows what. The boys and Herb were useless, but Herb doted over Sarah the same way he doted on Mother, Mallory and Brenda. She was "one of his girls."

Mother was mother. Always there. "I raised this crazy brood," she reminded Sarah, "and there's nothing about mothering that I don't know." Like any new mother, there was a lot about mothering that Sarah was happy to learn. Mallory learned right along with her.

Sarah was loved. She was part of the family. It was Robert's family, but as time passed, she felt like it was as much her family as his. Living in the family home with them, she was there a lot more than Robert was. She was Mother's daughter and "sis" to Mal and "sissy" to Brenda, whom they both called "lil' sis." Herb called her "Girly," probably because she was anything but, though no one understood Herb's nicknames. All the kids had one.

He called Robert "Horse." Robert never knew why. "I've never even been on a horse." Sarah knew. Robert was bigger and stronger than the rest and had a competitive drive that often led to others being bruised more than was required. He loved physical contact.

Mal was "Kiddo," and Brenda was "Lassie," which she hated, but that never mattered. Herb called everyone by their nicknames unless he was angry. Then he couldn't figure out what to call them, which made everyone laugh and broke the tension. Herb was incapable of staying mad. He loved everyone, even people he'd just met. His family loved him. His people at the company loved him. He turned hiring over to Justin because Herb hired anyone who came in the door.

Most of all, Mother loved him and he loved her. They were in their late forties, and even though Mother had lost her nice figure, Herb hugged and snuggled and cuddled with her at every opportunity. Herb had put on quite a few pounds, and Mother teased him about it, but then she'd seduce him on the couch by breathing into his ear, which was his kryptonite even though he hardly needed any, and they'd sneak off in the middle of an evening. They'd return smiling less than a half hour later. Everyone grinned, but no one said anything.

***

She had to admit to herself, as she stared into the darkness, that she'd been very happy back then. She took a deep breath, turned onto her side and was asleep in minutes.

FORTY-SEVEN

In the morning after they ate breakfast, meditated and went through their yoga, Sarah looked her girls in the eyes. "I want the two of you to know that my situation is not your father's fault. Sure, I've been afraid of him, but I still had control over my decisions. Not doing what you know in your heart is the right thing to do is your own fault. What happens as a result of your decisions are your responsibility, no one else's. No one makes your decisions, especially once you grow up and move out on your own. At that point, your decisions are yours, and you have to live with the consequences of those decisions. I am.

"I lied to myself. I tried to convince myself that what I knew was not a healthy relationship was really the best thing for me—for us, to keep the family together. Then lies piled upon lies, and eventually my whole world began to unravel. Never again. Never again will I lie to myself and do things that I know, in my heart, connected to the universe of souls who love me, are not right for me. Good things happen when you stay in harmony with the world, with the spirits who love you."

"What about us, Mommy? Were we bad decisions?"

"No, my sweet Janie, you two are proof that the universe loves me with all its might. You are the happy ending, the silver lining. You two are the most wonderful things that have ever happened to me, and I wouldn't trade any of my dumb decisions if it meant losing either one of you.

"When your father and I made the two of you, things were pretty good between us. The decisions I'd made at the time, the things I allowed to happen, bothered me, but there were a lot of great things in our lives too. You were the result of happiness. Both of you were. You have to know that."

Sarah got up on her knees, toddled over to them and gave them big hugs. They laughed at her funny duck walk and smiled as she hugged them. She plopped back down between them and continued.

"Things got bad when your father's drinking started to get out of hand. He got sicker and sicker and lost control of it. That's what the disease of alcoholism does. It takes your soul out of the equation. Your soul is where love comes from. Your brain takes over. Even though you feel love, because your soul is still there, of course, you can't do things to show how much you love. You drink alcohol instead. Your father spent our money on booze instead of doing the things he needed to do, that his soul knew he needed to do, for himself and his family. He felt bad about that, apologized afterwards, promised never to do it again, but in the end, he couldn't stop himself.

"When I threatened to do something to interfere with his access to alcohol, no matter how much he loved me, he lashed out at me, and lots of times, he hit me. Sometimes really hard. Early on, he felt bad. He'd run to me and hold me, apologize and kiss me, but eventually, his brain was so in control that he couldn't even feel remorse anymore.

"We tried to get him help. I should've done a lot of things, looking back—things I knew in my heart were right for me, for us, but I was too frightened. The decision not to do what I knew was right was my decision, and I've been paying the price ever since. Finally, I did what I needed to do."

She paused and the morning air was deathly silent. A small breeze blew, gently rustling the leaves. The birds began to sing, and the forest came to life. Nature revived her as she soaked it in. She took a deep breath, as did both girls, cleansing her mind from the negatives in her life.

Sarah changed the subject to the many good times they'd had on their adventures. "Remember when we . . ." The rest of the morning was spent recollecting their various trips. Jazz brought up the time Sarah was bucked off the horse in Arizona. Janie nearly fell over laughing as she remembered her mother covered in cactus barbs, sitting in the dirt in that corral. They began to plan their next one.

After lunch, they packed up and made sure they left nothing that would indicate they'd ever been there. The smoke house was dismantled. Their campfire was doused and spread out. Rocks were returned to the stream. The remaining smoked deer meat was packed up with them. When they had their packs on, Sarah spent a moment to scan the clearing. A lot of healing had occurred in the last three days. She breathed in the fresh air, closed her eyes and thanked the spirits of the woods; when she opened her eyes, a ray of sunshine, focused by the trees, fell right on her. She bowed. It was the right thing to do, then the ray was gone, blocked by a cloud. Rain was coming; she could feel it. It would wash away any remaining evidence of their stay.

She turned and encouraged the girls to move quickly. The rain arrived just as they put the last pack into the car. Both girls made it into their seats, but she was caught. Instead of running to her door, she walked deliberately through the downpour. She bent back, stretched her arms wide and faced the sky. First Janie and then Jazz jumped out to join her. They grabbed her hands and made a circle. They too leaned back and faced the sky. They closed their eyes and let the rain wash everything negative away, all the fears, pain, anger, jealousy, hurt and, most of all for Sarah, her hatred. She felt the growing power of positivity flow even stronger into her and into her girls. She shouted out loud to the universe, "Om Namah Shivaya," and the girls repeated the mantra.

FORTY-EIGHT

On Tuesday morning, she felt better—not free of the guilt, anger and fear she'd been living with for so long, but better. She'd slept well. It would've been better to stay out in the wilds, but they had to come back, and here was where the tension existed. Nonetheless, she could tell the girls were happier and freer as she watched them board their bus. Janie always ran onto the bus, but this time Jazz did as well, calling out to a girlfriend she spotted. Sarah went for a run, worked out in their basement gym, took a nice long shower and dressed for the day. The weekend had been restorative. She needed that positivity. There was a lot to do.

Robert had put the house in a trust for estate tax purposes. Sarah's first stop was to their bank to visit their safe deposit box. The banker, whose name was Carol, was sweet and helpful, leading her right to the box and entering her control key. She pulled the box out and set it on the table, then left Sarah alone to review its contents.

She opened it and found the trust for the house, insurance policies on the house and cars, their life insurance policy, some pieces of particularly fine jewelry, which she planned to put in the auction, their passports, wills, trusts and powers of attorney, marriage license, the deed to the house, an envelope containing some foreign currency left over from various trips and a few other items. She gathered it all together and put it in a manila envelope.

In Carol's office, they closed out the safe deposit box account, and Carol agreed to exchange the foreign currency for American dollars at the current exchange rates. Carol handed that duty off to a teller, who returned with a little less than $1,000 cash about fifteen minutes later. *Not bad.*

She asked Carol if Robert had any other accounts with the bank. She showed Carol the marriage license and the power of attorney as to Robert's finances. Sarah and Carol confirmed with the hospital that Robert remained in a coma and clearly wasn't capable of handling his own affairs. It turned out he did have an account with them, titled only in his name. She asked to see it, and the banker pulled it up on her screen.

"I'll need the username and password," Carol requested.

Sarah scrambled for the other scrap of paper in her purse. She found it and typed in the information. It worked. The account contained $84,683.

She maintained her cool. "I need to close that account. We need the money." She showed her the foreclosure notice. That was enough to convince Carol that, with the power of attorney, Sarah could withdraw the money. She received a cashier's check, took the money to her new bank and deposited it into her account.

She called an estate attorney who was a friend of Shawny's. Sarah met her early in the afternoon and instructed the attorney on how to change their estate documents. She confirmed that the joint house trust provided that either of the trustees had the power to sell the house, their personal property and do other things governed by the trust. That meant that Sarah did not need Robert to sell the house or hold the auction.

She removed Robert as a beneficiary, personal representative and as attorney for her affairs.

"Who do you want as your personal representative and power of attorney, Mrs. Robinson?"

Sarah was taken aback but lingered on the name she used. "And, I want to change my name back to James. Can you do that for me?"

"Sure. Best to do after the divorce is final. It can even be a part of that decree." The attorney was very matter-of-fact with a slight southern Virginian accent. "Now, as to the matter of your personal representative and power of attorney. Who shall I say name for those?"

A sense of panic rose through her. She had no one. No one she trusted. Why hadn't she considered this? Her stomach turned in knots, she felt hot, flushed.

"Are you alright, ma'am?"

"Um, I'm sorry. I don't have anyone. I guess it can't be my eldest. She's only 11."

"No, ma'am. Must be an adult. At least 18 here in Virginia."

She wasn't prepared for this. Robert's was her only family. *What about Mallory? I can trust Mallory to do the right thing, to care for the kids. To keep them from Robert.* "OK, my sister-in-law Mallory, I guess. Can I create something that keeps the children away from their father? Something that protects them? He's stark-raving mad, violent and an alcoholic."

They went over the details, discussed options, and the attorney promised she would do what she could. Sarah made an appointment to sign the new docs early Wednesday morning.

"That was a lot harder than I thought," she said aloud, clutching the steering wheel in the parking lot outside the offices.

She called Margaret, the realtor, with the news about the trust and e-mailed her a copy. It turned out that three families had viewed the house over the weekend. They were all interested. Margaret expected at least one offer by the end of the day. Margaret e-mailed the trust to each of the brokers representing the three potential buyers so that they could complete their offers properly and had confirmation that Sarah had the legal right to act on behalf of the trust to sell the house. Margaret also sent copies of the trust to the bank and title company.

Sarah next called the hospital to check on Robert. Even though she'd called with the banker only a few hours earlier, Sarah wanted to know more. Robert was not doing well. His liver and kidneys were struggling.

"They aren't failing, yet," the nurse explained, "but that's still a distinct possibility. Withdrawal is hitting him hard, which, given his years of abuse and what he put himself through last week, is to be expected. The doctors brought him out of the coma on Sunday, and he screamed and fought to get away. He began bleeding again and seemed not to care. That sort of outburst is extremely bad in his condition. We had to sedate him, and the doctor's decided to keep him in a coma for now so he can heal. It's for his own good."

Sarah's heart raced as she listened. She'd been there so many times. "He's a very violent man, nurse. It's good to take precautions. Any idea when they might take him out of the coma?"

"Not at this point. He's still in withdrawal and medically unstable." He was still in ICU and would be for at least the rest of the week, even if he recovered enough to be awakened again.

Why'd they even try? Sarah wondered. "Please, take your time. Don't rush this. His future depends on taking this slow and safe," Sarah added.

"We will, ma'am. We'll be careful with him."

Tuesday evening, Aunt Mallory came to visit with her much younger children. The girls loved their cousins. Mallory knew generally the things Robert had done to her over the years. Although they didn't discuss any of the forthcoming changes, Mallory suspected what would happen. She'd seen the "For Sale" sign out front. The divorce and all the other stuff, Mallory preferred not to talk about. This visit was short and sweet and all about the girls. Sarah meant to tell Mallory of her new position in her estate docs and with regard to the girls but never found the right time to.

As Mallory left, she'd promised the girls they'd go shopping soon. When the two women reached the front door, Mallory took Sarah's hands in hers and looked her in the eyes. "Sarah, we'll do anything to help you out. You got that? Anything. You call me and I'll be there. If you need someone to care for the girls, for running errands or getting out, whatever you need, I'm here. Got it?"

Sarah believed her and nodded as tears came to her eyes. Mallory gathered Sarah into her arms and held her. "It's going to be OK, sis. Don't you worry about a thing." She pulled back and studied her face closely. "You hear me?"

"I do. Thanks, sis. You cannot know how much that helps." Mallory had been angry at her oldest brother for years for what he'd done to Sarah and his daughters as well as the havoc he'd so often caused.

After Sarah signed the new estate documents on Wednesday morning, she met with her divorce attorney. Sarah updated her on everything she'd done. They chatted about the weekend with the girls. She made Shawny promise not to bring the incident involving Jazz into the dispute unless absolutely necessary, and after receiving that commitment, Sarah told her about Robert's molestation of their oldest.

"Sarah, I have to ask, why aren't you filing sexual assault charges against Robert?"

"I considered it, but other than Jazz, there's no remaining evidence. He'll deny it. Hell, he probably has no idea he even did it. I can't drag Jazz through that nightmare again. We spent the weekend getting that darkness out of her soul. I can't put it back there."

"OK, I understand. I hate our system, but what can you do? We'll keep it under wraps until we absolutely need it, and even then, we'll have a long and hard discussion about it, including with Jazz, before we bring it up."

"That's exactly what I want. Thank you, Shawny."

Sarah called Margaret. There was an offer, and another was imminent. "We have some time. Let's see what I can reel in today to help our leverage." Sarah agreed to wait.

After she hung up, she sat in the idling car, staring at nothing.

FORTY-NINE

By Wednesday evening, a contract for their house was finalized and signed. The bank had agreed to the deal and provided all the notices the title company needed. She and Robert would get nothing from the sale, but at least they wouldn't be sued for the difference. A banker was assigned to the case, and he'd handle most everything from that point forward. Sarah would just have to sign the closing documents. That'd be in about a month. Robert would be out of his coma way before then, and she could only hope he wouldn't challenge the deal and screw it up. Margaret and Shawny both assured her that the bank and divorce judge would never let that happen.

Sarah and Margaret reviewed several rental options online. Sarah decided she wanted a house and selected three she liked, all located 40 miles northwest of D.C. in Frederick, Maryland. They'd all visit the houses on Friday.

Late Wednesday evening, a nurse from the ICU called. Robert's condition had stabilized enough, and the doctors had decided they'd bring him out of his coma overnight. He'd be fully conscious in the morning, and depending on his condition and behavior this time, they'd let Sarah know if a visit was feasible after the girls finished school. She dreaded that call.

As she was heading to school on Thursday, their last day, to pick up Jazz and Janie, she called the ICU to check on Robert. A man, consulting the notes, responded, "Let's see. Fully awake. I guess he had a rough night. Seems to be in reasonably good spirits as of about an hour ago."

"What does that mean, 'reasonably'?" Sarah asked.

"I'm sorry, ma'am, I'm not sure. My shift just started. That's not really what it says here. That's what I interpret it to mean. Haven't seen him yet."

"OK. Thank you. We may come to visit him this afternoon."

The old school seemed to stare down at her as she drove up. The sky was grey and overcast. Ominous clouds rose to their west. Parents and school buses waited for the children to run out the huge front doors, but at that moment, the broad concrete apron and stairs were empty. This would be their last day at Jackson Rose Montessori. It would be their last day under the supervision of Principal Martenson, whom Sarah loved as a person, as an administrator and as an educator. There was no one better to teach her children.

How will they adjust from the open classroom Montessori system that allowed each student to learn at her own pace to the structured public school system that moves kids along the same standardized path from grade to grade regardless of their individual capabilities? How will Janie deal with "ordinary" kids in a traditional classroom? She'll be light-years ahead. How will Jazz deal with the insensitivity that pervades the public system, from teachers to administrators to the students?

Sarah had gone to public school. She'd been smart and different. It'd been hard. She'd felt alone often, even in the crowd of students. She was afraid for her girls in that world.

The bell rang and the students poured out of the big doors. Sarah stepped out of her car and walked around to the passenger side so the girls could see her. The girls sprinted across the wide concrete divide. They flew into her arms, and she hugged them tight. All three climbed into the car.

"Girls, I have several pieces of news. First, tomorrow we are going to look at several houses for our new home. How does that sound?"

The girls were more excited than she'd expected. This change was high on Sarah's priority list, but she thought it'd be more disruptive to

Jazz and Janie. Apparently not. She hadn't addressed the school issue yet. *I'll get to that.*

"That sounds fun," Jazz replied.

"It's a new adventure," Janie added.

"Great, and yes, it will be a fun new adventure." Sarah hesitated. "OK, now the other news."

"The bad news, right, Mom?" She couldn't hide much from Jazz.

"Just news. Your father is out of his coma. He seems to be in good spirits and would like to see you guys. We can visit him this afternoon."

The pause was thick with tension, and Sarah turned to her girls.

"I'm not ready to see him yet, Mom." Jazz was looking down at her hands in her lap.

"Janie?"

"I don't know, Mom. I'm kinda scared to see him in the hospital. Hospitals have lots of sickness and stuff. We could catch something."

She turned on the car and pulled out. Sarah took a deep breath and thought about how to handle this and all the changes headed her daughters' way. Once they saw the dramatic difference in the size of house she could afford when compared to the one they were in, along with the location in relationship to their current school, the changes to their lives would become real for the first time. Sure, the house was under contract to be sold, but they still lived there, had their same rooms, had all of their stuff and everything had pretty much stayed as it had been for all of their lives, except that the huge dysfunction in the home was gone. It was the only home they'd ever known.

The rest of the drive home that afternoon was quiet. She pulled into the big garage, which now only housed her car. The Mercedes had been totaled. She was going to have to work out the insurance settlement. One more thing she had to deal with. She was sure he didn't remember that he'd destroyed it. She also suspected no one had told him about the crimes he'd been charged with, none of which were major or would lead to jail time. Her heart sank. *He's getting out.*

He was lying in a hospital bed, completely oblivious to the disaster he'd created and what waited for him upon his release. And she certainly wasn't ready to bring him up to speed.

The girls were adamant. They did not want to go see their father. Jazz made it clear: "Seeing him is not the right thing to do in my heart. It will not help to keep me in harmony with the universe. I'm not going!"

"Me neither, for the same reason!" Janie followed her sister up the stairs to their rooms.

Sarah couldn't overcome that argument. It was her own philosophy she'd taught them and the same way she needed to approach the situation. What did she know in her heart was the right thing for her to do? She took a deep breath and decided to meditate on it.

Within minutes, her spirit was released from within her to mingle with the spirits of the universe. She felt the answer. She had to visit Robert. She didn't have a clue what would happen next, but she knew she had to go.

She sprinted up the stairs and called the girls. They were both in Jazz's room. "Girls, I meditated on what I need to do, and it was clear: I need to go visit your father. Any change of heart in here?"

They both shook their heads.

"OK, I'll head over on my own, which is fine. Really, it's the right thing for me to do. Jazz, you're in charge until I get back. You know the drill. While I'm gone, figure out what you want for dinner. Whatever you guys want is fine with me. I shouldn't be long, I hope."

"What're you going to say?" Jazz asked.

"No idea. None. I'm being called by the universe to do this. You guys good?"

They looked at each other. "Yep."

"OK. I'll call when I'm on the way home. Oh, hold on." Sarah ran into the girls' study room and grabbed the printouts of the houses she was interested in. She handed them to the girls. "These are the houses I liked. They're a lot smaller and pretty far away. We can talk about them tonight when I get home. They're on your computer. I love you two. Wish me luck."

"You'll need it," Jazz added.

"Thanks."

FIFTY

"ICU is on the third floor. Take the south elevators, which are around the corner, down the hall and on the right. When you get there, follow the signs."

The receptionist was friendly if impersonal. Sarah found her way to the elevators. She stood in front of them, staring at the button for several seconds until a couple with long faces, holding a balloon and a stuffed animal, arrived. They ignored her and pressed the up button. The up arrow lit, the elevator dinged, and the doors opened. The couple got on, pressed a button, walked to the back and turned to face the doors. When they looked up, she hadn't moved.

The man looked at his wife, who asked, politely but with a bit of urgency in her voice, "Are you coming, ma'am?"

Hands sweaty, her throat constricted, she took a deep breath. *Here goes.* "Yes, I am. Sorry," and she walked in. It was hard for her to press the "3" button, but she managed it. *These people must think there's something seriously wrong with me. Maybe there is.*

After ascending, the elevator dinged again, and the doors opened. Right in front of her on the wall was a sign with "ICU" on it in big threatening letters, pointing to the right. After stepping off, the doors closed. She couldn't move. She tried a deep breath, closed her eyes, another breath, centered herself as best she could, sighed and faced the big letters. *Follow the signs.* She did. Right. Then left. Her steps more difficult. Then right.

ICU. The letters seemed to scream at her. Two big white doors with small windows. She was again paralyzed. She inched closer, put her right hand on the smooth metal doors and stared through the window in the righthand door. White. Antiseptic. Busy. *He's in there.* She snapped her hand down and stepped back, recoiling. Heart pounding, breaths short, she felt faint. Deep cleansing breath. Nothing. Another breath, another failed attempt to center herself. *Sarah, you can do this!* She put out her right hand, touched the door, held it there for a second, then she pushed it open and forced herself through.

"Hello, I'm Sarah. May I help you?" the receptionist asked. There it was—"Sarah"—right on her name badge. Somehow that made her even more uncomfortable.

"I'm also Sarah. Sarah Robinson." The other Sarah just stared at her. "My husband, Robert Robinson, is here somewhere."

"Oh, sure. Mr. Robinson is awake and in room 3642. Right down that hall there, go left, and his room is on the right." She looked at the screen. "Oh, you have to go with a nurse. I'll get you one."

A few seconds later, a pleasant-looking plump woman in her fifties rounded the corner.

"Hello, Mrs. Robinson. I'm Amanda Graves, the nurse practitioner on duty. Come with me. Robert is alert and seems to be in pretty good spirits. Are your daughters with you?"

"No." Though nervous, she mused briefly over someone named Graves working in an ICU. It eased her nerves a bit and allowed her to grin as she followed Ms. Graves into the room.

"We're not going in just the two of us, are we?" Sarah asked, as her stomach rebelled and her heart raced.

"What's wrong?" Nurse Graves put a caring hand on her shoulder. "Are you going to be OK?"

"It's just that he's extremely violent. I'm divorcing him and selling our house before it's foreclosed upon. He's hit me, beaten me for years. For the first time ever, I hit him back. That's where he got all the cuts. He fell into a table. My daughters want nothing to do with him."

"I'll get some orderlies." She called over a couple of good-sized guys and explained things to them. "OK, they understand what we're up against. One was here last time they brought him out from the coma, so he completely understands. I think we're safe. You ready?"

Sarah looked at the two men and took a deep breath. "Sure."

Nurse Graves turned and led them into the room. "Robert, you have a visitor. You up for one?" The two men walked to either side of the bed, flanking Robert, who seemed not to notice them.

Robert sat up. "Absolutely. Sarah, it's so good to see you." He held out his arms for a hug, and Nurse Graves stepped aside.

Sarah stood transfixed. She couldn't approach him. "How are you doing, Robert?" she asked stiffly, glancing at the nurse. Even if Robert couldn't, Nurse Graves and her team were feeling the tension in the room.

"Pretty good. Still some problems with my liver and kidneys. They say it'll be several more days before I can get out of here. Feet hurt, so I'm stuck in this bed. I guess I stepped on some glass. My shoulder hurts. Other than that, pretty good. I could use a drink. Did you bring anything?" He smiled. Sarah didn't. "How are the girls? Did they come with you?"

"They're doing fine. They couldn't make it today. Sorry about that. Your condition changed kinda suddenly."

"I understand. Those girls are so busy. Is Mother coming by?"

Sarah was taken aback. She almost blurted out that Mother was very ill and bedridden, but another thought occurred to her. "Robert, do you know today's date?"

"Sure, it's February 18."

The faces of everyone in the room acknowledged the anomaly. "What year?"

"Why would you ask me that?" Robert looked around at the others, all obviously waiting for an answer. "What's wrong with you? You all know what year it is—2015."

Sarah turned to the nurse. "Ms. Graves, do you have a minute?"

She nodded and they walked out into the hall.

"Where are you going?" Robert yelled. A bit of a skirmish could be heard between Robert and the orderlies as they worked to keep him in his bed.

Robert was still yelling for, and then expletives at, Sarah. Her heart was already beating quickly, and now her flight response was in full mode. She wanted out, took Norse Graves' arm and moved her down the hallway toward the exit. "Nurse, February 18, 2015, is one day before Robert's mother was diagnosed with terminal cancer. She's been ill for a few years, but in 2015, there was still hope. That was dashed on the 19th of February when test results showed that the cancer wasn't shrinking but was spreading. That news sent Robert into a tailspin. How on earth do we deal with this?"

The nurse considered this new information as they stood at the ICU doors. The commotion and vitriol were increasing back in Robert's room, and more help raced past. "We're going to need a psych consult. It was obvious to me that you had no real desire to be here." Another orderly ran past them. "Now I understand why. We'll take care of it. You should go, and we'll handle it from here. The psychiatrist will likely want to talk to you. Does he have any other family who'll want to see him?"

"To tell you the truth, I'm not sure. He has family. Lots." She paused. "It's been a rough several years."

"Yeah, I get it. We had a similar situation in our family. Very tough to deal with. Unforgivable, no matter what condition he was in. OK. I'll call the psychiatrist. You go home to your daughters. I'll make something up for Robert. He's in a dream world anyway. He may not even remember you were here. I'm going to give him a sedative. We'll handle it."

"Thank you. Let me know what you need from me." Sarah shook Nurse Graves' hand and pushed through the exit doors.

It was a lot easier to leave than it had been to come in.

FIFTY-ONE

"How'd it go, Mom?" Jazz was waiting in the living room for her.

"Your father's still a mess. I'm glad you guys didn't go."

"Tell me."

Sarah hesitated but decided Jazz could handle it. "Your father thinks it's February 18, 2015. That's the day before we found out that Mother's cancer was incurable. He's stuck in the past. It was weird. I don't think he remembers anything since then. They've called in a psychiatrist to see what they can do for him."

"If I were him, I wouldn't want to remember anything since that day either," Jazz said. "He lost, like, two jobs that year. We got kicked out of the Club. He's been drunk pretty much ever since."

"You're right, honey. He wasn't all that great before that, but after we got the news about Mother, he fell off the cliff. They may need me to tell them what's really happened so they can tell how far out of whack his memories are. Does he just have some dates mixed up, or is he living in a fantasy world?"

The two sat there for several minutes, gazing absently at the floor.

"It'll work out, Mom."

"Yeah, just a lot to deal with," Sarah confessed to her oldest.

"We'll be OK."

"You know, Jazz, I'm the one who's supposed to be soothing you with those words." They both grinned a bit then sat in silence for a few

177

seconds, Sarah staring at the floor and Jazz studying her. Finally, Sarah looked up and broke the tension. "OK, how about dinner? What should we make?"

Just then Janie came bounding up the stairs from the basement playroom. "Mommykins, you're home." She ran and jumped into Sarah's arms.

"We were heading to the kitchen to make dinner."

"Let's go out. I feel like Chinese."

"That's funny, you don't feel the slightest bit Chinese to me." Sarah squeezed Janie's arm. "What do you think, Jazz?"

Jazz pinched her sister on the butt. "Nope, not one bit."

"Moooommmm." Sarah put Janie down, who then snarled at Jazz before laughing uproariously and falling onto the floor.

"Actually, Mom, Chinese food does sound good."

"I am too tired to cook," Sarah conceded.

"We can celebrate the last day of school, Mommy," Janie said from the floor.

"OK, Chinese it is. How about Ma's where we can eat out on the patio? It's beautiful out."

They agreed.

Sarah was surprised that Robert didn't come up once in the dinner conversation. Jazz brought along the printouts of the houses they were going to visit the next day and some research on Frederick, Maryland. They went over each place in detail.

While Sarah was at the hospital, Jazz broke it to Janie that they weren't going back to Jackson Rose. Sarah was pleased that the discussion focused on the public schools, the various private schools, parks, wilderness areas, festivals, museums and other cultural institutions near the houses.

"And this one's a Montessori school. It goes all the way through high school. And see back here—they give scholarships to worthy children of families who can't afford the tuition." Jazz smiled.

Sarah was impressed and nodded. "We'll have to visit, see if we like the place and find out what it takes to get in."

It was amazing the additional information Jazz had dug up on each of the houses, their histories, owners/landlords, what the houses rented for and pictures from other sites, including Facebook, Instagram and other social media Sarah had never heard of. The dossiers were complete. Jazz was nothing if not thorough.

Jazz had also uncovered another house for rent on a social media site for the neighborhood. The rent for the house was in their price range.

They were moving. Tomorrow would be a big step in that direction.

FIFTY-TWO

"Hello?"

"Mallory? How're things?" *How lame.*

"We're fine here, Sarah. What's up?"

"Well, Robert came out of his coma last night, and I went to visit him this afternoon. The girls didn't go. It's a good thing. Mal, he thinks its February 18, 2015."

"Wow. Really?"

"It's right before we got the news that Mother's cancer is incurable. Remember, Mal, they thought she maybe had six months?"

"She's showed them. Mother's tough."

"It seems his mind has erased everything that's happened since then."

"Hell, sis, given all the crap he put you and the girls and all of us through since then, I'd just as soon forget it too. So, what now?"

"They're calling in a psych consult. I have no idea what will come of that. They told me that the psychiatrist may need to talk to me, and I was hoping, maybe, you'd come with me. I don't know if I can handle it alone."

"Of course, honey." Mal paused. "I wonder if he even remembers stuff that happened before February 2015." Sarah could hear Mallory sigh. "OK, I tell you what. You have enough to do. I'll call the hospital in the morning, find out what they need from us and then tell the rest of the family."

"Thank you so much."

"What're you doing tomorrow?"

"The girls and I are looking for a new home," Sarah answered.

"Where are you looking?"

"Frederick, in Maryland. It's a nice community, good schools and several houses the girls like in our price range. We need to find something. This house closes in about a month."

"Wow. I'm sure you'll miss that house."

"Probably, but the last several years have been hell, Mal. I think we all need a fresh start. The girls seem to be looking forward to it. So, I'm not sure we'll miss it. I still can't go into the study. I went in while the cleaners were here and once to rearrange for the realtor, but since then, the door's been closed. I have lots of great memories with the girls here, but there are more bad ones with Robert."

Mallory sighed again. "Sis, you know we're here for you, no matter what. We have plenty of room, and you can stay here if you need. If the house search doesn't work out, you have a place with us. You worry about your new reality. Let me worry about Robert. I'll keep you updated. You OK with that?"

"Thank you so much. You can't imagine how much I appreciate you taking this off my shoulders. Let me know when and if I need to be at the hospital. We may have to take you up on the offer to stay with you. We'll see. Everything's a mess."

"Sis, your world's been a disaster for years. This is a huge change, but it probably should've happened a long time ago."

"Yeah, everyone keeps telling me that."

"Hang in there. Love you." Mal hung up.

It was so great to have a sister, even if not by blood. She settled into a big chair, her phone and hands in her lap. This was the hardest part. Robert's family was her family. She had no one else. No parents, siblings, grandparents, aunts or uncles or even cousins. She was the last in the James family tree. The children of Robert's brothers and sisters were Jazz and Janie's cousins. They were all younger, even than Janie, but her girls loved them and loved to be around them.

If Robert "recovered," whatever that meant, and showed up at the family holiday gatherings, would I be invited, would the girls be included? Of course, they'd include the girls. If I'm not invited, the girls would be crushed, but would they go without me? Would the girls go alone with Robert?

Sarah's thoughts spiraled from there. *Would Robert be sane and safe enough to have weekend custody without me? Would the girls go with him? Am I losing a second family?* She was going to be alone again. That, she realized, was the main reason she'd stayed with Robert all these years. The fear of losing the family was so penetrating that she'd ignored the other stuff. She could not abide the abuse toward her girls, though. Their situation had to change, and she had to trust that the universe would make the family part work somehow.

This time, she assured herself, she was strong enough to handle it.

FIFTY-THREE

The drive to Frederick took over an hour, which was probably a good thing, Sarah thought. They met Margaret at the first house. It was a lot smaller than their current house, of course. But being in the actual space was eye-opening. This was the house they'd liked the least, had the lowest rent and was the smallest. She'd arranged it that way on purpose so that the house they liked best, the biggest, would be last. It was still smaller than the first floor of their current house, but it was big enough.

After the first house, Margaret treated them to lunch at a quaint bistro on a lovely lane filled with other small businesses. None of the houses they were considering were near this wealthier part of town, but the lunch was nice and, best of all, free. Sarah had made it clear to Margaret that there would be no discussion or mention of Robert. Margaret respected that request. Early on during lunch, it was decided that the first house would be removed from the list.

Jazz regaled Margaret with her dossiers on the other houses, the schools and nearly everything else there was to know about Frederick. Margaret was impressed. "Young lady, these are amazing."

As Jazz began to show Margaret her research, Sarah turned to her youngest, who was uncharacteristically quiet. She'd been on her phone the entire time. "Janie, you OK?"

Sarah was worried she was really struggling with all of this. Janie took a deep breath.

"Well, I Googled the school Jazz mentioned, Jarmellson Academy, and I connected to two girls my age who go there. We've been discussing CRISPR-Cas9, which is a really cool gene-splicing technology being used in horticulture and for all kinds of things. It finds specific gene segments that are creating a problem, uses the Cas9 enzyme to cut the section out, and then they can either attach the two ends or put a good gene back in. Poof, the cell is cured. These girls are going to a camp in a couple of weeks at the school where a scientist is coming to talk about it. Can I go?"

Wow, that came out of left field. "Um. Get me the details—dates, times, costs—and we can look into it Monday. No school, so we can do it together."

"You bet, Mommy." And she returned to texting with her two new friends.

Sarah had never realized how truly bright Janie was. She needed to get the girls into this school.

The next house needed a lot of work but was acceptable. However, everyone preferred the third house, the one Jazz had found. Sarah and Margaret would reconvene over the phone that night and make some decisions.

FIFTY-FOUR

Janie jabbered on incessantly about Jarmellson Academy, the camp, CRISPR, her new friends and some botanical science event that neither Sarah nor Jazz could keep up with. As Janie rambled on and Sarah listened intently, occasionally interjecting an intelligent question, Jazz focused the entire drive home on her phone. The Academy's camp that Janie wanted to attend began in a couple of weeks, and being about plants, Janie was beyond excited. After a 50-minute drive, Sarah was still not sure of the details from her 5-year-old. She'd figure it out later. As they pulled into the driveway into the spot where Robert had bled on her car, Sarah's stress levels rose. She needed to get out of this house as soon as possible.

"Mom, I hate to even ask, but I've been texting with some girls from the Academy that I found on Facebook, and, well, they want to meet me at the Frederick Mall tonight at like 7:00."

"It's already almost 5:00."

"I know, Mom, but I'd love to meet these girls and start making friends in our new hometown. After dinner, could you drive me back out there?"

"Let me think about it. Alright, you two, out of the car. We've got a house to rent." She paused for several seconds as she considered Jazz's request. "And Jazz, if you're going to meet your friends at the mall in two hours, you'd best get cleaned up and dressed properly. Sheesh, Janie, do you think that sister of yours is worth another trip out to Frederick tonight?"

"Sure, Mommy. And we can go hiking up behind the new house and see what's up there. Wha' d'ya think?"

"OK, we've got a plan. A plan with a lot of driving, but it's good to start familiarizing ourselves with the new town. Now, go change. I'll start dinner and call Margaret."

Sarah called Margaret, who helped her complete the rental application online. Her credit was still great. Still employed, her income was strong. They could afford the rent on their favorite house. Margaret assured her she'd be approved.

The three sat at the table. Sarah again took their hands, focused on the center space between them and said, "It's been a crazy ride, these last few weeks and months and years, for us. Thank you for guiding us into our next life together, free of all obstacles and burdens." Again, she had no idea to whom she was directing this gratitude—the universe of spirits, perhaps—but it felt good. They chatted about Frederick, the new house, the Academy, the botany camp, the two girls Jazz was going to meet and the girls Janie had connected with.

The drive back to Frederick seemed quicker. They found the mall. Jazz spotted the two girls instantly. "There they are, Mom. Stop," she yelled, and Sarah pulled to the curb. Before Sarah could say anything, Jazz bolted out the door, saying, "Thanks, Mom, I'll call." The girls were cute and athletic and greeted Jazz warmly. They turned and sauntered, like adolescents do, into the mall. Jazz was dressed perfectly, like the other girls—a little trashy, with a hint of luxury, all mixed in an eclectic look that somehow worked.

"Oh well, Janie, there she goes."

Sarah patted the front seat, and Janie squirmed between the front seats and into the passenger seat and secured her seatbelt. "Off to the wilds of suburban Frederick."

The sun was setting, but that'd never bothered the Robinson girls in the wild, especially a wilderness between two sets of subdivision houses. They didn't even use flashlights. The moon was bright enough, along with the unwelcomed, albeit soft, glow of the streetlights. They followed the creek as it meandered nearly a half mile each direction from the house they were after. They walked to the big lake to the east and back, then up to the main road to the northwest and back. During the walk, they stopped and listened to sounds from the woods. Janie bent down and looked at plants. They flicked water at one another, joyful and carefree. *What a change.*

"Let's see what's up the hill," Sarah suggested. They climbed the hill on the other side of the creek. In the soft twilight, lit by the luster of the moon, sifting through the branches and leaves above, they found their way. Over halfway up, atop an outcropping of rocks, a six-foot-wide, eight-foot-long oblong ledge loomed over the deepest part of the woods. Without a word, Sarah and Janie sat lotus style and slipped into meditation. No mantra, they simply focused on their breathing and the sounds of nature. The breeze through the trees. The rustle of small animals. The undulating purr of cicadas. Janie would also be feeling the spirits of the plants around them. It was a peaceful time. The spirits of the woods danced with theirs. No purpose. No desires. No pain or sadness to throw off. Just peace and quiet and love.

The peace was broken by the sound of her phone, vibrating in her pocket and playing the ringtone designated for Jazz.

"Hi, honey. How's it going?"

"Awesome, Mom. We're ready to leave. Can you come and get me? Same place."

"Be there soon." She looked across to Janie. "Your sister's ready."

"Mommy, this place feels like home."

"It sure does, honey, it sure does."

Jazz was still chatting with her two new friends when Sarah drove up.

Before Sarah could even say hello, Jazz started, "Mom, I want to play soccer. There's a soccer camp Karen and Bridgett are going to. Can I go?" It was the first time Jazz had shown an interest in sports, but she was in great shape, very coordinated and it sounded like a great release for her. Jazz seemed nervous and excited at the same time.

"Sure. Why not? Soccer. Who knew?" For the first time in a long time, Jazz dominated the conversation on the drive home. She talked

187

about the girls, some others she'd met and showed off a few things she'd purchased.

"Did you meet any boys?"

"Mooommmm," she replied, even as they shared a smile. "Well, yes, there were boys at the mall, and we met a few. They'll be in eighth grade at Frederick Middle School, the public school, next year. They seemed nice. A couple were cute."

Sarah smiled to herself. *Good start in the new world.*

FIFTY-FIVE

On Saturday morning, Sarah found herself with nothing to do. No tasks to occupy her mind. She felt lost and frightened. She wandered in the early morning light around her room and then down the stairs and around the main floor. Jazz especially, but Janie on occasion, liked to sleep in. This was one of those weekends. It'd been a long one for all of them, or perhaps it was the calm with Robert out of the house. No fights, banging and yelling. No horrid stress.

Sarah made coffee and stood in her robe staring out the sliding door into the big backyard, green and luscious. There were a few weeds in the gardens now, but she didn't care. The sky was blue. She slid the door opened, walked out onto their red cedar deck under the huge old oak tree and, clutching her coffee near her chest, plopped down into one of their comfortable chairs, the kind with fabric stretched between steel.

She set the cup down on the round table beside her, took her lotus position, closed her eyes and listened. No mantra. No desires. Just listening to the birds, the leaves, the squirrels. She could feel the soulful power of the ancient tree, much younger than the one with whom she'd shared important time after her parents had passed, but a being who'd been here long before this house or neighborhood. It was one of the few old trees that were saved.

Her mind wandered into the vastness of the spiritual universe. She didn't engage with it as she sometimes did. She just felt it.

Warmth.

Calm.

Gentleness.

Her muscles relaxed for the first time since the camping trip. What became clear, what she heard and felt as clear as anything she'd ever experienced, was that she was doing the right thing for her family, but behind it was a touch of foreboding. Something she couldn't put her finger on. She felt like maybe she wasn't going far enough, but as stress began to interfere, as she began to try to figure out what was going on, the connection faded and then was lost.

Her eyes opened and she said aloud, "Sarah, you know better. Just be."

Before she could try again, Janie skipped out the door. "Hi Momsy, what's for breakfast? I'm starving."

Sarah gathered the spritely youngster into her arms and held her until Janie wriggled free with a huge grin.

"What do you want, Ms. Janie?"

"Pancakes. Can we?"

Sarah smiled and remembered how her father had made pancakes for her as a child. Cheap, easy and fun. "OK, young lady, pancakes it is. Now I have to remember how to make them."

They spent the morning looking up the recipe, making and failing at pancakes before they got it right. Jazz ambled down the stairs and smiled at the mess in the kitchen. She got herself some juice and sat at the table to watch, giggling and making fun at their attempts.

The pancakes were good enough, and the morning, even cleaning up, was something frivolous they all needed.

Later that afternoon, Sarah, Jazz and Janie visited a Soccer Star store. The helpful female attendant, Tammy, who'd obviously played, went through all the gear Jazz would need to play competitive soccer. Tammy was patient, showing Jazz the stylish way to wear everything, when to wear what and advice on what to expect from veteran soccer players on her first few days. Jazz left with more knowledge, a little more fear and growing excitement along with new soccer "boots," shin guards, a ball, several pairs of shorts, practice shirts and socks, scrunchies and rolls of colored gauze to hold her hair back in a proper ponytail.

Since neither of them knew the first thing about soccer, they also bought two books recommended by Tammy. One focused on skills—how to kick, pass and head the ball, including several advanced maneuvers, how to perform them, and when and why to use them—and even a little about their histories. It had a ton of pictures and detailed instructions. It also went over the rules of the game, from time to fouls to etiquette.

The other detailed the strategy of the game, positions and what each was expected to do, lineups and the advantages of each, set pieces and more. Tammy suggested they watch the English Premier League or German Bundesliga, both of which were on early weekend mornings, to get a feel for how the professionals play the game. She also mentioned that the U.S. Women's National Team was playing a friendly game the following Saturday night.

Jazz explained as though she'd been following the team for years, "The girls talked about that game. The U.S. Women are playing Norway, who apparently is pretty good." Tammy nodded.

Jazz texted her friends that she had her equipment. "Mom, they're getting together on Tuesday night for a kick-around, like at 7:00 at Frederick Municipal Park," she read from the text. "Can I go?"

"Sure, sounds fun. Janie and I can check out the Academy. I'll try to make an appointment."

"Yay," Janie burst in.

They all crashed on the couch that evening and watched a movie all the way through, uninterrupted, something they'd seldom, if ever, done. As Sarah lay her head down that night, she thought, *Maybe normalcy is possible.*

FIFTY-SIX

The landlord responded around 10:00 Sunday morning that her application had been accepted. Once she signed the lease, the place was theirs. The only wrinkle was that the landlord wanted the lease to begin on Friday, six days from now.

Sarah wasn't paying the mortgage on the old house anymore since it was under contract and the bank was handling the deal, so they could do that. This would be better. Sarah and Margaret texted back and forth, working through minor details on the lease. She wasn't a contract attorney, but she knew enough—perhaps too much. She worried the details would end up messing up the deal, but at 4:30, Margaret told her they had a lease.

Sarah hung up her cell and fell back into the secretary's chair in front of Jazz's laptop waiting for the final contract to arrive. It took forever. Exhaustion settled in. She took a deep breath. Running around had made her feel like she had her head on straight and kept her mind off the inevitable—dealing with Robert. *When he gets the divorce papers, he'll go ballistic. When he finds out the house is sold, he'll be uncontrollable. When he gets out and starts drinking again—well, she didn't want to even think about that. One step at a time. We need to be somewhere he can't find us before then.* She stared at the screen.

What's taking so long? She carried the laptop, open and active, downstairs to get a cup of coffee, walked around the living room with it still

192

open, sat in one of her big chairs and stared at it, finished her cup, got up and poured another and returned to the upstairs study. Nothing. *What's taking so damn long?*

Then, *ping*, the e-mail popped up. The owner had signed. The deal was real. She called the girls, and they came running into the room.

"We're moving to the house we liked best this Friday. How about that?"

"Yaaaayyyy!" The two girls danced around the room. Sarah hugged them.

"OK, now to make it final." The two girls crowded around her as she went through each page, clicking on the electronic initials and signatures until she finally reached the end.

"Wow, Mommy, that's a lot of stuff to sign."

"OK, girls, here we go. Want to push 'Send' together? It's *our* house, after all." They all put their hands on the mouse, Janie on the bottom, then Jazz and Sarah on top. "Ready, on three. One, two, two and a half."

"Mommmmmy!"

"Three." The mouse clicked and the screen notified them that the documents had been successfully sent. The girls cheered, hugged and danced around the room. A few seconds later, when she received confirmation of the deal, Sarah printed it and the fully signed lease. She put it all into the manila file she'd been using for the house, which included Jazz's dossier, and set it on the desk with emphasis. "Done deal!" She feared Robert, but he'd have no idea where they were.

Sarah realized it was approaching 5:30, and she hadn't even eaten lunch. "I'm starving. Let's go out for dinner to celebrate. What d'ya say?"

"Yay!!" was the universal response.

"Get cleaned up, change clothes, and let's get outta here." They all ran to their rooms. Excited, they all got ready quickly. Janie, of course, was ready in seconds. Sarah freshened up her makeup and hair, changed into a simple blue dress and slipped on some pumps. She and Jazz arrived in the hallway at the same time, complimented each other, and they were off.

They met Mal and Sam, her husband, and their young children for dinner at a quaint Tuscan restaurant. After greetings, Mallory jumped right in. "So, tell me about this house."

"It's perfect," Jazz started.

"It's got an awesome huge yard that backs up to these great woods with a creek running right behind us and a hill that's full of woods," Janie continued.

"It's common ground, so no one can build on it," Sarah noted.

"Nice." Mal and Sam smiled at the family's excitement.

Jazz and Janie started talking between themselves about the woods and what they would do there, and Sam reluctantly got up to change the baby, giving the sisters a few minutes to talk.

"In my heart, I knew this was the right house for us. It's big enough. The woods behind it sealed the deal. The girls went gaga over them."

"Sounds wonderful, Sarah. I'm so happy for you." She patted Sarah on the shoulder.

FIFTY-SEVEN

The next day, Mallory called. The psychiatrist, Dr. Mary Underwood, had asked if Sarah would come to the hospital and spend a few hours with her going over things so that she could get a better read on how to treat Robert. Sarah and Mallory headed in together. As they sat in the psychiatrist's office, after introductions, Dr. Underwood brought them up to speed.

"Robert is still stuck in 2015. He's becoming increasingly agitated, even violent. His father came to visit, but he didn't stay long. I guess he's not doing well either." The two women nodded. "So, no one else has visited, and Robert wants to see you and the girls and can't understand why you haven't come around. He's demanding to know why his mother hasn't visited. Not sure why his father didn't explain that, but perhaps that's why the visit was short. Of course, we haven't yet told him his mother's dying and bedridden. He has no memory of her in that condition. He's demanding alcohol and to be allowed to leave."

Sarah and Mallory looked at each other and then back at the doctor. "You're not discharging him, right?"

"Oh my, no. Late Friday evening, he struck an attendant while trying to escape and had to be restrained to his bed. By Saturday afternoon, his liver and kidney function were improved enough to move him to the psyche ward. He fought with the orderlies and had to be sedated. As you know, he is a big man. In the psyche ward, they can restrain him under a

195

psyche consult. The staff there is better prepared to handle his outbursts, violence, confusion and general condition. It's been a rough weekend for Robert."

Mallory asked, "Why has no one called Sarah or me or anyone in the family until now?"

"It was better that we handle him in this condition without a lot of distractions. Your presence would only be more confusing for Robert and, honestly, for you. You're in different times. He's living in your past like it's the present. You'd be hard-pressed to recollect that time well enough to deal with him in his current state. We're not even sure if what he believes actually happened. That's why you're here. Anyway, he's been sedated as of Saturday night and is pretty incoherent right now. He'd be too violent for visitors and caregivers if he weren't."

The psychiatrist paused, creating an uncomfortable silence, so Mallory spoke. "OK, so what can we do? What are we here for?"

"Yeah, we're here to help, as best we can," Sarah added, realizing how hollow it must have sounded.

"I need history, background. I need to know what's real, what may have caused Robert's break with reality and any other details you can think of."

"Before we begin, I am divorcing Robert. This conversation needs to be protected by doctor-patient privilege or some other privilege. I don't want what we say here to be dragged into court because Robert is the patient and, therefore, has the privilege. We're both attorneys. I need to be protected."

Dr. Underwood pressed a button on her intercom system. "Nance, can you come in here? Bring patient admission forms please."

Sarah and Mallory completed the forms, which included statements as to their rights regarding the information being shared.

"My sister, the lawyer," Mallory said as she signed the form. Sarah smiled.

"No problem. You're now both patients of mine, so we can continue. I need the background; I don't need to share it with anyone. And if I need to, I'll get your consent. Agreed?" The two women nodded. "OK, Mallory, you're his sister, why don't we start with you? What was Robert like as a child?"

Mallory and Sarah spent a bit over two hours with the psychiatrist bringing her up to speed. The two smiled and laughed about the wonderful times at the beginning when Sarah became part of the family: the "day out" with Mother, punking the younger brothers, shopping together, the births of Jazz and Janie, the big family brunches on Saturday mornings, holidays and other events.

Sarah talked about her weekends and summer trips into the wilderness with Jazz and Janie. Mallory knew about the trips but didn't know anything about what they did. They had a lively discussion about how they survived. The doctor and Mallory were amazed.

Mallory then turned to the doctor. "And then our mother was diagnosed with cancer."

Dr. Underwood broke in. "Let's take a second. I couldn't help but notice, as you reflected on all the wonderful times the family shared in those early years, that Robert was, at best, a passive participant. In fact, after Mallory finished telling me about his childhood, and you went over the tragic way you and Robert got together, neither of you even mentioned his name. I presume he was at the Saturday morning breakfasts?"

"Of course," Mallory said. "No one missed them unless you were out of the country or something."

"I presume he was at the births of your children?"

"Sure. Of course, he was there. He was right there with me as they were born. He held my hand. He told everyone in the waiting room about the births and the names we'd chosen."

"Actually, Sarah, he was in New York on business when Janie was born. Mother was in with you. She told us about the baby. She called Robert to tell him, but he wouldn't take the call. He was in a meeting or something. Remember, he didn't even come home for three days after Janie was born."

Sarah looked at her sister. She sifted through her memories for that day. Then she turned to the doctor. "Mallory's right. He wasn't there. He wasn't around much, really." Sarah paused. "And when he was, it was less and less pleasant."

"We all helped Sarah out with the girls when they were really young. Mother picked them up every day and cared for them while Sarah went to work. I'd stop by to help her out. I didn't have my first child until 14 months after Janie was born, so it was fun for me to go through the process with Sarah's girls. Robert worked late a lot."

Sarah continued the story, "Robert would come stumbling in drunk most nights—well, really every night, even back then before Mother was diagnosed. He was late and drunk at Jazz's fifth birthday party, and I was angry. That was the first time he hit me. He knocked me down in the living room, then he stormed into his study and slammed the door. He apologized later that evening, and we moved on. Where was I going to go? I'm an only child. My parents are both dead. I have no other relatives." Tears surfaced in Sarah's eyes. "Mallory and Mother and Herb and . . ." She began to sob. Mallory put her arm around her. Through her tears, Sarah added, "They're my only family. They're my girls' family. They're all I have." The tears flowed more strongly, dredging up her fears and conflicts.

"We tried to get him help." Mallory still held Sarah around her shoulder. "The entire family had an intervention one Saturday afternoon. Mother took Sarah and the girls out somewhere. Dad led it. He called Robert a drunk. That was probably not the right way to start an intervention. Robert became enraged, threw a vase against the wall, shattering it. Then he cussed us all out, told us we had no idea what he was going through and stormed out, shouldering right through our brothers. Even they couldn't stop him."

"I remember that day." Sarah began to pull herself together. Her anger at him tended to help. "The bastard went to Pappa's, his favorite tavern, as usual. I had to go over there and drag his sorry butt into my car and bring him home. He almost fell out the door trying to get out while the car was moving. Luckily, I'd made him put his seat belt on. What a nightmare. It was not the first time I had to do that." She paused, recalling the painful memory. "He smacked me in the car, trying to get away. I had to fend him off while I was driving."

FIFTY-EIGHT

"**O**K, so even in the good times, Robert was not all that involved in your life, Sarah. Would that be accurate?"

Sarah's eyes clouded and fell from the doctor's. Mallory pulled her chair even closer and put her other arm around Sarah's shoulders. The tears flowed again, and she couldn't do anything to stop them. "We were never normal, Mal," she croaked out. "I couldn't make . . . a good family." Mallory guided Sarah's head to her shoulder, and Sarah sobbed.

"Cry it out, honey. Just cry it all out." The psychiatrist sat in silence, waiting for Sarah to pull herself together.

Sarah lifted her head off Mallory's shoulder, wiped her eyes with her right hand, cleared her throat and said, for both to hear, "Damn, I really am a head case. Good thing I'm her patient now." The doctor cracked a smile, and Mallory giggled softly.

"Mal, I don't think I ever really loved him. I never did. I loved you guys. I loved Mother and Herb and you and all your crazy, wonderful family. I was in love with *you*, not him. Maybe he knew that. Maybe I drove him away. Maybe I drove him to drink. It's all my fault. Oh my god, Mallory, what have I done?"

The psychiatrist broke in, "Sarah, *Sarah*, none of this is your fault. Everything you did was normal. Maybe you loved him at the very beginning. It's hard to tell at this point, but he was your husband and the father of your children. You did what mothers do. You protected your girls, and you tried to make your family work.

"His disease is his disease, and this one, alcoholism, has ruined more families than yours. An alcoholic, especially one in the depths of the illness, is selfish and very hard to love. So, your responses and actions are perfectly normal defense mechanisms, and I see them all the time." The doctor paused. "Sarah, you are suffering from a condition referred to as battered woman syndrome. You had no way out. Over time, you rationalized things, doing whatever you could to make yourself believe that the marriage was working or at least might be saved, to protect your children and their lives. Your symptoms and actions are right on point with this condition, including your final lashing out against Robert."

The therapist stood and leaned across her desk. "So, Sarah Robinson, this is *NOT* your fault. Do you understand?"

Sarah nodded, glancing at Mallory, whose eyes were filled with empathy. Mallory squeezed her sister's shoulders. Sarah felt new strength and turned to the doctor, now standing erect behind her desk. "Yes." Sarah wiped away her tears and took a deep breath and tried to center herself. She raised her head, straightened her shoulders and addressed the doctor, "I do understand. Thank you."

"Good." The doctor sat back down. "OK, this has been a lot. Do you want to move forward, or is this enough for today? Can you handle the next part? From where I'm sitting, it doesn't get any better, does it?"

"Worse." Sarah looked at Mallory, who looked back at her lovingly.

"Honey, you don't have to keep going. We can do this another day." Mallory touched Sarah's shoulder.

"No, Mal, I think I need to get all of this out. I've been helping the girls get through it. I think it's my turn to get it all out. I'm making a break from this. I need to put it behind me. Is that OK, doctor? Do you have time?"

The doctor looked at her cell phone. "We'll make time." She pressed the com button on the old phone system on her desk.

"Yes, doctor?" came the pleasant voice of the receptionist.

"Nance, can you call Mrs. Washington and Mr. Smith and reschedule them? Tell them it can't be avoided and apologize."

"No problem."

FIFTY-NINE

"OK, we have lots of time. We are closing in on the time frame Robert is currently living in. Who wants to start? Mallory, you mentioned, before I broke in, that your mother was diagnosed with cancer. When was that?"

Sarah was thankful Mallory opened the next part of the story. She went through the pain everyone felt upon learning Mother had cancer. She went over the efforts Herb made to find a cure, trying every treatment anyone suggested might work. Nothing did, but it seemed to prolong her life, though Mother was now a shell of her former powerful self. Mallory turned toward Sarah.

"I guess it's my turn. Robert was drinking more and more. A few months before they determined her cancer was terminal, he lost his job with the big firm but managed to catch on with a smaller litigation firm. He'd come home drunk and violent. Sometimes he'd barge in and, well, make me have sex with him."

"He raped you?" Mallory said, disgust on her face.

Sarah stared at her. "I gave in. It was better than being beaten, and most of the time, he was too drunk to perform."

"Sarah, that's rape," the doctor said.

Sarah looked at her then back at Mallory. That had never dawned on her. She couldn't process the idea. "It was survival." Finally, she continued, "Well, more often, he'd pass out in his study and leave me alone.

By February 2015, we weren't sleeping together anymore, but I guess we could be civil to each other. Before he got fired, I'd still dress up and go to the Club with him and to dinner parties and such to 'impress clients.'" Sarah made air quotes with her fingers, a smirk marring her face. "He could make it through some of them, but as time passed, he'd get drunk and become belligerent, ruining the evening for everyone. Then he'd blame it all on me, which was never good."

Fists and pain invaded her mind. Her heart began to race, and her stomach clenched. She slumped over, and Mallory grabbed her before she fell to the floor. The doctor raced around the desk and helped her up. Deep breaths helped her push the images and pain from her mind, from her body. She slipped back into the chair, and the two women helped her sit up straight.

"Sarah, I think this might be enough for today," the doctor said, crouched in front of Sarah, hands gently on her shoulders, eyes gazing directly into Sarah's, as though trying to read what was inside them.

"No!" Sarah declared. "I have to get through this. I need to. My girls depend on me, even if I only get past this enough to make decent decisions. So sit down; let's continue." Sarah sat up, her eyes stern.

The doctor nodded, rose and returned to her chair. "OK."

Sarah continued, wiping tears from her eyes. "So, January 2015 was the last decent month he had, I guess, by his standards. He'd won a case and received a nice chunk of money in the settlement. But in mid-February, the tests came back on Mother showing that the cancer had spread. She was given six months to live. I don't know, but that seemed to kill him. Maybe he really needed me then. I didn't have it to give him."

Mallory broke in. "No, Sarah, this is not your fault, and it was not Mother that sent him spiraling out of control, as if he could get worse."

"What do you mean it didn't?"

"He didn't care about Mother, or her illness or any of us, then or pretty much ever. Robert was an asshole. All he cared about was himself. I'm sorry to say this, honey, but you were his trophy wife. You're tall, pretty and well-mannered and were trained by Mother on how to act in polite society." She took a deep breath. "Honey, and I'm sorry to have to be the one to tell you this, but he fucked anyone in a skirt. He had one-night stands, girls he kept in other towns and a few he entertained in D.C. at his apartment. That money you thought he'd won on a case was the last loan Herb gave him to keep you all afloat.

"A day or so after Mother's diagnosis, the family made a decision that Robert needed to get his life together and they were no longer going to support him until he stopped drinking. Robert was a falling-down drunk, and Dad finally cut him off. We all agreed and stood by Dad's decision. *That's* why he fell apart."

Sarah stared at her for several minutes. "Of course. Of course, he was having affairs. He was out all night and over weekends. How fucking stupid am I?"

The tears poured out again, this time rejecting the affections of Mallory. Mallory understood. She was the bearer of really bad news. Bad news she and the family thought Sarah already knew. It was so much. Airing everything out had blown up on her, and Sarah slid off her chair to her knees and wailed. Mallory jumped out of her chair and put her arm around her. Sarah shifted her body into Mallory's and accepted the love. They sat there on the floor for what seemed like hours, though it was only minutes. Visions from memories raced through her mind. "Oh my god, what an idiot I've been!" she screamed up at the ceiling.

Then, like a light had been flipped on by that release, she stopped and looked into Mallory's eyes. After a few seconds, she said, "I did know." Sarah's voice was low but became stronger as she continued, "I did know, Mal, and I just didn't care. I think I wanted it that way. Over time he forced himself on me less and less. Of course, I didn't want him touching me. I wanted it that way."

She took several cleansing breaths, which barely worked but allowed her to sit up. She crawled back into the chair. She wiped her eyes and turned to the doctor. "I did know. I knew. By then, the fact that he was hardly ever home was the best part of our marriage."

She turned to Mallory. "I had all of you to love and care for me and the girls. You all knew our family secret, but that brought you and me even closer. I did know. Of course, I knew. The affairs made him the bad guy and me the beloved sister who was being mistreated. It was what I needed. I'm sorry." Her heart rate slowed as the realization settled over her.

"Oh goodness, sis, we didn't love you because of that. We cared for you because we loved you. You're as much my sister as Brenda is, maybe more so. You and I are closer. We've spent time together since you came into the family. Sure, we knew Robert was being his usual asshole self, but sisters band together, and that's what we did, bringing you into the fold."

Sarah looked her in the eye and loved her more than she ever had. She took Mallory's hands in hers. "Thank you so much, sis. I love you too. It's been so great to have a sister, a family." They hugged. Then Sarah turned to the doctor, cleared her eyes and straightened up, and in a more matter-of-fact tone said, "I did know. I've been lying to myself for so long.

"And the revelation about where that money came from changes everything. I thought, for these last couple years, that Mother's illness and impending death threw him off the deep end. We all mourned and struggled and did everything we could to make her remaining days as wonderful as possible, not to mention trying to help Herb through it all. However, now that I think about it, Robert was never there."

"And Mother beat the odds," Mallory chimed in. "She's way outlived the prognosis. It's been a blessing. Everyone's been around except Robert. You, Herb and I have always been there for her."

Mallory explained to the doctor, "Mother's in hospice now. She's lost most of her faculties, a lot of weight, and we're not sure what's keeping her alive. Even the doctors aren't sure."

"Remember the day when you, Herb and I were with her? She came out of the fog, clear as ever. I'll never forget that moment. She was so funny." The memory brought a sad smile to Sarah's face.

"She was her old self for a few seconds before she faded," Mallory remembered.

"She took my hand in hers and looked me straight in the eyes. I thought she was going to impart some deep bit of wisdom or something. Instead, she asked me for some escargot. We laughed so hard, I thought it would kill her." Sarah turned to the doctor. "Then she pulled Herb to her, told him she loved him and thanked him for trying so hard to save her life, then she slipped back into the fog then off to sleep. She's never done that since. We all hugged and cried. The machines started beeping, and nurses came rushing in. We thought she would die right before our eyes. We were pushed out of the room. They stabilized her. Herb was inconsolable. We all cried, but we tried our best to be there for Herb. Mother has always been his rock. She's everything to him."

SIXTY

The psychiatrist prompted, "Let's go back to your mother's final prog-nosis and go through the realities of the next couple years since Rob-ert seems to be living at the beginning of that time frame."

The two women went through that first month or so, Mallory filling in information that Sarah didn't know relating to the family. There were fights over money and his behavior. Sarah rehashed their recent past together, the times he'd hit her, the explosions at dinners, the Club and at home.

As Sarah moved closer to the present, the memories became in-creasingly painful. Sarah was glad Mallory was there. They held hands throughout. Sarah broke down and cried a few more times. Mallory learned of things she and the family hadn't known, not the least of which was the molestation of Jazz.

"Fucking asshole. We should put him in jail, Sarah!" Mallory was aghast at that story but was sworn to secrecy, which was not, by a long shot, her forte.

Finally, Sarah went over in detail the events of the evening and morning that led to his hospitalization. At this point, Sarah was all cried out. She sat up straight and summarized for the doctor what steps she was taking and what would face him, including the misdemeanor criminal charges, when he was released from the hospital.

As she finished and stood, a weight lifted from her shoulders. She could feel it. Mal half-grinned at Sarah's reaction. The doctor seemed to understand as they shook hands. The afternoon, while incredibly pain-ful, was freeing in a way. She wasn't happy. She wasn't sure what she felt. Nothing more than unburdened, but it felt good.

As they left the doctor's office, she said to Mallory, "Mal, I needed that experience. I've lied to myself for so long. I feel like a fool for staying with Robert. I'm moving forward. I'm doing the right thing. Honestly, I no longer care what happens to him."

"Good for you, sis. It's about time, but I love you for keeping hope, for staying in the marriage as long as you did, trying to make it work, but now even more for having the strength to get out and move on with your life. I'm here for you. You're my sister and always will be." She held her arms wide and Sarah walked into them. The two hugged for several minutes.

"I love you, sis."

"I love you too, Mal."

SIXTY-ONE

The next morning, Sarah turned her focus on packing up the huge house. *What should she take with them and what should they sell at the auction?* Anything to keep her mind busy.

Mallory called. "Sis, let's do lunch. Yesterday was intense. I feel like we need to debrief or something. I've been wired ever since."

Sarah realized that with all the new information, she'd been tense as well. "Sure. A nice chat would be great."

They met at a quaint coffee and sandwich shop in Georgetown. They talked about the discussion with the psychiatrist, working their way through the revelations and pain of the last several years. After ninety minutes of rehashing the previous day's discussion, with no tears whatsoever, Sarah refocused the discussion on the future. She told Mal about the Academy, both girls' new friends and planned activities, and the impending move. Mal was so happy for them. Then she asked her to be her personal representative of her estate and to care for the girls if anything happened to her. A tear appeared in Mallory's eyes as she accepted. They hugged and parted, important issues resolved and a vision of a brighter future established.

That evening, Sarah, Jazz and Janie drove out to the fields in Frederick Municipal Park to meet the other girls. They'd promised to help her with the basics before camp. There were nine girls knocking the ball around when she arrived. They had two small portable goals set up and some cones in a rectangle. The two girls Jazz had met at the mall sprinted to the car as they saw her getting out.

"Jazz, welcome to Frederick."

"Home of the Jaguars."

Sarah got out and walked around the front of the car. "Hello, ladies. I'm Sarah's mother, Ms. Robinson."

"Hi, Ms. Robinson, I'm Bridgett."

"I'm Karen."

"Very nice to meet you both." The preteens stood there awkwardly, not knowing what more to say to the adult.

"Well, bye, Mom. Come get me in . . .?" She looked at Karen for help.

"About 90 minutes."

The three girls sprinted back to the group. Sarah watched as Bridgett and Karen introduced Jazz to the other girls. Jazz had read both books from cover to cover in the three days since their purchase and had practiced a little in the backyard so she wouldn't "feel like a total geek."

They started simply, passing the ball back and forth around the circle of girls with the instep of their feet, just like the book instructed. Jazz stood with her back to Sarah, Bridgett and Karen on either side of her, helping her with her form. She seemed to be picking it up pretty well. A little stiff, but she was getting it. Sarah was happy that Jazz was making friends. She'd been so melancholy. Of course, now she knew why. Sarah would help lift that burden off Jazz's back if it was the last thing she did.

Sarah and Janie took a visit to the Academy, speaking to the headmistress, Ms. Jansen, who was firm but friendly and clearly a feminist, which Sarah appreciated. It was late, so Sarah thanked the headmistress for meeting with them. They discussed the admittance process as they toured the facility.

"Well, I received a call from Sadie Martenson at Jackson Rose, and she told me I would be nuts not to take your girls. She actually used the word 'nuts.' We're old friends. They'll have to take the entrance exam, but if they're anything like the girls Sadie described, they shouldn't have any problems. The schedule for the exam is right here. We have preparation classes they can sign up for, which I recommend." Sarah brought up finances, and Ms. Jansen went over student aid and scholarships. When Ms. Jansen stood, Sarah and Janie followed her lead. Ms. Jansen took Janie's hand and looked her in the eye. "We look forward to having you, and your sister, in the fall."

When they returned to the field to pick Jazz up, the girls were playing a pickup game. Sarah and Janie got out of the car and leaned against it to watch. Jazz was doing fine. She was athletic and graceful enough, and a quick learner. Sarah could see that many of the girls had advanced skills that Jazz would have to learn, but if she knew Jazz, she'd practice constantly until she could match or exceed them.

When they finished, the girls congratulated one another and a few hugged Jazz. Other parents were arriving. Sarah met the woman who pulled up behind her but almost immediately forgot her name as the girls jogged over toward them. Jazz was jubilant as she climbed into the front seat.

"Mom, I'm pretty good at this. It's so fun. The girls are great. This is the best idea you've had in years, moving up here. I'm going to love it."

"Me too, Mommy. The Academy is so cool, Jazz."

The three talked about soccer, the visit to the Academy, Frederick and their new home all the way back to the house. In their minds, Frederick and the new house were already home.

Over the next couple of days, they packed and sorted. Sarah kicked the soccer ball with Jazz in the backyard, and Jazz asked to join Sarah on her morning run. Sarah shortened the run and slowed the pace, but Jazz did a decent job of keeping up. On Thursday, they ran a little farther and faster. Jazz was winded by the time they returned but had loved it. The three did yoga every morning and meditated after that. They were focused, and she could feel their spirits gaining their freedom.

On Wednesday, the psychiatrist called. "Hello, Doc. How's Robert doing?"

"No real progress. He's still stuck in 2015. He's not even advancing the date as the days pass. Every day is February 18, 2015."

"What does that mean?"

"I've been thinking, and I feel like maybe Robert needs to be shocked into reality. He needs to find out that it's 2017, his mother is terminally ill, he's an alcoholic who almost died and has been cut off by his family, and that you are divorcing him and moving away."

"All of that?"

The doctor breathed deeply over the phone. "Can a few of your brothers and sisters come down early afternoon? We'll take it one fact at a time and see how he responds."

Sarah called Mallory, who was available, then Brenda, who could join them, but her husband Jim couldn't.

"That's OK, lil' sis. Just family, I think. If he's in 2015, he won't even know Jim."

Brenda agreed. "I'll be there. This should be interesting."

Sarah also got ahold of Justin, who would be there. Stephen, the middle brother, was at his home in Chicago, and Danny was in school in California, but both Dr. Underwood and Sarah felt the three siblings should be enough.

SIXTY-TWO

They met Dr. Underwood in the main lobby of the hospital. Sarah introduced Brenda and Justin. Sarah and Mal briefly summarized the discussion they'd had with Dr. Underwood on Monday.

Dr. Underwood took over. "Robert is stuck on February 18, 2015, which I understand to be a significant day in the life of your family—the day before your mother's condition became unquestionably terminal. Correct?"

"That's also the day before Herb told Robert that I was going to take over the business and their estate," Justin noted. "He was pretty pissed off about that. He threw a complete fit in our dad's office. Herb told him that if he'd get off the booze, we could revisit these arrangements. He even gave him the name of a prominent doctor who helped people with addiction problems. Robert threw the paper on the ground, walked to the liquor cabinet, grabbed a full bottle of bourbon and stormed out the door, slamming it behind him. That was February 19, 2015. I don't know how much Mother's condition had to do with his choosing the 18th as the date to be stuck in."

While the overall information was common family knowledge, that event, on that date, was a revelation. "We kept it to ourselves. Robert was a big enough mess already. I'm sorry now we didn't say anything." Everyone reassured him they understood.

Dr. Underwood interjected, "OK, another new piece of data. How do we want to handle this? I think one bit of news at a time, and let's see what he does with it. Since perhaps your mother's condition is not the driver as much as his relationship with your father may be, why don't we start with your mother and see if it changes anything in his perception of things? Mallory, do you want to talk to him about what happened with your mother after February 18, 2015?"

Mallory nodded.

"Then, if he handles that, Sarah, why don't you walk him through your relationship since then? Let's see where that takes us."

"OK." Sarah stared at the floor, trying to breathe, while the doctor addressed the siblings.

"Sound like a plan?" They all nodded, though it was obvious none of them wanted to be there any longer than necessary.

"This is going to be fun," Justin muttered.

The rest nodded in agreement.

Two big male orderlies led them in. There were two already in the room. Robert smiled brightly as they all filed in, each with as close to a smile as they could muster plastered on their faces.

"It's about time my family came to visit. What gives? I've been in here forever."

No one moved to hug him.

Dr. Underwood began, "Robert, what day is it?"

"Why does everyone keep asking me that question? It's February 18, 2015, of course."

"Robert, it's time you got through this block. Today is May 26, 2017."

"What are you talking about?"

"Your family is here to try to help bring you into the present. I'm going to tell you that the last two-plus years have not been good for you, which is why you chose February 18, 2015, as the day to stay in. For you, it's been that date every day since you were awakened from your coma. If you have any chance of returning to a normal life, you need to get past that date and caught up to the real present day. Do you understand?"

"NO! What the fuck are you talking about?"

Sarah stepped forward to the edge of the bed, glanced at the orderly, who nodded, and put her hand on Robert's. "Robert, Dr. Underwood and the rest of us have your best interests at heart. You have to move forward or you'll stay in this bed for the rest of your life. Do you want that?"

"No. Fuck no. They need to let me out of here. I'm sorry, honey. What are they talking about?"

Sarah decided to violate the plan. "Robert, it's May 26, 2017. Jasmine is 11. She'll be 12 in 24 days. She'll be starting middle school. Janie's 5." Sarah paused. She wasn't sure Robert knew the ages of his girls, even in 2015. "She'll be in first grade in the fall."

She remained calm and focused, but she couldn't generate any love or positive emotions toward him. In her heart, she didn't really want him to recover. "Robert, you're an alcoholic. Over the last . . ." she paused to think, "seven or more years, and especially since February 18, 2015, your drinking has ruined our marriage and your relationship with our daughters. You've beaten me many times. The girls are not here because you've beaten them and sexually molested Jasmine, which I just learned about."

His head was obviously spinning. She looked at Dr. Underwood, who nodded.

"Robert, Mother is sick, dying of cancer, bedridden. You haven't even visited her in two years." She paused. "She's lived longer than anyone expected."

To everyone's surprise, there was almost no emotional reaction from Robert about this news. He simply didn't seem to care about Mother's condition.

Sarah looked back at the doctor and the family. She took a deep breath and nodded to Justin. Mallory put her hand on his back and guided him forward. He moved under the pressure but against his will. His eyes revealed sheer terror.

Sarah smiled and took Justin's hand, guiding him to the bed. "OK, your turn."

Justin's voice was creaky. "Hello, brother. You look pretty good for the mess you've made."

Something in Robert responded. He scowled at Justin. "What the fuck do you mean, brother?"

"I can't do this. I just can't." Justin pulled away and stormed just outside the doorway.

Sarah took a deep breath. This had to work or nothing would. "Robert, you instigated a long-running feud with Justin and Herb on February 19, 2015. That was the day Herb confirmed that Justin was going to run the family company and Herb cut you off financially. Right now, you're stuck in the date before that significant event. Do you remember any of that?"

"No. You're wrong. None of that's true. Herb loves me, and he promised me that I'll take over the business when he retires. You're still the nasty liar you always were!" He grabbed her hand, hard, and twisted. She tried to free herself but couldn't. Two orderlies came to her aid and ripped Robert's hand from hers.

Justin barged back in from the doorway. "Robert, goddammit, all of that's true, and it's just the tip of the messes you've caused over the last few years. Herb cut you off from representing the estate and the business and everything on February 19, 2015, because you're a fall-down drunk. You lost your job, cheated on Sarah, ignored your girls and spent money wildly—mostly Mother and Herb's money. Don't you remember that huge fight in Herb's office? You stormed out and slammed the door. No one saw you for three days."

Robert began to cry. "You fuckers. You're all liars and cheats. You stole my legacy. You stole my livelihood, you asshole." Justin backed up. The past was flooding back to him, faster than perhaps he could process it. The orderlies restrained him. The siblings wanted to leave, but Dr. Underwood asked them to stay.

"Robert," the doctor's voice was soothing and calm, "do you know how you got here? Why you're in this hospital?"

"I got hurt somehow."

"Right. Good. Do you know how?"

"I guess someone beat me up. I'll get that bastard when I get outta here. You can bet on that!"

Sarah spoke up. "I beat you up, you asshole. You hit me one too many times, and I hauled off and laid you out in your study. You broke your precious Asian figurines when you fell on the glass coffee table. That's what gave you the gash on your arm. But did you try to help yourself? No. You got another bottle of booze, cut your feet to pieces on the glass and drove off. You bled all over everything. Then you tried to beat me again in the morning, but I escaped. You totaled your Mercedes into the side of Pappa's and nearly died. Luckily for you, some cops found you and you ended up here, alive."

"You fucking bitch. I'm going to kill you. You fucking whore bitch . . ."

She ran from the room and the other family members followed. Orderlies held him down, and Dr. Underwood injected a sedative into his IV. He was out in seconds.

The doctor walked slowly into the hall. "Well, that didn't go exactly according to the plan, but if that didn't shock him into the present, nothing will. It was a lot for him to process. Imagine living through more than two years of your life in a matter of minutes. Then imagine it was as big a nightmare as Robert's life has been during that time. We'll see what comes of it when he wakes up in an hour or so. I'll keep you posted. He's a violent man, that's for sure. Thank you all for coming in. I had no idea how that would go." The doctor looked a bit horrified. "Now we know. I'll keep you posted," she repeated, clearly shaken. "Still through Mallory, right?" They nodded.

The family headed to the elevators.

"I had no idea he molested Jazz," Justin said as they entered the elevator.

"I had no idea Herb told him he wasn't getting the company on the 19th," Brenda said.

Mallory replied, "He is one fucked-up guy. I can't seem to feel sorry for him though. Is that bad?"

They all shook their heads. None of them knew how to feel. They hugged and kissed one another as they exited the hospital. Sarah felt included as true family. She was not sure whether Robert still was.

SIXTY-THREE

Sarah took her time driving home from the hospital. She stopped at a small coffee shop to collect her thoughts. Robert was dangerous. She'd known this, of course, but he'd threatened to kill her, right in front of the family and the doctor. The threat frightened her. She closed her eyes and centered her soul. She wouldn't mention the encounter to the girls. They were already afraid of him and didn't need more of that negativity as they were starting to heal.

Jazz had another kick-around that evening. They headed out early and had dinner at Stanley's Diner on Main Street, a landmark in Frederick. The food was fried and horrible for them. It was fun and something Robert would never have permitted. They were determined to do everything he wouldn't allow them in the past. Girls playing sports was on that list.

Janie and Sarah watched the entire workout. Janie was sitting in the grass texting with some of her new friends. Sarah leaned against the car. Jazz was clearly a beginner, but pretty good and getting better, Sarah thought. Of course, Sarah was both biased and had no experience with the sport. Regardless, Jazz was having fun, which was all that mattered.

A mother of one of the other girls introduced herself. "Hello, I understand you're Jazz's mom. I'm Maxine, but people call me Maxy. Sandy, the redhead, is my daughter." Sarah followed her finger.

"Sarah," she answered and stood. Several other mothers came over, introduced themselves and who belonged to them. She was a bit overwhelmed. She realized that while she had a few acquaintances, she had few—maybe only one—real friend, Mallory. She'd bottled herself up in their uncomfortable cocoon for so long, straining to find a way through, that she hadn't needed other entanglements, or perhaps didn't have the time or emotional room for them. She wasn't sure.

Sarah tried and made more acquaintances, but the conversation inevitably turned to things Sarah knew nothing about. One of the women, Susan, helped to translate. Sarah liked Susan. Perhaps she'd even made a friend. She and the girls now had plenty of new numbers in their phones from their new hometown. It was becoming more a home to them than the old neighborhood had ever been, and they didn't even live here yet.

Jazz chatted with several of the girls when the workout was over. Sarah and Janie waited patiently. The long drive home was full of chatter, not one word of which related to Robert. Sarah wasn't completely sure that was healthy, but for now, it seemed right.

Sarah sat alone in the living room in one of the big chairs that would be sold. The girls had friends in Virginia, but it was as if they were eager to start over. That seemed unusual for girls their ages. *This situation, our situation, Robert, must have been unbelievably horrific for them to be willing to uproot their lives like this.* A sharp pang of guilt drove deep into her heart. Despite what the doctor had said, she couldn't help blaming herself, at the very least, for not taking this step sooner.

SIXTY-FOUR

On Thursday, at Sarah's urging, the girls planned to spend the day with their best friends in Virginia. Both of their friends' mothers had stopped by to pick them up. Sarah had the huge house to herself. Boxes were strewn everywhere, but they were largely packed and ready for the movers to come the next day. Sarah was just finishing a box of kitchen items when Dr. Underwood called. "Sarah, how're you doing?"

"Fine," she lied.

"Well, while I doubt you're really fine after what you've dealt with this week, I do have to ask you a favor. Would you be willing to come in and talk to Robert again?"

"Why?"

"I feel like we're making progress with him. He's in the present, sort of, but he hasn't come to grips with his alcoholism. He has no memory of it. Would you be willing to come in and tell him some of the things he did while drunk? I'm asking the others to come in as well, but one at a time this time. Are you free this afternoon?"

Sarah had no desire to ever see Robert again. "Not really, we're moving tomorrow." She took a breath. "OK, I'll come in for a brief visit only. I guess, if he does recover, I'll have to deal with him for the sake of the girls. I may as well start now. How about 1:00?"

"Fine. See you then. No guarantees, and he will be restrained, but maybe we can make progress. Thank you."

"Doc," Sarah hesitated. "Do you have time before that?"

"I can make time. Do you want to talk some more?"

"I don't know . . . I feel like I need to talk before I see him again."

"Alright. How's noon?"

"Thank you. Am I spoiling your lunch?"

"No. I usually eat at my desk, and I'm trying to lose some weight, so no. Really, no. It'll be fine. See you at noon."

"Thank you." Sarah hung up, put the phone down on the kitchen counter and stared at the wall. She wandered, lost, into the foyer. She stopped and stared at the closed door to his study. Her right hand on the wall helped steady herself. She tried to think of something good, positive. *Nothing. Nothing but fear and anger.* She closed her eyes, turned right into their spacious living room, opened them and sat down on the large cushy sofa that had not made the list of items that could fit in their new home. She took a deep breath, then looked around the room at all the stuff Robert had to have to keep up the wealthy façade.

She slouched back into the soft cushions and stared into space. She didn't move, didn't meditate, didn't think and really didn't see. Her mind was dead—dead tired physically and emotionally. She sat there, unaware of how much time passed. A voice called to her from the back of her mind. *Sarah, this is not your fault.* It became stronger. Felt familiar. *Sarah, this is not your fault.* Sarah closed her eyes. *Sarah, this is not your fault,* came the phrase. Who was it? *Repeat after me, young lady: Sarah, this is not your fault.*

"Mom!!" Sarah said, perhaps out loud, perhaps to herself. It didn't matter. She could hear her own mother, deep in the recesses of her mind. Then it felt as real as if she were standing right in front of her. *Sarah, this is not your fault. Sarah, I've been watching you your entire life. I've never left you. Repeat after me, young lady: Sarah, this is not your fault.* She repeated the affirmation over and over, finally speaking it aloud to the empty room: "Sarah, this is not your fault."

"No, it is not."

Sarah bolted to her feet and turned toward the foyer. It was Mallory.

"Sister, you have got to answer your phone. When you didn't answer, I freaked out and busted my tail over here."

"How'd you get in?"

"Well, you're going to have to replace a pane of glass in the back door of the garage. I'll pay for it." Mallory walked over and plopped down onto the couch beside her. "You OK? You were mumbling when I came in, then you startled me when you yelled." Mallory wiggled her head a little to lighten the mood with the silly gesture. "'Sarah, this is not your fault.' And, my dear sister, it is not."

Sarah took a deep breath. "I guess I'm OK. It's been a lot, and someday soon, Robert will get out. What then? The doctor wants me to talk to him again. I don't know if I can, Mal. I don't really want him to recover. What if he does? Then what?"

There was a long pause as Mallory put her arms around Sarah and held her close. After several minutes, Mallory said in a soft voice, "I don't know, sis. I don't know." She hesitated as though she was considering the situation. "Hon, we'll deal with that when it happens, but it doesn't seem like that will happen terribly soon. He hasn't even addressed his criminal charges."

Tears streaming down her cheek, Sarah looked into Mallory's eyes. "But they're all just misdemeanors. Drunk driving and stuff like that. He, or Herb, will bail him out if they even set bail, and he'll be free."

"Does he have any money, sis?"

Sarah thought about that for a second. "No. Not that I know of."

"Well, Dad's not going to give him any more, especially after I tell him what he's been doing to you and the girls. After the outburst in the hospital, he'll be charged with all of that, too, I imagine."

"Maybe you're right." Sarah was sure none of that would come down on him. However, she was able to compose herself as the two sisters hugged.

Mallory took Sarah by the shoulders and stared into her eyes. "It's going to be OK. You understand? It's going to be OK."

Sarah nodded, not yet convinced but feeling better.

"I hope so, Mal. I hope so."

SIXTY-FIVE

After a long talk about where she was emotionally, Sarah stood with Dr. Underwood outside Robert's room. They held hands. Dr. Underwood allowed her time to summon some courage. The white walls of the hallway seemed to be closing in. Heart pounding, she breathed deeply several times, trying to center herself. It didn't work.

She verified that the orderlies were on guard and relented. "OK. Let's go in."

Dr. Underwood led her into the room. "Robert, are you up to a visitor?"

"Sure. Sarah, I'm so sorry about the other day. You said so many things that I'm sure aren't true, and then everyone else was laying a lot on me, and it was just too much. I'm sorry."

"Robert, you're sick. Very sick. You have to come to grips with that. You have a disease. It's called alcoholism. It's not your fault, per se. When you drink, you—"

"Shut the fuck up with this bullshit alcoholic shit." He sat up. The orderlies moved. He put up his hands and lay back down. "Sarah, you know that I can completely control my drinking as well as you. This is really starting to piss me off."

"Robert! Goddammit, I really couldn't care less whether you ever get better. In fact, with what you've put me through over the last several years, I'd hoped against hope that you would've died in the study or on that sidewalk outside Pappa's, but you didn't. So, you shut the fuck up and listen to me." His face registered shock. She'd never spoken to him this way and seldom cursed. "You're a full-fledged alcoholic drunk. You have no control over yourself when you take that first drink, and you can't stop yourself from taking that first one. Every birthday, every anniversary, every holiday, with me, the girls or the family, have been ruined by your drunken outbursts and selfish infantile behavior. I really don't care if you recover. It's best for me if you stay in here for the rest of your miserable life. But if you hope to get out and see your children ever again, you need to take responsibility for your own life. You're a fall-down drunk, Robert, an alcoholic asshole, and you either get help or you'll never see me or the girls again. Do you understand?" Her face, now a mere foot from his, was red with anger.

She backed up and moved away from the bed. He was thinking. Maybe she'd reached him.

"Just get the fuck out of this room," he exploded. The orderlies grabbed his arms. "When I get out of here, you'd better be in Cuba if you want to get away from me. You're dead, bitch. You killed Mother. You turned Herb away from me. You took my brothers and sisters from me. Now you want to take my girls from me. Well, fuck you. No way. *Ever.* You're a dead woman. You can count on that!"

"Fuck you, Robert! I hope you rot in here, you fucking bastard!" Her heart was racing as Dr. Underwood ushered her out the door, down the hall and out of the psyche ward. They could hear him screaming at her, battling the orderlies, until they breached the outer doors of the ward. Dr. Underwood patted her shoulder gently until she calmed down.

"Well, if that doesn't at least start the process of realizing he's an alcoholic, I'm not sure what will. The outburst is not unusual. We'll see what happens as he lies there thinking about his life now." The doctor put a hand on Sarah's shoulder. "I realize him recovering is not high on your list of priorities, but helping him heal is what we do. So—"

Sarah interrupted, "Doctor, you cannot let him out of this hospital! He'll kill me and maybe the girls! Drug his ass into the stone age. Just make sure he does not get out of this hospital!"

"So long as he's this violent, he'll be here." The doctor paused. "But if he improves, we can't hold him forever. We're not a prison, Sarah."

Sarah stormed out of the hospital, tried to calm her nerves with deep breaths, which failed her, climbed into her huge car, which she cursed at, and sped out of the lot. Angry and frightened, her heart racing out of control, she stopped in the parking lot of the coffee shop near the hospital but did not go in.

I need my teacher. She hadn't visited the ashram in several years.

Sarah called the main number. "We have a session in 20 minutes," said the pleasant male voice. "It's a group session, if that's OK?"

"Fine. Yes! Get me in." She hung up without even giving her name. Her mind was cluttered with hatred, dread, chaos, the flood of changes she'd been experiencing and nearly every negative emotion one could imagine. A man turned without his blinker, and Sarah screamed out the window at him. She honked at a woman talking on her cell as the light changed—not a polite tap but a full-on honk. She was mad, frustrated, frightened out of her mind and not sure where to turn.

The ashram was in a strip mall, taking up the final two bays, next to a sub shop. She pulled in and headed toward the building, ripped open its ugly aluminum and glass doors and stepped inside. There she was transported into a world of 18th-century Indian images. Darker, comforting. Soft, multicolored silk fabrics adorned the walls alongside pictures of the many gods and goddesses of Hindu, all cardboard and a bit worn, but lovingly framed.

Maharishi Prema, which means "love," she remembered, was a strong woman, who, like Sarah, was only part Indian.

Guru Prema greeted Sarah as she turned from removing her shoes. "Sarah, I could feel the weight of your soul before you even crossed our threshold. You are very dark today. Darker than usual, and, my dear friend, that's saying something."

The two weren't really friends, but Sarah appreciated the sentiment. "It's a very long story, teacher."

The guru waited; when it became clear that Sarah was not going to unload her soul to her, Maharishi turned and guided her and the others into the back room, referred to by the group as the temple.

The teacher stood before the seated group and began, quietly but with a penetrating, spiritual power. "Shanti, or true inner peace, comes when we let go of the material, emotional and personal things that plague our lives, even those things we love in our lives. We tend to hold onto both very tightly, but it is in the letting go that we gain clarity of vision and can see the path we are to take, if only a single first step. It is by bringing true unburdened peace to our lives that we are able to see, to feel, to understand."

The teacher and her pupils took the lotus position, or as close to it as their bodies would allow. Sarah entered the position with ease.

The guru led the chant, one Sarah knew well:

Om Asato Ma Sad Gamaya
Tamasoma Jyotir Gamaya
Mrityor Ma Amritam Gamaya
Om Shanti Shanti

which essentially means:

Guide me from the unreal to the real;
Guide me from the darkness to the light;
Guide me from fear of death to immortality of soul;
Let there be peacefulness all around us.

As Sarah repeated the mantra in her mind, she remembered the voice of her mother, guiding her through mantras, including this one. She felt it, heard it, sensed her mother with her, hugging her, her maternal soul enveloping Sarah in its bosom. She felt warm. It calmed her. She let the spirits move Robert from her mind, take the terror and clean it from her soul. Her heartbeat slowed. Her breaths followed. Sarah's muscles relaxed. Her soul seemed to float at the edge of her physical being, near the universe of spirits, and she could feel her mother and father there, pouring love into her.

As the mantra approached 108 repetitions, she settled back into herself. As the session ended and the others began talking to one another about how wonderful it all was, she sat alone quietly and gazed at the shrine at the front of the room. It was a picture of a Bengal tiger. It seemed real to her at that moment, providing her with strength.

She stood, bowed to the tiger, then to the teacher, then to the other three walls because it felt right. Sarah relaxed and stood erect, stretching back, staring at the ceiling, then erect, seeing the world within the little temple. She felt better, freer, but still uncertain as to the next steps to take—the path, or at least the beginning of it, she'd been promised.

Maharishi Prema touched her on the shoulder. "Sometimes, when we are so deep in the hole we have dug for ourselves, the first steps must be those that get us out of it. That path out may not be easy. In fact, I feel it will be fraught with trauma for you, Sarah, but you know that it is what you must do. When you have reached the edge, you will know the way. It may not be the path you now hope for, but if you have faith in the spirits of the universe, they will guide you along the right journey for you and your loved ones. You will know because your heart will know." The guru stared knowingly into Sarah's troubled eyes, smiled in a way that reached into her soul with warmth, a sense of calm and an odd sense of reverence that Sarah couldn't quite grasp. The teacher then lifted her hand, nodded in a manner that seemed almost deferential, as though Sarah were the superior rather than the student. The guru's eyes returned to Sarah's. In a quiet voice, almost imperceptible, she said, "You are a special one, Sarah. You will see."

The teacher turned and began to attend to the many others who wanted to speak with her.

By the time Sarah walked back into their house, one she now hated, she was as centered and positive as she could possibly be.

She busied herself with tasks. She was digging herself out of the hole she'd dug. That was the first step. Step one. *Get past step one,* she kept saying. *One task at a time.* It kept her mind and her hands busy, which helped.

She arranged for all the utilities and, most important, the cable to be turned on in the new house. She made sure she had the channel that carried the U.S. soccer team's games as well as the ones that carried the English and German games. Sarah compiled the bills and created a spreadsheet so she could figure out how to pay them.

One task. Then another. Keep busy. Make dinner. Off to soccer. Find something to do.

First step: Climb out of the hole. Next step: *I'll know it when I'm standing at the top of the hole. Climb, Sarah. Climb.*

SIXTY-SIX

On Friday morning, the movers arrived at the old house to collect everything they were taking to the new house. It was delivered that afternoon. The movers placed each piece of furniture where it belonged according to a plan drawn up by the three girls. Each labeled box was set into the proper room. Sarah thanked and tipped the movers before she and the girls began unpacking in earnest.

Keep busy, Sarah reminded herself, *and we will get to the edge of the hole. Then I will know what to do next.*

On Saturday morning, the estate sale company arrived at the old house in force to prepare to auction everything else that afternoon. Robert's personal belongings were in the garage. A company was coming to move them to a storage unit. It was amazing how quickly the estate sale company had everything verified, cataloged, tagged and prepared to be sold. Although Sarah was not present at the sale that afternoon, she'd be pleased when she later received the check from the proceeds—over $45,000. The bottle of scotch alone went for over $5,000. It would be a nice chunk of change for their new beginning.

One chapter closed. She felt as though she was nearing that glorious edge. The bottom of that hole was now well behind her. She could see light above her for the first time in . . . well, she couldn't remember how long. Those early years at Mother and Herb's house, maybe?

Sarah, Jazz and Janie unpacked, finding a place for everything immediately. By the time Mallory, her husband Sam and their children arrived about 10:00 A.M. on Saturday, nearly everything was put away. Sam was helpful in handling the heavier items. Mallory spent most of the time keeping her children occupied. They all went to lunch at a no-frills Mexican restaurant in Frederick. Robert hated Mexican food and, for that matter, Mexicans, legal or otherwise, and even though he was seldom home for dinner, the girls hadn't ever had Mexican cuisine. Now that they were out from under his thumb, they were eating Mexican, cooked by a very nice Mexican couple.

By the evening, the house looked pretty put together. There were still some boxes to go through, but they were out of the way in the basement or garage.

That evening, Sarah ordered a pizza and salad from a local pizzeria a friend of Jazz's had mentioned. The delivery girl was sweet. Sarah tipped her too much.

Jazz found the soccer match between the U.S. Women's National Team and Norway, and they all crashed in the family room with the extra-large pizza and huge salad, which was way more than they could eat. It was spread before them on the coffee table, a place at which they'd never dined. Another taboo broken. They sat back and listened to the British announcer on a U.S. telecast introduce the teams. Now they would see what this game was all about. On the opening play, a Norwegian woman slammed into a U.S. player and sent her flying.

"This doesn't seem very friendly. I thought this was a friendly match, Mom?" Jazz stared at the TV as the player was helped up by her teammates, words were exchanged between the two teams, and the referee restored order.

"That's what the guide says. That's what Tammy said," Sarah answered.

Janie chimed in, "I'd hate to see them when they're not being nice to each other."

Sarah breathed in deeply the peace that surrounded them. For the first time in as long as she could remember, she felt truly at home.

SIXTY-SEVEN

Her phone vibrating on her dresser woke her. It was 2:04. "What the . . .?"

She slid out of bed and ambled over to the phone. "Yes, hello. Do you know what time it is?"

"Ma'am, I'm sorry, but this is the police. Your husband is Robert Robinson, correct?"

"At the moment, yes he is. We're getting divorced."

"I understand, but he has broken out of the psyche ward of the hospital, and we wondered if you might know where we can locate him. We've been told he's very dangerous." His voice was dispassionate, like this was just anyone.

Her mind snapped into focus. "What are you saying? Robert's out? Hell yes, he's dangerous. He threatened to kill me just this week! He's huge and mean and a hard-core drunk!" She paused to try to compose herself. "Have you checked all the bars and taverns in the area? Liquor stores or open grocery stores?"

"We're working that angle. We have officers looking into places that're still open."

"Well, he's not here. I'm calling the Frederick police. Can I have them call you?"

"Sure." He gave her his direct number, still way too calm.

"Thank you. He's threatened to kill me several times." She reminded him. "Please find him. Check our old house." She gave him the address.

"It's going to be sold in a few days by the bank. All the locks have been changed, and he doesn't have the new key. He thinks he has liquor there. He doesn't, but he might go there." Her mind was racing, heart thumping in her chest.

"So, if he's there, he's probably stuck outside somewhere."

"I don't know. He's crazy strong, violent. If he wants in, he'll get in. Does he have any money? How's he getting around?"

"He stole a car."

"How the hell did he escape from the psyche ward, for crying out loud?"

"Don't know, ma'am, but he created quite a ruckus, broke several things and injured at least one person, so we're trying to find him."

"You have to find him! He's going to try to find me. He'll try to kill me. Do you have the numbers of his brothers and sisters?"

"No, ma'am." She put him on speaker and read them off to the officer.

"Try them. Maybe he'd go to one of them. Who knows? My money's on the taverns or liquor stores, though. He's an alcoholic and a nasty one."

"Thank you, ma'am. That's all very helpful. We'll keep you posted," he said, still as relaxed as if she were reporting a lost cat.

"Please find him, sir. You need to take this seriously. He's insane. He wants to kill me. Find him! Let me know as soon as you know anything. He's crazy and violent and hates me." Sarah was rambling. She couldn't stop her imagination from racing through horrific scenarios.

"We will. Thank you," he said politely and hung up.

"Sir, this is serious—" she implored before realizing the conversation was over. After staring at her phone for several minutes, she called the hospital.

"Hello, how can I help you?"

"Psyche ward. It's an emergency."

"Ma'am, I can't patch you through there; we've had an emergency up there."

"That's my goddam husband. *He's* the emergency. Now connect me right now."

"OK, ma'am, calm down. I'll connect you."

"Psyche. How can I help you?"

"Hi, this is Sarah Robinson. I understand that my husband has escaped from there this evening. Can I talk to someone who knows what happened?"

"Just a moment."

"Hello, Mrs. Robinson, I'm Nurse Jason. How can I help you?"

Sarah took a deep breath. "Hello. I learned my husband escaped from there this evening. Can you tell me what happened? I'm afraid for the lives of myself and my girls. The police are involved, but I need to know what you know."

"He seemed to be fine yesterday and all day today. At about midnight, when we went in to give him his meds, it happened. He'd been pleasant all day. He was on something that helped. I can look it up."

"No, I don't care. What happened?"

"I don't know, he bolted. He punched the doctor, pushed an orderly into the wall, knocked the tech down and sprinted out the door.

"He was on a rampage, running through the department, knocking people over and creating chaos. The doors were locked, of course, but he grabbed the receptionist, put his arm around her throat and dragged her to the door. He threatened to strangle her if they didn't let him out, and he started to. The orderly unlocked the door, and your husband dragged the woman into the hall. He threw her back into the orderly, and he tripped on her as Mr. Robinson sprinted down the hall and down the steps that led outside.

"He pushed down a young nurse's aside and took his car. Then he was gone. Where he went after that, we have no idea."

"Damn it." She stopped to think for a few minutes. "OK, nurse, is there anything else I need to know? Is he on any drugs that could make him crazier than he already is? Anything?"

"No, he was on the sedative, and we were about to give him a dose, so right now he's not on anything."

"Does he have any weapons? Anything he stole from the hospital?"

"Not that I know of. He didn't have a weapon here. He seemed so pleasant all afternoon, and then he exploded. He took us all by surprise. We're so . . ."

Sarah hung up.

How could he find us? Who knows we're here?

She called Mallory. "Mal, sorry to wake you, but Robert's escaped. I don't know where he is, but no doubt he'll find some booze as quickly as possible and then try to find us to kill me. If he contacts you or shows up, don't tell him where we are, OK?"

"No, of course not. I'll keep a watch out."

"The police are gonna call. I gave them all your numbers."

"OK."

"Mal, can you call the siblings and let them know? Tell them to not tell Robert where we are. Who lives closest to the hospital? Justin, right? Would he go there? Does Justin know where we live?"

"Who knows, sis. Yeah, the family all know where you guys live now. We were all at Justin's this evening."

"Alright, please call everyone else, and I'll call Justin myself. Thanks, Mal. Lock up. You're not that far away either."

She hung up and dialed Justin's cell phone. No answer. She tried the land line. It beeped quickly. "Damn."

She hung up and called the police officer back. "59th precinct, how can I help you?"

"Can I speak with Officer Mares please? It's urgent."

"Just a minute, please."

"Office Mares."

"Officer, this is Ms. Robinson. I think Robert's at Justin's house. He's not answering his cell and the land line beeps like it's been disconnected. I'm afraid he's there. If he threatens him, he may tell him where we are. Can you please check it out ASAP?"

"We're on it. I'll get someone there immediately. What's the address?"

She gave it to him, and he hung up. "Fuck, fuck, fuck!" she said out loud. He had a car. He could take a car if he needed another one. He could take their booze. It would take him 45 minutes to get here. Hopefully she'd hear from the police or Justin or someone well before that.

She hung up the phone and called 911. "Frederick police, what is your emergency?"

She went through the entire story. "Call Officer Mares at the 59th. Send someone over here right away. I think he may have gotten the information from my brother. I'm concerned for him, but the police in D.C. are on their way over there now."

"He threatened to kill you?"

"Yes, ma'am. He's said several times that he'd kill me. Given his nature and the likelihood that he's drinking as he's driving here, I think he means it! Please hurry!"

"OK, I'll send someone right over. Should be five, maybe ten minutes, tops."

"Thank you. Please hurry."

Another call beeped on her phone. It was an ambulance service. She hung up and answered it.

"Oh my god, Sarah, you have to run! It's Brenda. He's coming, and he's crazy, and he has one of Justin's handguns. He shot Justin. We were over there together. We're in the ambulance. Oh my god, he made Justin tell him where you are. He shot him when he wouldn't at first. He's coming. Run, Sarah. You have to get the girls and run, right now!"

"Oh lil' sis, I'm so sorry. Can you tell me how long ago he left the house?"

"Like maybe half an hour. He took Justin's car, the Charger, so he's flying. He knew where Justin's gun was. Then he smashed our phones and ripped the land line out of the wall. He took two bottles of booze. I'm sure he's hammered by now. Get out. Run. Hurry."

"OK. Love you. Thanks." *Damn! He's close.*

She ran into Jazz's room and woke her. "Daddy's coming and he's mad. Get dressed—fast." Sarah grabbed three flint knives Jazz had made that adorned her dresser.

She sprinted out of Jazz's door and into Janie's room with the same message. Janie was already out of bed and began dressing quickly. Sarah ran to her room, tossed the knives on the bed and pulled on some jeans and a sweatshirt. The girls were waiting for her in the small hallway leading to the front of the house.

SIXTY-EIGHT

The crash of glass startled them. "Honey, I'm home," Robert called.

"In here, hurry." The three raced into her bedroom. Sarah shut and locked the door. She put a hand to the door. "Damn," she muttered. It was a weak hollow door that, she knew from experience, wouldn't stop Robert for long.

Bam, crack. "Fuck!" He'd kicked open the front door, fell through it and down the single stair into the family room. She turned, grabbed the phone she'd left on her dresser in her haste to get dressed, then sprinted to the window. The girls followed. Jazz saw and grabbed the knives. "Mom, you might need these."

"Where are you, sweetie blossom? It's your loving husband."

The gun shot rang through the house as it ripped a hole at an angle through her door. They heard the bullet slam into the drywall a few feet from them, leaving a gaping hole. She found the latch to the window and unlocked it then tugged on the window. It was old and moved slowly. She tried to evenly balance both sides so it would slide better and managed to get it up a couple of inches, but it hit the flipped-out clips designed to keep outsiders from opening the window.

"Shit." Adrenalin pulsed through her.

"Where are you, sweetheart? Do you have our lovely children with you?" He was coming down the hall.

"Hurry up, Mommy, he's coming." Janie was crying and starting to panic.

A thud sounded from near the door. He'd likely lost his balance, bouncing off one of the walls but not falling.

"I got it. I got it. We'll be OK." She pushed the window back down and fumbled to push in the clips.

"Come on, sweetie. Where are you?" He was at the door. His knuckles rapping on the hollow door rattled through her spine. An eye peered through the hole in the door. "Hello, girls. Fuck." He'd lost his balance and tumbled back, crashing against the far wall.

Sarah ripped the window open and pushed the screen out. Janie dove through and Jazz quickly followed, rolling in the green grass behind the house. The door smashed open, and there in the frame was Robert, a nearly empty bottle in one hand and a sinister black handgun in the other, still pointing at the floor. "There's my little wifey-poo."

"Girls, run. Run for help." They sprinted toward the house next door.

Sarah turned and snapped one of the knives at Robert. It grazed his right shoulder just as he'd raised the gun and fired. The knife caused him to miss well to her left. The bullet again smashed a hole in the drywall. Sarah dove through the open window. Her knee caught the sill. She landed on her face in the grass. Sarah rolled, pulling her legs out from the window as another gunshot exploded into the side of the opening. She crawled to her left as fast as she could, opposite the way the girls had run. She'd protect them as much as possible.

Robert poked his head out the window. "Come on, sweetheart. Take it like a man. You're dead. I'm dead. We're all dead." He shot at her and hit her in the left calf. The crack it made as the bullet hit her fibula rang through her body. She screamed in agony, rolling to her butt, reaching for the leg as the excruciating pain raked through her.

He was big and struggled to get out of the window. She regained her focus. Running was no longer an option. His huge frame loomed over her, blocking the light from the next house. She released her leg and faced him, sitting on the ground.

"You motherfucker! What the fuck is wrong with you? You hit me and beat me, fine, but hitting little Janie—what kind of man does that?" She threw one of the knives at him. It hit him in the left arm.

"Ouch." She'd hit him but didn't inflict any real damage. She held onto the last one in her right hand, readied for the opportunity to strike.

He took a step, stumbled on the uneven ground but didn't fall. She scooted away backward on her butt as fast as she could, dragging her leg. It was bleeding profusely. Each movement sent shots of pain through her leg. She kept going.

"I never hit Janie."

"She says you did, you child beater. I believe her. She's not a raving, violent, drunk asshole like you are. She's a little girl. She's your daughter, and you hit her. You're a drunk and a child molester!"

He shot again. This one hit her in the right shoulder. Again, the crack as it tore through her shoulder bones ripped through the air. "Arrgghhhh. Fuck. Ugh." The force of the impact knocked her down and sent the knife into the darkness.

She closed her eyes for a second to force the pain back as much as possible, then pulled herself up on her left hand, her right dangling beside her. "Goddammit, you big drunk-ass pussy. What's wrong with you?" She had to distract him, prolong this process. "You're a child molester, Robert. You sexually molested Jazz in her own bed." She paused, closed her eyes, took a deep breath to control her reaction to the intense pain. She could feel her soul and her connection to the spirits of the world center her. She could bear it.

More important, Robert stopped. She continued, "Yeah, I know all about the floozies you've been fucking all these years. Then you try to get your rocks off on your own daughter. You fucking bastard child molester!"

"I never touched Jazz." She pushed herself back toward the edge of the house with her left arm and right leg. Pain tore at her body, demanding she stop. She did, closed her eyes and took another deep breath. The spirits calmed her and gave her strength. Her mother's voice calmly instructed, "You can do this. Control your body." She could feel her mother and the natural spirits she'd taught her to connect with helping her, giving her strength. She opened her eyes and continued to move away.

"She says you did. She described it in detail, how you jizzed all over her nightgown as you humped her. She's traumatized! Thank heavens you were too drunk to penetrate her, you pervert!" He stood there, gun at his side, trying to recall the incident. It seemed to shock him, causing him to stand still. She took the moment to again close her eyes, breathe deeply and ask her spirits to give her the strength to scoot around the corner of the house. Inches at a time. She was about to reach her destination.

"You lying cunt. I never touched our girls," he screamed. She could hear his footfalls approaching.

She pulled herself around the corner and leaned against the house. The fires burning in her leg and shoulder were nearly unbearable, even with spiritual help. She was bleeding and could feel herself fading. He shot again. It crashed against the concrete and caromed off into the darkness.

"Jazz says you molested her. You more than touched her—you scarred her for life. You're a fucking pervert child molester and you goddamn know it!" Sarah took deep breaths to gain some control. Slow the heart, reduce the pressure, minimize blood flow. With each breath, she could feel her heart and adrenalin slowing. The spirits were there, trying to help her. Sarah focused her mind away from the raging pain signals, but now her brain was struggling to function. Her connection to her body was fading. "Stay focused," she whispered.

He stumbled around the corner and stood tall above her. She could only make out a silhouette. The moon and the stars behind him began to blend into fuzzy, glowing dots. He took a long swig of a bottle and threw it into the darkness. Her body was done. She was helpless.

"Why do you hate me?" he asked. Although the statement came out of left field, she seized the opportunity.

"Robert, honey, I don't hate you."

"You hate me 'cause I'm a no-good loser."

He was right, of course. He staggered and raised the gun and pointed it right at her head. He stumbled closer. The barrel seemed as though it would swallow her as he put it on her forehead between her eyes. The cold steel registered, but she couldn't understand it. She gathered everything her mind still had and looked up at him with the most loving, endearing eyes she possibly could. The moonlight made her face glow. She hoped that helped the mood.

"Sweetheart, no. I stayed with you because I love you so much. I knew about all the affairs, but I loved you and stayed with you. Think about it, honey. Through all of them, who was always there for you when you finally came home? I was." She could see him begin to think. She needed him to think. Thinking for drunks took time, and time was what she needed most.

After a few seconds, she continued, "When you got drunk and passed out at Pappa's, who came and picked you up and brought you home and tucked you in bed? I did." She again gave him several seconds to think about it. The gun dropped several inches and he staggered a half step back.

"When you got into fights at the Club, who smoothed things over for you? I did." She paused again. It was working. He was remembering. "When you had that fight with your family, who was it that helped you home and then called Herb to work it out? I did." The gun dropped a few more inches. She had no strength to grab it or do anything. She could feel the blood leaving her.

"Why did I do all those things? Because I love you so much." The gun dropped farther. It was still pointing at her chest, but it was getting heavy. This was her opportunity to escape. *Move, body.* It wouldn't, couldn't. Every movement, even with her good left arm, was painful and clumsy. She was losing blood and, with it, control. She would not last long. *Where are the cops?*

"Honey, if you would stop drinking, we can love each other again. Do you think you could stop drinking?"

He lowered the gun. Then he backed another step away. The glow from the back window shown on the left side of his face. She forced her mind to focus. His look was one of confusion and deep sadness. He fell to his knees and started to cry. His hand, still holding the gun, lay on the ground. She could feel herself fading into shock from the pain and loss of blood. Other than the faint sounds of his sobs, the air was eerily quiet. It was as though even the bugs were holding their breath.

The world was out of focus. She thought he was raising the gun. Where was he aiming?

Sirens broke the quiet, helping her regain a little focus. He shot. She cringed. No new pain. He'd shot at something across the back of the house. Adrenalin brought her nearly back. *Not at the girls!* She tried, swung her weak left hand, but he was too far away. She couldn't focus. A bang, pinging off the concrete foundation, burrowing into the ground in front of him. A puff of dirt. Sounds, images she tried to reconcile but could not.

A voice, a female voice. She didn't recognize it, couldn't understand it. Her mind was fogging.

Robert's gun, flash, bang. Not at her. At the voice. Bang. Thud. "Ugh!" Robert grabbed his shoulder, falling back, twisting to his left. He stayed upright. The gun swung around, toward her.

The huge gun barrel, like a giant concrete pipe, dark, like the hole she'd dug, coming at her. It was going to swallow her. Cold, between her eyes. Black metal. A huge hand. Black metal and a huge hand. Darkness. It was all she could see. Black and massive and dark. *It's going to swallow me whole.* Gigantic dark, black hole.

Sirens. A yell from someone, somewhere. A moment. Gun at her forehead. Helpless against the siding. She closed her eyes and took another deep breath. She focused herself inward, calming her body with her spirit. Her breathing became slow, rhythmic and even. She again slowed her heartbeat, reducing the beats to lower the pressure and slow the flow of blood. The spirits were there. Her mother had taught her these skills. She took herself deep into meditation, but his scream broke the trance. She was too weak to hold it.

"One more shot and I blow her brains right into the side of this fucking house."

A voice said something. No more shots. She moved her left arm, but it wouldn't obey, and her body slid that way down the side of the house. When she hit the ground, unthinkable pain seared through every nerve in her body. She wanted to die right there. Robert reached for her. Nothing was real.

"I'm so sorry, honey. I'm sorry I ruined everything. If we both die, we can be together again in heaven. We can start over." He grabbed her sweatshirt and pulled her back up. Terror.

Scream! Nothing. Darkness, fuzzy moon, darkness. Huge dark form, wavering back and forth. Light. Dark. Bright light.

Deafening bang. Pain exploding. Then nothing. Darkness.

SIXTY-NINE

She tried to open her eyes, but the light was bright. "Is this heaven?" she mumbled. She heard a scurry of activity and lots of random voices. She tried to open her eyes again. Everything was bright. White. She couldn't focus. She heard beeping. Steady beeping. Dots appeared above her. She could sense movement. Shadows moving quickly all around her. Voices. Flowers. The sweet smell of flowers. *Heaven?* She sensed people.

She smelled medicine, sterile and horrid. She grimaced and closed her eyes.

She paused. Her mind began to awaken, reconnecting to her soul. She opened her eyes again. This time ceiling tiles came into focus. The dots had grids. The light above her was dimmed. She heard a voice. She couldn't understand it. Then she heard it again. "Sarah, can you hear me?"

She moved her eyes to the sound but had a hard time forming the words. She mumbled, "Yes," but she couldn't tell if anyone heard her. She felt something cold entering her arm. She felt better. Things began to clear.

Flowers. There were flowers everywhere. And smiles. She felt warm hands touching her, holding her hands, stroking her face. It was Jazz. She was there. And Janie, to her left. She began to cry. Her mind was clearing. Her spirit was settling in her body, reconnecting. Her perspective changed, and she could see the faces. After a few seconds, they became clear. Everyone was there. She smiled.

Her first words—her first thoughts, always—"Jazz and Janie, I'm so glad you're OK."

"Oh, Mom, we're so glad you're OK. We were so worried. All of us." Jazz leaned in close.

"Mommy," Janie interjected, "Daddy shot you three times. He almost killed you, but the doctors said you're really tough and are going to be fine." Janie didn't mince words.

"I will be, honey. I'm going to be fine." Mallory and Sam, Brenda and Jim, Stephen and his wife Sally were in from Chicago, and Justin was there with his girlfriend Marcia. Danny was there with another young man. Herb was there. Mother, of course, was not. But, otherwise, the entire family encircled her bed. *Her* family. She wanted to hug her girls and them at the same time.

She couldn't move. The pleasant voice spoke. It was the same voice she'd heard as she was waking up. "Sarah, lay down. You're not out of the woods yet, young lady."

Sarah found the nurse to her right, next to Jazz. "You're old," was all her mind could muster. There were giggles from the family, and the nurse smiled.

"Sarah, you lost a great deal of blood. We've replaced it thanks to many of your family who donated." She turned and smiled at them, and all were smiling back. "You've had three surgeries. The first took several hours. Your vitals have stabilized, so we've guided you out of sedation. You've been asleep for the last three days." The nurse turned to the equipment beside her. Sarah's mind cleared more, and after a few seconds, Sarah was completely present.

Jazz spoke next. "Hi, Mom. You're a total mess. You have three bullet wounds, several broken bones, a bunch of parts that had to be repaired, and your leg and shoulder are in casts. You have bandages everywhere. But you're going to be OK." Tears came to Jazz's eyes, and she put her head on Sarah's chest. Sarah ran her fingers through Jazz's hair.

"I'm going to be fine, honey. Good as new. Remember what we talked about. All that stuff is just machine parts. My soul is perfectly fine. I'm all here. They can fix or replace everything else."

"I know, Mom, but we almost lost you."

An IV tube entered her left bicep. It was heavily taped down. She had a catheter, which felt weird but was necessary. She had a breathing tube in her nose and was hooked up to a whole host of monitors. "I'm sure I look pretty scary, though."

The family chuckled, and Jazz lifted her head and smiled.

"Just lay back," came the soft words of the nurse. Jazz and Janie each took a hand. All her brothers and sisters found a place to put a loving hand on her.

She cried tears of joy and smiled as broadly as she had ever smiled in her life. Margaret, Shawny, Ms. Martenson and even Susan, whom she'd only met a few days ago, were all there. They all slipped through and told her to get well. Shawny said, "I am so looking forward to raking that bastard over the coals." Everyone laughed. "Glad you're going to be fine, sweetheart. You'll be just fine."

"Mommy," Janie broke in, "this is Ms. Randolph. She saved your life by shooting Daddy. She's our new neighbor and a retired cop. She shot at Daddy in the dark." The nice woman, probably in her seventies, stepped through a small opening in the family. Her sweet-looking husband was beside her.

"Glad you're OK. Just clipped him. Sorry I didn't get him or get there earlier."

Sarah smiled. "Thank you for saving my life."

"Mommy, she was so brave. After Daddy threatened to blow your brains out, Ms. Randolph slipped through the back of the yard in the dark toward Daddy. Daddy didn't see her. Daddy was going to shoot you again, but Ms. Randolph shot Daddy first."

Ms. Randolph continued the story, "Your husband's gun dropped when my second bullet hit him, but his finger contracted, pulling the trigger a third time."

Mal continued, "You have a broken left fibula and right clavicle and quite a bit of soft tissue damage from the first two bullets. The one in your leg hit an artery, and you lost a lot of blood. The last shot broke several ribs and punctured your left lung, right below your heart. It also just missed your aorta. The doctors said you were very lucky. Looking at you, sis, I'm not sure how they rate lucky around here." There was another chuckle from the family.

"Right now, I'm the luckiest and happiest woman in the world. Thank you all so much for being here. Thank you, Ms. Randolph."

"Call me Dahlia. Nice to meet you, ma'am. I'm glad you're going to be OK. Sorry I couldn't get there sooner."

"That's OK. Call me Sarah. You saved my life. You risked your own. Glad to have you as a new neighbor and friend. Thank you so much."

Justin stepped forward. "Your house is being repaired as we speak. It'll be good as new when you're ready to go home. So don't even worry about that, sis. It's on the company."

"So, where's Robert?" Sarah asked.

There was a hush over the room. Justin broke the silence. "He got away. He has two minor bullet wounds. They'll still need treating. They should have him soon."

"It's been three days. They haven't found him yet?" she asked.

Justin looked at the others. "Not yet. He scrambled into the darkness as the cops tended to you. They only sent one car, two cops. They called the ambulance and stayed with you. Robert apparently stole a car from some drunk guy down the street who was coming home late, which is ironic, and got away."

Mallory stepped in, "They're on it. They'll catch him."

She caught Herb's eye. He dropped his gaze immediately. *There's more to this than they're telling me or than they know.* The beeping sped up.

"OK, everyone, this is not helping. Sarah needs to rest. Time to leave," the nurse interjected.

"Mom," Jazz broke in, "Aunt Mallory and I have been planning my first birthday out here. You should be out by then. We're inviting all our new friends. I'm so excited."

"So am I, Mommy," Janie chirped. "The Academy is so awesome. This is a great place. Get better, Mommy."

Sarah smiled. "I will, sweetie. I will."

"Alright, alright. Enough for her first day. She's going back to sleep. She'll be on a normal schedule starting in the morning, and you can come in less of a horde then." Everyone laughed as Sarah smiled tiredly. The nurse began to usher everyone out. Each of her siblings stopped by her bed, kissed her either on the forehead or cheek, told her how much they loved her, and each called her some form of sister. Herb left without saying anything to her. Brenda was last, lingering at the foot of the bed. Mallory and Justin stopped near the door. Mal ushered the girls out, then both came back toward the bed.

Tears began to stream down Brenda's cheeks. "I'm so sorry I didn't warn you sooner, Sarah."

Justin broke in, "Sarah, I'm so sorry I told Robert where you were. I'm so sorry all of this happened."

"Justin, how are you?" Sarah asked.

"Not bad. Bullet went through my thigh. I guess that's good. I'm great, really. Patched up and walking without a cane as of today."

Sarah turned to Brenda. "Lil' sis, this was not your fault. You called as soon as you could. We'd all be dead if not for you. You didn't cause this. You saved our lives. I'm in your debt."

Brenda hugged her and cried. "No debts between sisters. I love you, sissy." It'd been a long time since Brenda had called her that. It felt good.

"I love you too, lil' sis."

Justin grinned, squeezed her hand, nodded and headed out of the room.

Mallory walked over, put an arm around Brenda and guided her out of the room. "I've got the girls, by the way. I've even gotten them to soccer camp and Academy every day all the way up in Frederick. Since when is Jazz such a soccer player?"

"Since last week. Thanks, Mal. Love you."

"Love you too."

"Alright. How're you feeling?" the nurse asked.

"Right now, wonderful."

"Well, it's late—9:30. Most of them have been waiting all day. The doctors ordered a few tests earlier. You're looking pretty good for the wounds you suffered. Lots of love, I guess."

"Yeah." Her smile was deep and joyous. She'd never felt more loved.

At that moment, even with all her injuries, her life was as perfect as it had ever been. She asked the nurse to give her a moment. She closed her eyes and settled into the world of her spirits. They were warm and happy. She thanked them. She saw the face of her smiling mother. They'd all been there for her. Love flowed through her body.

Darkness oozed across the peace, blocking out the beauty, the feelings of love, tightening the muscles of her body. *Panic.* Robert's face appeared, looming, menacing, close. Bourbon filled her nostrils. He was still out there, loose. He'd kill her the next chance he had. He knew where they lived. Sarah's mind raced. What did she know? *Herb.* Herb couldn't look her in the eyes or touch her. Herb was helping Robert. The firstborn, the golden child. He and Mother, no matter how sick she was, could not let Robert go to jail.

She had to get out. Take the girls and escape in the dark of night. She'd tell no one. Not even the girls. New place. New names. New looks. *Where will we go? Not Cleveland. Somewhere else. Somewhere he'd never think of.* Visions raced through her mind of her girls' faces when they found out they'd not be going to the wonderful Academy or playing on the soccer team, enjoying their new friends at a birthday party, seeing their beloved grandparents, aunts, uncles or cousins, or living in their new house with the woods in back. She began to cry. Her heart raced. She tried to get up. She needed to act now. He'd kill her right here in the hospital.

The nurse put a soft hand on her shoulder. "Sarah, you've been overstimulated by all this attention. It's time to put you back to sleep." Before Sarah could react, the sedative the nurse had plunged into her IV started to take effect. She could feel love and fear and guilt and panic swirl within her as she faded off.

ACKNOWLEDGMENTS

First Steps is my second novel, the prequel to the Reset series. Much of it was part of the original Reset manuscript, which editor extraordinaire Andrew Doty, of Editwright, convinced me was really more than one book. As I've gone through this writing and publishing journey, I've learned so much from and met my editors and mentors through my memberships in the St. Louis Writers Meetup Group, St. Louis Publishers Association and the St. Louis Writers Guild. I recommend these groups to any aspiring author.

I am deeply grateful to my genius editor, Karen Tucker of Comma Queen Editing, who helped me finish Reset and has worked through all the versions of First Steps. She has masterfully guided me to a superior story, told, I hope, with depth, sensitivity and some degree of skill. I love the cover my book designer, Jamie Wyatt, put together, reflecting so nicely the elements of First Steps. Thank you, Jamie, for your diligence and creativity.

I want to thank my wife, Barbara, who not only puts up with me, which I imagine is no easy task, but also read many drafts of First Steps. People advise that a wife is a poor editor because she loves you and will say whatever you want to hear. Barbara is not that way. She tells me what she thinks, and her counsel is incredibly valuable. It is our deep love for each other that allows that degree of honesty.

This book is about a battered woman's escape and how she deals with the aftermath. It was critical that this resonate with women who've survived that situation. I want to thank my many beta readers who read all or parts of First Steps over the last four months, especially those who themselves were victims. In particular, thank you to Karen, Elena and Dee Dee for their touching and emotional stories that helped me shape Sarah and her experiences in First Steps.

Thank you to all. I'm so proud to be supported by so many wonderful people.

ABOUT THE AUTHOR

Ned Lips discovered that his first book, *Reset*, was a metaphor for how we all go through resetting our lives. Since learning the lessons from his own book, he has put aside nearly all other activities and has reset his life to follow his deepest passion, writing stories. He writes a blog on how he's reset his life and tries to impart the wisdom learned in his nearly 60 years of successes and failures, largely following the paths others had set for him, and how he's reset his life to exploit his own superpowers.

Ned is a father. In his past lives, he's been a serial entrepreneur, an attorney and a host of other things. His wife, Barbara, always points out that Ned transforms every job into the one he really wants to do, no matter the job description. It's been an interesting journey.

Reset was Ned's first published novel, the first in a series. As an entrepreneur, he determined that self-publication made the most sense. *First Steps* is the prequel to the series, setting up the traumatic life from which Sarah emerged and the strength she developed in overcoming that life.

Ned has written for decades, including poetry, short stories, magazine articles and several books in various stages of completion. Ned was a columnist with *The Moderate Voice*, an e-zine, and has ghostwritten more than 25 articles for well-known experts in their fields. Ned has been involved with several not-for-profits and continues to dedicate time to helping others. He's been married to Barbara for over 12 years and has two wonderful daughters making their own names in the world.

Visit www.nedlips.com for Ned's blog, updates on the *Reset* series and more!

Made in the USA
Columbia, SC
25 August 2019